FRAGMENTS OF MEMORY

FRAGMENTS OF MEMORY
A STORY OF A SYRIAN FAMILY

by Hanna Mina

translated by Olive Kenny and Lorne Kenny

with an introduction by Khaldoun Shamaa

Interlink Books

An imprint of Interlink Publishing Group, Inc.
Northampton, Massachusetts

This edition first published in 2004 by

INTERLINK BOOKS
An imprint of Interlink Publishing Group, Inc.
46 Crosby Street, Northampton, Massachusetts 01060
www.interlinkbooks.com

Originally published in Arabic as *Baqaya Suwar*, Damascus, 1975

ISBN 1-56656-547-2

The painting on the cover, *Cemetery from the East* by Suraya Al-Baqsami, is courtesy of
The Royal Society of Fine Arts, Jordan National Gallery of Fine Art, Amman, Jordan

This English translation is published with the cooperation of PROTA (the Project of
Translation from Arabic); director: Salma Khadra Jayyusi, Cambridge, Massachusetts, USA

Printed and bound in Canada

Table of Contents

Acknowledgments

Hanna Mina is one of the Arab world's major novelists, particularly famous for his delineation of real life tableaux from the modern Syrian experience, especially the life of sailors and the sea. The present novel, however, is unique among his multi-faceted work in that, while it characteristically excels in the depiction of the malaise of a life lived under great stress, the experience it presents has two further qualities: first, it is mostly the experience of the author himself during his sadly deprived childhood, and second, it is an experience tied to a mode of life prevalent in the early decades of this century that is no longer in existence. It has been one of PROTA's main aims to bring out in English translation a number of novels depicting life in the Arab world of a bygone era, and place the events and experiences of this era on record not only for students of literature, but also for those generally interested in issues of social history and individual human interaction with change— issues particularly marked in the modern Arab world in the wake of the many political and social revolutions, and, in particular, the advent of oil.

Work on *Fragments of Memory* has been a labor of love, and my heartfelt thanks first go to Olive and Lorne Kenny for volunteering to translate this long and difficult text. Many thanks go also to my friends, Amin Abd al-Hafeez for checking the translation and Professor Elizabeth Fernea, that untiring searcher for good Middle Eastern texts suitable for presenting to the English speaking reader, for her work in editing the English text for style. Khaldoun Shamaa, the well-known Syrian critic, who is thoroughly acquainted with both Mina and the Syrian literary scene, has very kindly written the introduction to this novel, for which I owe him much gratitude. My thanks also go to Ayman el-Desouky for translating Mr. Shamaa's introduction.

—*Salma Khadra Jayyusi*
Director of PROTA (Project for the Translation of Arabic)

Introduction

In his attempt at articulating the feelings of hatred that the nineteenth century had towards "realism," Oscar Wilde saw them best expressed in the image of that savage, primitive creature that Shakespeare called "Caliban" — a play on the word "cannibal" — in one of his plays. He envisaged the waning century beholding itself in the mirror, just like the Shakespearean creature, unable to control the feelings of fury and rage aroused in it by such a sight.

Wilde's observation, however, was not only directed at "realism" as a literary trend with certain aesthetically defining features. It was also, and more specifically, directed at a common feature that characterizes the realist novel in all its different conceptions and tendencies. This "common feature" consists of the realist novel's insistence on documenting the darker, more negative aspect of human existence.

The important role that the Syrian writer, Hanna Mina, played in founding the Syrian Writers Association and the Arab Writers Association — both of which espoused the ideals of socialist realism and clearly had ideological intentions — was, one might claim without running the risk of exaggeration, firmly grounded in the realist tendencies prevalent in Syrian literature at the time. In fact, the Syrian novel witnessed four major movements in the three decades from the forties to the sixties:

1. A romantic movement, with Shakeeb al-Jabiri as one of its most distinguished members.

2. A classical movement, which attempted a mediation between the realist and romantic tendencies. Abd al-Salam al-'Ujaili and Sidqi Ismail are among the best representatives of this movement.

3. An existentialist movement, represented by the works of Mutaa Safadi.

As to the fourth, the realist movement, it was notably ideological in its intentions. It derived its intellectual and aesthetic bases from the political literature of socialist realism, as well as from the vari-

ix

ous, disparate renditions of the latter's political ideals into the language of the novel.

This brief and schematic review of the various novelistic trends in Syrian literature might, however, appear to the general reader as unconditionally and uncritically reliant on the terminology and conceptual tools of Western or European literature. But this can be explained by simply referring to the general process of acculturation which gave rise to the modernist movement in Arabic literature. What I mean by "acculturation" here is the appropriation, by the individual or the group, of certain cultural values through the immediate interaction with a different culture and the subsequent insights that might be obtained as a result of this interaction. Some of the insights obtained in this process (of interaction with a different culture) pertain to various values, techniques, and textual strategies, and the transformations they go through as they enter into the experiences of the appropriating culture. It is in this manner that Syrian literature, which occupies a prominent position among the various Arabic literatures, has appropriated, in various degrees, many of the major movements in both European and American literatures. The close connection between the rise of the novel—considered an extraneous European literary genre—and the existent realist tendencies might not therefore require much explanation.

The sense of moral and social commitment which reigned over Syrian literature, beginning with the forties, made the experience of "realism" in the novel intellectually conscious of its own position. For instance, Hanna Mina's persistent claim that the novel ought to reflect social reality does not only issue out of political commitment to Marxist ideology: such a claim also derives from a sense of commitment toward expressing the wretched social circumstances under which the impoverished classes—the majority of Syrians—found themselves living and suffering, following the collapse of the Ottoman Empire and throughout the period of the French Mandate. This period also witnessed the confused beginnings of a modern Syria (with its present geographic boundaries).

In other words, the novel, only generally understood, seemed at first to be the one genre most suitable for the articulation and transformation of both personal and social realities—seen as two sides of the same coin. Such, for instance, seems to be the case in *Fragments of Memory*, in which the autobiographical style is successfully blended with the third person, objective narrative. And since the protagonist in this novel belongs to the masses, and not to the ruling class, it becomes only a matter of simple inference to see how this kind of autobiography could turn into a paradigm for expressing social reality. For, in such a context, there is no sense in differentiating between the "I" of the narrator and the author himself. Third person pronouns are hardly ever used in this kind of narrative; for the "I" of the narrator, the nucleus of autobiography, lies at the center of the narrative and is immediately present throughout. The fictional world that emerges from the narrative is the creation of this "I," which stand for the author himself. In *Fragments of Memory*, however, we are not faced with the narrative account of a purely personal history, as is generally the case in biographical works. Nor are we faced with a spiritual autobiography in the manner of al-Ghazali's *The Deliverer from Error*, or Aurelius's *Meditations*, or St. Augustine's *Confessions*, or Rousseau's *Confessions*. Rather, we are faced in *Fragments of Memory* with a narrative technique that comes very close to such autobiographical works by Gorky as *My Childhood, In the World*, or *My Universities*. In this kind of work, the dividing lines between autobiography and the novel are blurred, and the writer's only sense of measure is his honesty of expression and his intimate and insightful knowledge of society. In this way, such problematical issues as may arise in relation to the complex world that the language is able to create begin to lose their substance. As one of the historians of the Arabic novel once put it, Hanna Mina

> ...has continued to use a vivid realism that makes no concessions to such devices as flashback or stream of consciousness in order to recall the past. The narrative sequence is uncomplicated and the impact is often similar to the heroic saga...[1]

Such an understanding of realism makes it appear at first sight as perhaps too simple and direct an expression of reality, so much so that it almost fails to draw the line between the novel and autobiography. It almost reminds us of H.G. Wells's over-enthusiastic but

---

[1] Roger Allen, *The Arabic Novel: An Historical and Critical Introduction* (Syracuse: Syracuse University Press, 1982), p. 73.

pertinent exclamation: "Who would read a novel if we were permitted to write biography all out?"

Hanna Mina's realism, however, is the expression of an attempt to mediate between the autobiographical and novelistic techniques; an attempt which very often lends itself to the kind of conventional mastery that avoids any ostentatious attempt at parading the various techniques used in the novel of realism. The narrative structure of *Fragments of Memory* does not desperately seek climactic moments that are problematized and then resolved. It offers a picture of reality that is simple, direct, and quite emotional, sometimes to the point of melodrama. It is very often the case that the writer manipulates external events and uses them as masks or symbols of the narrator's—also the main character in the novel—inner psychological states. The writer here is primarily concerned with communicating his experiences in the most direct and simple way possible. He does not engage himself in the controversies over aesthetic techniques and structures that characterize the maturing Arabic narrative genres in the period following the Second World War. This aesthetic reconsideration of narrative techniques sprang from serious research into traditional Arabic narrative techniques in an attempt at developing a narrative performance that is distinct from the traditional European narrative genres.

It is perhaps important to mention at this point the fact that *Fragments of Memory*, the first edition of which came out in Damascus in 1975, belongs to the stage in the writer's career in which he no longer concerned himself with "realism" as an ideology or as a philosophy or aesthetics, as was the case in his first three novels. Realism, as he saw it then, was something that paralleled or equaled reality itself. Reality, in other words, was seen as transcending in its richness any realist conceptualization as such, be it aesthetic or philosophical—regardless of how the author might see himself in relation to these issues. And, despite the loss of faith among some contemporary critics in the ability of literature to reflect reality purely and simply, the image of a writer able to communicate his experiences aptly and in a powerful and unforced simplicity is what comes forth in *Fragments of Memory*. This kind of style helps in communicating an image of Syrian society in the thirties and forties through the struggle of an impoverished family—of an origin that is neither rural nor urban—which moves from the city to the countryside, only to be forced back unwillingly, groping for survival.

Hanna Mina's life, as a matter of fact, parallels in its rhythm and details his aesthetic performance. He was born in Latakia, the only Syrian port on the Mediterranean, in 1924, and soon moved with his family to the port of Al-Suwaydiya, in the Iskenderon province— which shortly thereafter was captured by the French and annexed to Turkey, despite the fact that the majority of its population was of Syrian Arab decent. His family moved to the countryside not long after this, and stayed there for a number of years. He started school at the age of eight and completed his primary education in 1936. It was at that time that the experience that he describes in *Fragments of Memory* with absolute accuracy, directness and charm began. Extreme poverty forced him into employment as a dock worker, a hairdresser, and a journalist. He was forced out of school after the completion of his primary education. Hanna Mina is thus a self-made, self-taught writer.

In 1942, Hanna Mina wrote short stories for Syrian and Lebanese newspapers and literary magazines, all of which were lost. In 1947, he moved from Latakia, where he worked as a hairdresser, to Damascus, where he began his career in journalism. In 1954, he helped found the Arab Writers Association and played a major role in shaping its realist orientations and in promoting the idea of a political commitment on the part of the writer: one of the most influential ideas in the Arabic, intellectual mid-fifties sphere. In the same year, he published his first novel, *Blue Lamps*, inaugurating a new phase in his career, in which he devoted himself exclusively to the writing of novels. And despite the fact that he published thereafter many short stories and critical essays, the novel remained his principal and most favored literary form.

For the past two decades, Hanna Mina has been working as a civil servant in the Department of Authorship and Translation, one of the departments of the Ministry of Culture in Damascus. He is now a consultant in the same department, and a member of the Union of Arab Writers. In 1967, the novel *The Sail and the Tempest* won the state's Promotion Award, and in 1990 he won the Uwais Award, one of the most prestigious awards in the Arab world, for his complete works.

Finally, I hope that the reader will find in this novel—in which autobiography blends with the novelistic narrative—a most pleasing introduction to one of the major literary trends in contemporary

Syrian literature, which is now witnessing substantial advancements in the sphere of narrative genres.

Khaldoun Shamaa
London

Fragments of Memory
Chapter 1

They were taking my sick father out on a stretcher.

And my weeping mother was following him.

When he was out of our sight, we returned to the courtyard of the house on the other side of the large, doorless gateway.

It was a spacious house with a dusty courtyard into which the doors of the damp, dark rooms opened. Leading up to these doors were stone steps where the women sat, the children cried, or the men might sit themselves down for some reason or the other.

The courtyard contained a motley collection of junk: along the sides were hearths and firewood, jerry can flower pots with jasmine growing in them, chickens and filth on the ground, a Ford car and a heap of oranges. A man sitting on the fender of the Ford, hand on cheek, was regarding the heap of oranges while the children, gathered in a circle around the car, stared at the oranges. A woman seated on a stone was offering her child a sallow, flabby breast.

I was born in this house. The date of my birth was lost, regardless of the fact that my father celebrated my birth by distributing boxes of *mushabbak*[1] that he made and sold every day, and my young mother smiled—as they said—at the news because I was the only boy after three girls and I would remain the only boy, as the siblings following me would die one after the other from malaria, measles and a state of poverty reaching the verge of starvation.

When I was older my teacher in the elementary school was amazed at the fact that the date of my birth recorded in the registry office was 1911.

"This isn't quite possible, my little chap," he said, patting me on the head. "At that rate you are older than I. There's a mistake here. Who made it?"

I was dumbfounded. It occurred to me all of a sudden that the teacher would throw me out of the school, and the police would beat and imprison my father because of this mistake. I was afraid, not knowing what to answer. The teacher dismissed me, kindly charging me to ask my father to come to meet him. I did so and he

---

[1] A pretzel-like biscuit dipped in syrup.

came that same morning. He bowed to the teacher, placing his hand on his breast. But I didn't hear what he said to him.

In the evening when I returned home, I asked my father but he didn't answer me. He couldn't read or write; none of the family could read or write; likewise the whole quarter. Ten years after my birth the village *mukhtar*,[2] semi-illiterate, had taken upon himself to register the family for the first time in the registry office in the city of Alexandretta[3] where we had moved.

My father didn't understand how the mistake had occurred and I'm not too certain about how much attention he paid to it after he found out. He probably cursed the *mukhtar* and scolded mother for looking upon the whole affair as a catastrophe. Apparently, he had gone to the *mukhtar*, accompanied by an elderly coffee-house owner, requesting the registration of his family, enumerating them one by one. Pulling his brass inkwell along with a reed pen out of his waistband the *mukhtar* had written down the names of the father, mother, and the children. He may have questioned Father about everyone's birth date or, wishing to display his good nature, he may have written them down on his own, Father meanwhile nodding his head in affirmation—as he used to do over any matter of which he was ignorant. The *mukhtar* took his record to the registry office and thus obtained an official family identification booklet for us. On the front was a picture of my brown-skinned father wearing his wine-colored fez. He brought the booklet home and Mother put it under the clothes in her bridal box—our only wardrobe—where it was forgotten until I was big enough to go to school and the teacher discovered the error upon enrolling me. However, the date of birth was not the only mistake: the family's origin was in the village of al-Suwaydiya near Antioch. Either the *mukhtar* was aware of this or my father told him so. Accordingly, the *mukhtar* had put down al-Suwaydiya as the birthplace of every member of the family, including me. This mistake is still on my identity card...and will remain there. But the year has been straightened out. It became 1924 according to the tes-

---

[2] Village chief or headman.

[3] Renamed Iskenderun when it was transferred to Turkey in 1939, Alexandretta was included in the French mandate of Syria.

timony of those present at my birth in the city of Latakiya in that house I mentioned and according to the dates of the family births inscribed on the leather cover of the Gospel (Bible) by my paternal uncle, the only numerals he recorded being those of the years.

Thus I came to bear my name and thus I learned the date and place of my birth. When I was older and returned with my folks to Latakiya, after we fled from the governorate in 1939, I asked my mother: "In which house was I born, Mother?"

"That house has been torn down, son," she replied sorrowfully. "It was a big old house so it was torn down."

However, that demolished house presents itself to me like the remnants of a dream. It was the beginning of my consciousness of existence. The vision of it remains fragmented; it comes together then separates; it appears then becomes blurred; it forms a continuous chain and then the chain is broken; it is turned upside down then set upright. Through time it was wiped out as pictures on graves are obliterated from the effect of sun, wind and rain.

Now the only visions of that house remaining are the foggy scenes of the heap of oranges, the Ford car, the sick father being moved on to a stretcher and the mother following him weeping as they took him through the gateway of the house. It could be that these scenes stuck due to Mother's talk about them and due to them being pieces in the mosaic of painful episodes in the life of the family. In turn these happenings were the beginning of a storm-tossed life of flight, devastation and agony.

I was three years old. Mother is certain of this while I find it strange. Perhaps the powerful impression things in the past triggered in my memory explains the recalling of the specters of that distant childhood. The past has always found a lively reception in me. It matures in my being, is clarified and becomes translucent as drops of clear water, regardless of all the profundity I live among in the present. I live every dream that precedes the future and builds a future for me. Seldom do I draw my subject matter from any source other than these drops; from that thing that has fermented, been refined and become alcohol liable to ignite and blaze up within me when touched off by the match stick of recall.

However, the spark of retrieval runs up against impregnable walls when I try recalling what went on before that day my father was carried away on a stretcher. Anything before that house or previous to that episode is a complete vacuum to me; scenes etched on the film of memory came from the words of my young mother, short of stature, her round lined face, with its delicate timid features never capable of showing her feelings. She talked to us, at length, my sisters and I, of her times and her memories. Her accounts enabled me to hang pictures drawn by others on the walls of the void preceding the house and bring together the scattered pieces of the pictures following it, even of the time when I was conscious of things myself. Things I saw and experienced with my family; that I saw and experienced through the long years of my childhood up to my middle age.

I profited as much from Mother's reminiscences of our private life as I did from Father's stories of our life in general. On dark winter evenings with the wind howling mournfully around the house and the feeble light of the lamp tracing apparitions of our memories and fears on the bare clay walls, she would tell us, in our father's absence, stories to entertain us and herself.

We lived in an abandoned field in the village of al-Suwaydiya. Father was, as a rule, on a journey or in Sahl al-Omq harvesting liquorice roots along with the rest of the poor. There was nothing near us, except houses scattered in the fields of mulberry bushes stripped of their leaves during most seasons of the year. A depressing sight in the daytime, an eerie one at night.

On those nights Mother would sit on an old mat, my three sisters around her, while I the one favored child in the family sat in her lap or laid my head on her knee. She would tell us the stories of "Dahir and Zahra," "Sitt al-Badur" and "The Girl and the Judge and the Dish of Honey,"[4] reminisce and then sing to us, or with us. If we went to sleep where we were, she would sing a sad song to herself until the tears quivered in her eyes and teardrops fell on her cheeks and down to her knees. More than once I was awakened by those drops wetting my face. At that I would come to, and raise my head from her knee in surprise. She would quickly wipe away her tears and stroking my hair would tell me to go to sleep again. I would close my eyelids upon the kaleidoscopic mirage like fantasies: a blend of love for "Dahir," pity for "Zahra" and hate for Qara Shoul[5] who separated them in life and sepa-

---

[4] Stories from *The Thousand and One Nights*.

[5] Qara Shoul, or the black ghost, who is the reprover (critic) in the story.

4

rated them—as the story says—in death. He dug himself a grave, between their two graves, upon which a thorn grew. In the spring when roses bloom, and a damask red rose grew on Dahir's grave and a white Nicaniya rose grew on Zahra's grave, each one leaning over to entwine itself around the other, the thorn on Qara Shoul's grave would presumptuously stretch out to interpose itself between them, piercing them, bending their branches so that they withered.

Mother's reminiscences were as long as the frightful nights and as bitter as the quinine water we used to get by boiling the quinine leaves. We drank it as a preventive medicine against the malaria that viciously clung to us.

As far as I can remember from these stories, Mother, orphaned by both parents, was raised by relatives in the village of al-Suwaydiya on the coast near Antioch. Her older sister, who disappeared in the *Safar Barr*,[6] was said to have married and lived in Greece. Mother continued asking about her and said that a man from Bayt Uqda knew her address and that she was going to get that address and write to her. But that never happened. Her only brother, the middle child Rizkallah, was conscripted under Ottoman rule into the Turkish army. From there he sent for his two sisters to come to him. They set out for Mersin with the women who were going there to join their husbands in a sailing ship that almost sank as it was buffeted by fierce waves for two weeks.

In Mersin Mother and her sister worked as house maids and their brother died of pneumonia.

"Your uncle, son, was a man amongst men: as lively, generous, and brave as any hero in a story. Everyone loved him, even death. Death loved him and took him. I was still young. After he and your aunt were gone, I was a piece broken off a rock: alone, a stranger in a land where people were lost fleeing from the war. I wasn't the only one who lost their folks through death but I was the only one, in this exile, who had no relative left. Our village was far away and the *Safar Barr* terrible. Columns of refugees filled the roads. I

---

6 Literally the departure or traveling by land (as opposed to the sea). This refers to the migration of people from the coastal region to the inland areas. It was a time of famine due to the British and French blockade during World War I.

worked as a servant for a station manager in a town called Baleemadak.

"Your uncle, son, took an oath not to eat the Turkish *qarwana*,[7] stuck to his oath and didn't eat it. He was drafted to forced labor as the likes of him were not allowed to bear arms. He disdained this forced labor, shirking it in various ways, and ran away. When he reached Anatolia he quickly got work at anything he could find: a hired farm hand, a laborer on the railroad, an overseer in a workshop...and sent for us to come. He also sent in search of other scattered families from our village. They came and turned their affairs over to him and they found, for the most part, food, shelter and hard work. But it was work at any rate. Your father was one of your uncle's followers. They were crazy about him, and stuck to him until he left us for our father Abraham's bosom."

I recall lifting my head from her knee to ask, "Who is Abraham? My grandfather?"

"No...Abraham is a saint. The priest calls him Father Abraham... You'll understand when you grow up... Don't interrupt me!"

I shut up as I was anxious to hear the rest of what she had to say. In my imagination Father Abraham had taken the form of a huge old man with a white beard, smiling eyes, and a boundless lap upon which sat or lay all those who went to him, not to return. Mother used to send into his bosom all those who vanished never to reappear.

When our neighbor died, Mother went to the funeral to cry with the women weeping around the coffin in which the neighbor lay in his shroud. I wasn't allowed to enter to look upon his face as he lay there like she said.

"Where has our neighbor gone?" I asked when she returned home.

"To Father Abraham's bosom."

"Where does Father Abraham live?"

"In heaven."

"Are there houses and bread and water in heaven?"

"There's everything there."

---

[7] The food of the Ottoman army: boiled water with a few grains of lentils in it. Father says that a diver was the only one who could get a grain of it.

"Why didn't he take his wife and children with him?"

"They'll go when their time comes."

"And Father! Why doesn't he go?"

"Don't say that...," she chided, "you're little...how would you live without him?"

"You'll go and take me with you."

She cried as she held me to her breast, "Don't ever say that again...I don't want you to go or I or your father to go...you are little...don't ask so many questions."

I heeded her and didn't ask any more questions but I couldn't understand why she didn't want us to go to the bosom of Abraham sitting in the blue heavens. His sitting up there really intrigued me; he didn't fall from the heavens despite the fact that nothing from earth was supporting him like the posts that held up the roof of our hut and the roofs of our neighbors' huts!

Mother continued uncle's story: "In summer he used to take us to *al-raghat*[8] in the cotton fields. He was our overseer and he alone of all the supervisors took a ration of bread for the children and if he saw a woman or girl was behind in hoeing the cotton he would go back from the head of the line to hoe with her until she caught up with the others... Ah...he was so good and awe-inspiring. He knew of the land of Anatolia, the chiefs and highway robbers. He could do the impossible...He would bring bread and distribute it with his own hand to the sick and orphaned. When asked where he got it he answered, 'God sent it...there isn't in his whole creation a worm in the rocks that he abandons.' So I don't understand why he abandoned him in his hour of need...

"One day when he was in the city he was arrested and conscripted. The men said, 'This time he'll definitely eat the *qarwana*.' But he didn't eat it. He fled across the mountains through the snow. He reached us on his last legs. He was coughing and had a burning fever. He threw himself upon the bed from which he did not rise. 'My oil has run out, brothers,' he said to those who came to visit him, 'and this little one,' pointing to me, 'is entrusted to your care!' The older men answered, 'Don't talk like that, Rizk, our beloved friend. Tomorrow you'll get up as strong as a lion.' He smiled at them, turned away...and asked for water... He was burning up inside and the fire was coming out of his forehead. They put

---

8 The harvest.

7

ice on his head but he flung it off, 'Don't torture me, I'm finished!' He became delirious. We were in the wooden room with the fire blazing, and steam rising from the kettle... Those present were sitting while I was kneeling by his bed weeping, imploring him to open his eyes and speak to me. I didn't know anything about death and it never occurred to me that he would die. It was difficult for me to believe that in that room he could so quickly leave me alone in the world.

"I went to the box and took out a handful of lentils wrapped up in a shirt and tried to prepare something hot for him. An old man came to me asking me to put that off until morning. 'He'll be hungry by morning,' I said. He looked the other way and went to sit down. I didn't perceive that he was weeping or that Rizk wouldn't be there in the morning. Another one came saying, 'Go and get some rest, girl, in our hut.' He asked his wife to take me but I refused telling him, 'Perhaps my brother will need me!' The others said, 'Leave her...let her stay.' So I stayed...dawn was about to break when I heard a rumbling in his chest as I was kneeling beside him.

"Bending his head towards me, he opened his eyes with difficulty and held out his hand. A man said, 'Give him your hand, Mariam.' When I gave him my hand, he drew it towards him, placed it on his breast then said in a weak broken voice, 'Mariam.' 'I am Mariam, Rizk,' I replied, 'speak to me my dear brother!' Trying his best to open his eyes he said, 'My dear little one, an orphan...' His grip on my hand loosened and his eyes closed...at the same time I saw his tears and wept. The old man said, 'Don't be afraid, this is sweat from his brow,' and lifted me away. After a little while weeping broke out and a woman screamed, 'Rizk has died.' Then they removed me by force from the house."

I went to sleep on Mother's knee before the story was finished. I heard the rest of it afterwards. My youngest sister also went to sleep so my two other sisters and Mother cried together as they always did at sad stories. When I grew older I learned that Father, who was from the same village of al-Suwaydiya and Uncle's friend, had married my orphaned mother who was alone in the world. She had been taken to the old man's hut, which she left as a bride to share Father's exile and misery throughout the *Safar Barr* and the First World War.

During this exile my sisters were born in towns and villages of Anatolia. Then after the end of the First World War the family returned to Syria. They went to Latakiya, not to al-Suwaydiya, due to the fact that my father's two brothers were there. And there in the big house with the large courtyard I was born on the ninth of March. After me, according to what Mother says, five more children arrived: two boys and three girls. But death loved them all and took them to Abraham's bosom where he sits in the blue heavens.

Chapter 2

The two men left with the stretcher upon which lay the shrouded body. I remember that exactly. Father was the one laid out on the stretcher and Mother was following weeping. When they took him out, we returned to the courtyard where the Ford car sat with the pile of oranges beside it. My mother didn't want to speak to the man sitting on the fender, nor did she pay attention to the pile of oranges. She went inside while I approached the man and looked longingly at the oranges. He gave me one. Taking it gleefully, I ran to Mother in the room. She looked at me and cried, then clasping me to her bosom, sat in silence. When I was bored with that, I returned to the courtyard to find the children encircling the pile of oranges and the man in the same place on the fender, his hand in the same place on his cheek, his skinny wife screaming abuses at him. He did not lift his head or answer her.

This man was our neighbor in that house. His name was Kiryakou, a mechanic by trade and a Greek by origin. Kiryakou had dreamed up a power plant before power plants were known in many of our communities. He tried to generate electricity from the well in the courtyard of the dwelling and spent a great deal of time on his experiments that were doomed never to be completed.

According to what Mother told me, he was a mechanical genius. That Ford had been in the junk yard. Its French owner had given it up in despair of any power on earth being able to restore life to it. So Kiryakou bought it and brought it back to life. It was in his power to resurrect any mechanical device whatsoever. Therefore, he was much in demand, considered one of the successful and one of those for whom everything their hands touch turns to gold. However, he was a failure, in debt and miserably henpecked in his own house. He maintained that his wife was the cause of his predicament and his wife swore that his power station was the cause of the situation. The neighbors had differing opinions on this point but they all agreed the wife was a *sharma*,[1] ugly, nosy and loudmouthed, who took advantage of her husband's weakness in

---

[1] An expression used for a woman who is not a good manager of her household. Literally it means a woman with her nose cut off.

Arabic to lash out at him. She would yell at one of the children in his presence:

"Damn your father!"

Kiryakou would reply, "Why don't you curse my mother?" (He meant his son's mother.)

"Damn your mother, too!" the wife would retort.

She would keep up her curses until she made him lose his self-control. He would throw anything he could lay his hands on at her or tear his hair in anger, and, leaving off his electrical experiment-ing, escape from the house to drink in some tavern. He would come home drunk after midnight greeting anyone he chanced to meet with "Calemera."[2] Then his wife would open the door and yell at him: "Calespera[3] you son of a...!"

They would start a fight that would generally end up by the wife running to the mouth of the well to wreck the apparatus of the experiments of the power station.

When Kiryakou got the Ford, the whole quarter was preoccu-pied with it. Its rubber horn hanging on the side was never silent. The men and women circled it in amazement. Madame Kiryakou rode in it with her husband on an outing to the seaside. For that day she gave up her reviling and talked at length about the car-riage that went without the clip-clop of a horse just as if the rider were sitting on a cushion of fine feathers. The neighbors asked her how she had felt, whether she had been afraid. She said that in the beginning she had been nervous but became quite at ease and that she had felt like someone on a swing being pushed forward while the trees along the road were rushing backwards on their own.

My mother said, "We were surprised at what she said. Over night Kiryakou turned into a magician in our eyes. An elderly neighbor said that an *afreet*[4] hidden under the hood was what made it go... Then we tried it. I didn't. The women didn't ride in it

---

[2] Good Morning—Greek.

[3] Good Evening—Greek.

[4] A genie.

11

but the men did...your father did too. It was the cause of our ruin and flight from Latakiya."

After that she talked to us about Father. She said that in Mersin he worked as a porter in the harbor and on the decks of the ships. He was strong. He could carry the heaviest sacks and bales. He was one of the outstanding ones in his gang and was nicknamed "the Egyptian."

"Why the Egyptian?"

"Because he went to Egypt!"

"And where is Egypt?"

"On the other side of the ocean...I don't know where. Your father went there on a ship. He left me in Mersin and went... He was stranded there. He didn't succeed."

"Why didn't he succeed?" (asked my oldest sister).

"Because God willed it so!"

"And why did God will it so?"

"Don't object to God's will! It's a sin," retorted Mother angrily.

My sister kept silent, feeling that she had committed a sin. So I asked: "Why did he go?"

"Because God willed it."

"God or that woman who gave him the glad eye? " asked my sister.

"God put that woman in his path."

"That woman" remains a bad memory to Mother. She was a relative, her paternal uncle's daughter, a widow who was intrigued with Father and got him... He claims that she hid his clothes in the boat, compelling him to travel with her as far as Alexandria... Mother was skeptical about it. Her husband's conduct gave rise to doubt, her cousin being a widow... At any rate he had gone and returned a failure, defeated. Mother rejoiced at his return and forgave him. To compensate her for that, he told her about Cairo, "the Center of the world"; about the scoundrels, the delightful sounds and how the fruit sellers sang out their wares in melodious voices. The neighbors used to come to listen to the stories of the Egyptian who had seen "the Center of the world" with his very own eyes.

Mother would reassure us, saying: "Yes children, he saw it...he went to lots of places...your father doesn't settle down in one place. He doesn't succeed but he never settles down. He says he is looking for a loaf of bread. Our neighbor in Mersin cursed her son one day by saying to him: 'May the loaf be an apparition as you run after it.' The son continued pursuing the phantom loaf and never caught up with it... He lived in poverty like us. Your grandmother was a good woman. She died in our house and her pure spirit came back to us as a dove that settled down on our roof. She was a saint, your grandmother was. She never cursed your father. But despite that he never had any success... The loaf went on being an apparition before him."

My sisters and I had never seen a horseman except in a picture at a neighbor's. He had large whiskers. In one hand he carried a sword and a shield in the other as he rode his horse, pursuing a man in front of him. Whenever I listened to Mother talking about the imaginary loaf, I wished, secretly, the loaf would turn into a horseman in front of me also. One day I even opened a bread box and hid behind the mats piled up in the corner, hoping every minute that the loaves would pop out and change into horses[5] with riders on their backs so I could run after them. I was crouching, holding my breath awaiting the wonderful scene that was to take place. It was summertime so Mother and my sisters were out picking mulberry leaves for the silkworms. I went to sleep where I was hiding and, instead of the loaf jumping out and turning into a horseman, the cat jumped into some of the loaves and tore some of them to pieces. When Mother returned to witness the scene she spoke to the girls about their carelessness. They searched for me until they stumbled upon me and woke me up. When I learned what had happened to the bread I didn't open my mouth. Mother didn't question me about anything as she feared that my sleep was some sort of illness. She immediately put her lips, which were the thermometer in our house, on my forehead. When she was sure I was all right, she kissed me in delight, forgetting the misfortune that had befallen our food for the day.

However, Father, in his pursuit of the imaginary loaf, enticed Kiryakou to join him in the race. That was three years after my birth when Father had left his work on the wharf, following a break in his right forearm, the result of a heavy box falling on him from the winch of one of the ships. At first he worked as a shoe-

---

[5] The Arabic word for a ghost or apparition is *khayal*; for a horseman it is *khayyal*. The little boy evidently got the two words mixed up.

13

maker, then a confectioner. He also cropped up in one of the villages as a mason building country houses. No house was ever completed because he built as he chose without plumbline or cord. The stones of the walls he built would fall down and join him on the ground in the evening.

In the interval between two jobs, he found the cheap taverns suitable places to rest from his pursuit of the "imaginary loaf." In these taverns he would relate to those, who, like him, had grown weary of the race, and think about what had happened to him and what he had seen in "the center of the world" and new schemes for further journeys. He would always meet up with someone to share in carrying them out.

Kiryakou, having despaired of ever finishing his power station, after one of his fights with his wife, teamed up with Father in a strange enterprise! They went from Latakiya to Kasab for dangerous merchandise. Kiryakou sold the engine of the power plant, Father gathered up what remained of Mother's jewelry, and on an evening when no one in the building heard *Calemara* or *Calespera* they set out in the ancient Ford on a secret mission. The tobacco that grew in the Kasab mountains was of exceptionally good quality. The smugglers, who were at the same time highway robbers, carried it down on mules from the mountains to al-Suwaydiya. Father's brain hatched up the idea of having the car compete with the mules. He induced Kiryakou to transport the contraband tobacco.

In this way they plunged headlong, unarmed, upon a journey in which they lost everything. It was virtually impossible for the Ford to traverse the narrow rugged mountain tracks to where the tobacco was. However, Kiryakou put all his mechanical skill into service for the trip, and they reached their destination in a state of exhaustion. They paid their money and got the tobacco. From there they started down to al-Suwaydiya only to have bandits attack them half way there... They threatened to kill them, robbed them of their goods, forcing them to carry it in the car to a village near al-Suwaydiya.

"Your father, son, was never taken by surprise. He was used to traveling in the mountains, to sleeping in the heart of the mountains with no thought or fear of death. He would spend the night in the middle of a forest inhabited by all sorts of wild beasts as if he were in his own house. Those who accompanied him and lived with

14

him said so and I learned it from them. I admonished him a great deal and he was often convinced but it was in vain. I warned him of the outcome, reckoning that he would never go back to making these trips. But he never gave it up. How many times have I asked myself: 'Why? After what? What's in his head?' But I never found out... Your father tried me severely and tortured himself more. I forgive him... It got to be such a habit with him that he wasn't surprised at the bandits holding them up and confiscating the load in the car.

"While Kiryakou quaked with fear and wept in sorrow over his goods, your father...this is what Kiryakoum said...rolled a cigarette and conversed familiarly with the highway men. He saw no reason for anger nor felt any objection to drinking with them. He was able to lay his head down and sleep as if nothing had happened. He even slept while the robbers loaded the Ford with firewood of the stone pine together with all the plunder they had on hand.

"Thus the car proceeded on its way with its load: tobacco, firewood, kettle, a horse saddle, walnuts, hazelnuts, shoes of a man who had been killed, a box of bridal finery and plunder of all sorts.

"The leader of the band squeezed in beside Kiryakou, three rode in the back seat and on each fender stood a man, his gun at the ready. Your father was at the back of the car on top of the sacks loaded on the parcel carrier.[6]

"'If Kiryakou hadn't been with me I'd have escaped,' he told me that himself. 'The car was climbing the hills slowly. All I had to do was jump into the dense undergrowth and disappear. In fact I considered doing that, but the sight of the wretched Kiryakou squeezed in there with a gun pointed at his head from the outside deterred me.'

"'At one of the bends in the road shots rang out. Bandits again. The Ford stopped. Kiryakou dove under the steering wheel. I threw myself onto the ground and hid behind the car to await the end of the fight. At first I didn't see anyone. They were barricaded behind the rocks and pine trunks. No sooner had the leader of the group opened the door than they felled him on the spot... He was struck in the head and dangled like a bird on birdline... After that

---

[6] A sort of trunk made of plaited ironwork.

the exchange of fire didn't last long...only a short while... We surrendered...we put up our hands...the wounded emerged, they stripped those who were still alive of their arms and tied our hands behind our backs with ropes.'

"Yes, son, that's what he said, and that's what happened... In those days death gleaned travelers just like a rooster picks up grains of wheat. Highway robbery was a trade. It was virtually impossible for a traveler to wear a new garment. How often the robbers stripped people of their trousers. If one of them had been able to drive the Ford, neither Kiryakou nor your father would have got back. They were forced to spare them. Kiryakou had to transport the new bandits who confiscated the load in the car, adding to it the plunder they had on hand... They forced him to drive after beating him on the head and tying your father on the back seat with his hands shackled with ropes.

"It was bitterly cold at the beginning of winter, the snow was being driven by the wind. The Ford stalled. Kiryakou wept on his knees when threatened with death, 'Don't kill me'—he entreated them—'I'll fix it.' He fixed it with God's help. Your father was thrown behind the car trussed up, wet and forgotten.

"In the end they released him in a village... The *mukhtar* was a good man who gave them shelter and food and went with them himself in the car to al-Suwaydiya. He gave them a pile of oranges as compensation."

These were the oranges I saw in the courtyard of the house that day just as I saw my father, whom Kiryakou had brought back sick with a chest ailment, carried out on a stretcher. Mother told us: "They took him to the hospital lingering between life and death. I cried very much that day. I was afraid he was going to die leaving me a widow and you orphans. I feared for you more than for your sisters. My pregnancy with you was the result of supplication as they say in church. And I bore you in great pain. The day you were born my inner parts smiled as I burst out with thanks to the Lord and intercession for you. Our grotto was lit up, I lit a candle before the icon, and stood humbly offering prayers of thanks. While I was confined to bed following childbirth, I was gripped by unbelievable fear for you, imagining that you would not live because you were so thin. You cried continually. I was advised to give you water from boiled poppy plants to drink so you would sleep but I refused... They told me that if you didn't sleep you wouldn't live. Some

16

months after your birth I was advised to take you to the mosque on Friday, stand under the minaret at the time of the call to prayer and slap you on the mouth with your father's slipper. I did that...

"I was forced to leave you at home with your little sisters and go to some rich people in Latakiya to breast feed their son who was your age. It was very painful for me to sell your nourishment, but your father was absent on one of his trips and we had nothing to eat. I couldn't work as a servant when you were nursing so I was obliged, in order to feed you, to sell half your food. Your foster brother was named Jule. I go to him when I am in want. He is rich, from an influential family. His mother comes from another important household. She was a kind lady. She asked to see you before her son nursed to make sure that my milk was safe. So I carried you in my arms with my handkerchief over your face and went straight to her, trusting in the name of Christ, and my hopes were realized. I sat on the steps until they allowed me to enter. You were sleeping and I prayed to God that you would go on sleeping until she saw you. And that's how it was. She lifted off the veil and she looked at you. She was beautiful and goodhearted. She was satisfied with looking at your face so I burst out entreating her not to refuse me. I accepted her conditions: her son should nurse first when there was ample milk, in the morning I must wash my breasts and keep my face away from the baby, I must eat the food given me in their house and not take it home with me. I fulfilled all the conditions except that one... The bite stuck in my throat when I was swallowing it and she understood that it was more than I could bear and gave me some for your sisters too.

"Truly if we ever go back to Latakiya I will surely take you to her and she'll put her hand on your head so you can see how pretty her white hand is. You must kiss it and bow to her husband, my little chap, and shake hands with your foster brother. They will give you some of his old clothes and one of his toys and maybe some money... "

We never returned to Latakiya when I was a child as Mother hoped. After the failure of Father's trip with Kiryakou and being hospitalized, the doctors advised a period of convalescence in a village. Mother had relatives and a small piece of land in al-Suwaydiya, so Father decided to set off for there. There, for the first time, I became conscious of my existence...the images etched on

17

the film of memory came to an end and the chain of events and sights commenced...

When we came back to Latakiya after our flight from the governorate, I was an adolescent. Mother didn't take me to the beautiful lady to see her son, my foster brother. She mentioned it often and wanted to do so, but I don't know what prevented her from carrying out her wish. After a long time—I believe it was somewhere in circumstances I can't recall—I saw that lady and her son. I learned their names after they had left. The lady was long past forty. There was a residual beauty... Although the still pretty face had donned the veil of maturity...the figure had filled out and become somewhat stooped...the soft white hand was plump and the green branch was beginning to take on the sallowness of autumn. As for her son, the only thing about him that impressed me was his large nose in an all too placid face... He bore no resemblance to his mother nor did he look like the picture of her I had conjured up in my mind, since she was pretty and had lifted the veil off my face with her white hand and, it was upon her lips, where the word of acceptance or refusal rested, that Mother's eyes had been fixed.

Whether I had actually seen them with my eyes or they had remained people of my fantasy, I would still entertain feelings of affection and gratitude towards them... We had shared bread and salt, "milk. " But the bread and salt and milk did not go on forever...my foster brother grew and was weaned; I grew and was weaned and Mother discontinued her visits to that house... However, she suckled other babies in other houses and served other people of a different disposition... After Father recovered from his chest condition it was decided to leave Latakiya...

So we traveled.

Chapter 3

I do not recall the means by which we traveled from Latakiya to al-Suwaydiya, nor do I recall our first days in this coastal village. I never saw its coastline, its sea, or its main market that Father called the town.

The village was the birthplace of my parents and their forefathers. It was our native town where we had relatives, none of which I ever got to know. Our grandparents were dead; not one ancestor was left. Thus, despite its being our village, we lived in it as strangers at its remotest border, and I don't know if it lay to the north or south. However, it was a long way from the sea, the administration center and the main market of the town.

My consciousness of existence in this village begins with this picture: a slaughtered cow hanging from the branch of a gnarled tree, a small olive grove, a fire, some men, and Father. That was on Holy Saturday.

Fifty days of fasting and the next day would be Easter. At dawn Christ would rise from the dead and then we would eat the cakes and eggs.

Ever since February, Mother had been gathering the hen eggs with great care. We were living and working as day laborers in a field belonging to the village *mukhtar*. It was a small field, empty except for mulberry trees. Our only duty was raising silkworms during the silk season. It was a raw deal that Father had contracted with the *mukhtar*... He didn't succeed here either but he was forced into it... He had to find shelter somewhere, so he agreed to take the abandoned field. The *mukhtar* opened a page for us in his debt ledger. The first thing he put down in it, against the account of the silk harvest, was five kilos of mixed sorghum and barley, a few meters of unbleached cotton and a few articles like salt, oil, kerosene and soap. He also advised Father to be a faithful share cropper[1] who knows his obligations and pays his debts. Father raised his hand to his forehead and then placing it over his heart said, "At your service, Mr. Elias!"

---

[1] The Arabic word is *murabi,* i.e. the *fellah* who takes a quarter of the income accruing from the land he works.

Our house was a rectangle built of unbaked clay bricks, divided into two parts by a wall. One part was for animals, the other for living in. Since we possessed no animals, that part remained empty. Hens that relatives had generously bestowed upon Mother ran around and pecked there. In one corner we piled up firewood and dung,[2] and in another near a small window high in the wall was a hearth made of stones and clay.

Father began, with the help of the family, the cultivation of the land and the care of the mulberry trees by borrowing a neighbor's animal. Before the work was finished, a messenger arrived from the *mukhtar* asking for Father. So he went only to be told that he must work in his fields first and that Mother must work in the *mukhtar's* house. Father raised his hand to his forehead, lowered it and placing it over his heart said, "At your service, Mr. Elias!"

Early in the morning on the following day they set out to perform their forced labor. My sisters and I remained at home. We played. We listened to our oldest sister telling stories and we went to gather straw and dry branches from the field, but we did not find any children in the neighborhood. The houses were far apart, scattered amidst the fields of mulberry trees that were separated by ditches. Upon reaching the boundary line, we retraced our steps carrying the straw and firewood we had gathered.

I never liked that bleak field. The autumn had stripped the mulberry trees of their leaves, withered the grass and turned everything a sickly color. Even the sun looked pale. The cold north wind blew constantly. Our parents stayed away so long that I cried, then went to sleep on my sister's knee. At sunset when we had bolted the door and huddled together on the mat, our parents returned so exhausted that they threw themselves down in the corner. Mother kissed me saying she had sifted such a large pile of wheat that her back was broken, the palms of her hands were burning and covered with blisters, and that she must go back tomorrow to do the washing and clean the *mukhtar's* house. She also said that his wife had told her that the *mukhtar* was paranoid: he washed his own clothes and would not allow anyone to enter his room or touch any of his belongings; he stayed in the shop adjoining the house until evening and when he was finished there he came to

---

2 Cow dung gathered and made into round cakes, dried to be burned in the winter as fuel.

have his supper, then went to that room where she couldn't go to him unless he asked her to.

Father didn't say anything. He leaned his back against the wall, his knee forming a right angle to his body, placed his elbow on his knee, his clenched fist on his cheek, while his eyes plowed furrows in the earthen floor of the room. Before we slept he said to Mother, "We're not going to do forced labor tomorrow."

She tried to dissuade him, reminding him that winter was coming on and if the *mukhtar* did not give us food we would starve, and on top of that we were in debt to him. So we could neither release ourselves nor leave. He continued his silence. He had already left...he was, in his imagination, on the road. The family was the pawn. Mother understood. Like him, she had heard about the *mukhtar's* cruelty, injustice and the hardship of life on his land. And like him, every limb of her body was aching with weariness. Facing her on the morrow and the day after and the day after that was never-ending forced labor. It would go on throughout the winter. She would be obliged to go to the *mukhtar's* house through the rain, mud and cold. There was no way out except to leave. But how and to where? Indebtedness to the *mukhtar*, unemployment, being helplessly cut off in this remote village in this isolation amongst the fields in an exile closely resembling perdition. All that made our leaving impossible.

She could have, like Father, struck out one morning alone as a hungry vagabond, but her little ones were here. She couldn't abandon them, she couldn't take them with her and she would never leave without them. But he had made up his mind without any consideration of us, and in the morning she would try to dissuade him by crying and saying, "Have mercy on us! Don't leave us alone," doubting that he would listen to her.

During the night a frightening thing occurred. Some rogues attacked a house in the neighboring field by knocking a hole in the wall large enough for one of them to enter. The owner of the house, a widow, became aware of the presence of the thief as he was collecting the household goods and got into a fight with him. In the darkness his companions, thinking she was a man, shot at her but struck their friend who fell to the ground screaming, "Ah...you've killed me!"

In such cases thieves usually pick up their man and flee so that he won't fall into the hands of the authorities and squeal on them.

21

For some reason or the other, the wounded thief refused to let them take him. Probably because they had treated him so treacherously, he yelled, "Don't you come near me or I'll kill you!" He shot at them, they returned the fire and that night shooting resounded until the wounded thief's ammunition ran out and they finished him off.

In the morning the police from the town arrived. The people, men and women from the neighboring fields, went to get the news and see the thief who had been killed. Father went too, but Mother set out for the *mukhtar*'s house to wash and clean. We stayed behind in fear and trembling, not venturing out into the field. Shortly, we heard voices approaching the house... It was the neighbor's children from the adjoining field, discussing the incident as they came towards our place. Mother had passed by them, asking that they come over to play with us. What joy to have people of the same age come on a day such as this, to feel we weren't alone in this dreadful forsaken world confined within the field boundaries! My sister opened the door to them. They were a brother and two sisters, the boy the same age as my oldest sister, a little past ten. He had wandered around in all the neighboring fields, seen the *mukhtar*, had hunted birds with a slingshot, heard the complete details of last night's events and knew the way to the nearby carriage road where the police had passed by on their horses and by which they would return with the dead thief wrapped in a mat.

The boy suggested that we go and sit by the side of the road to see the thief. We locked the door and went. We sat on the edge of an irrigation ditch waiting while the boy told us endless stories, always directing his words to my sister. We stood or squatted around her, listening so we wouldn't miss anything he said.

"Have you ever seen a thief, yourself, in your whole life?" I heard my sister asking.

He didn't answer right off. Being the oldest one among us, he affected the manner of the brave young fellow, probably having in mind that in the eyes of my sister his reputation depended upon having seen a thief. So to get himself out of the fix he was in he replied, "Thieves steal children, that prevents them from seeing one."

I looked at my sister to find her cowering. Silence descended upon us.

"What's a thief like?" I finally asked.

The picture engraved on our imaginations at that time was not drawn from the words but the fear: the dark color, the large mustache, the thick lips and big ears under the ghoul-like long hair framing the face. We borrowed from family stories about an *afreet*, the features of this particular person who would rob us of our sleep on the approaching dark winter nights. The boy's chatter did nothing but increase our terror, and the woman who had fought the thief took on a legendary bovine shape... To me, Mother seemed like a ewe in comparison to her, a ragdoll. We succumbed to a weight of feelings that robbed us of our peace of mind all day long.

When Mother came home in the evening and suggested putting stones behind the door, Father yelled at her, with us alertly drinking in his words, that thieves don't come to scare people but to steal animals, money or grain and that we didn't own any of those things. They knew that and had made a hole in that woman's house to steal her cow.

We dozed off that night listening to a story and hoping. Father told us that one of our neighbors had awakened one night to find thieves breaking a hole through the wall of his house. He jumped up, seized the gun and sat in the dark waiting for them. When the hole in the wall was finished, the thieves started debating who would go in first... After a short while one of them stuck his head in. The man aimed at him and shot. The neighbors, having been aroused, ran to offer their assistance but the thieves had fled. Finding blood at the gap in the house in the light of a lantern, they followed it a distance into the garden. Father ended up his tale by declaring the necessity of buying a gun when we raised the silkworms and sold the raw silk harvest next summer.

Some days later, in midmorning the following Sunday, Mother put on her best dress and went with Father to the town center to raise a complaint to "Basus al-Ameer"[3] against some relatives of hers who had taken possession of her father's bit of land and refused to pay her her share of it. This Basus was one of the town's elite whose words carried weight. He would go to the sea wearing a long flowing silk cloak. The barefoot, half-naked poor like us

---

[3] "Al-Ameer," meaning "prince," is a nickname.

would watch him and make up stories and songs about him. They would say: *"Nazila Basus al-Ameer labis mashlah al-hareer."*[4]

Mr. Basus heard Mother's complaint and sent word to the debtor requesting him to give her back the land or pay the price. But the following Sunday he changed his position siding with the adversary on the plea that she wasn't the only heir; that she had a brother and a sister. She brought witnesses to testify that her brother had died, her sister had gone to Greece and they had heard nothing more of her. The witnesses were of no use because the opposing party promised "al-Ameer" to reward him at the expense of our mother, the orphan.

There was nothing more she could do except take her complaint to the government in Antioch. In her circumstances this was impossible. Not because Antioch was far away, but because she didn't possess the expenses of making a case. And because the proverb said: "May God never let anyone enter the government doors." She had no other recourse except crying...she cried but what good did that do?

"Neighbor," said one of the neighbor women, "dry your tears. Tears don't work on "Basus" or the *mukhtar* either. Our neighbor whom the thieves came to rob didn't shed tears or get down on her knees before them. She surmised that she had either to die or give up the cow, so both the cow and she came out safe. That's life for you."

Our daily life here was a continual struggle to the last breath, day and night amidst the gloom, the wind, fear and phantoms. This "Basus al-Ameer" whose door was a refuge, his house a court of appeal where the "lost sheep" could come, was nothing more than myth that his friends had created. Mother had to give up her supplications and tears. Wasn't she quaking like a ewe before a wolf? And fear always leads to the slaughter house. However, Mother was afraid and she left "al-Ameer," hopeless.

Across the fields came our parents, returning to us who were terrified by the memory of the thief. It was afternoon, the way was long so they had stopped over at a relative of ours hoping he would remember them so they could get a drink of water and rest awhile.

---

[4] "Basus al-Ameer went out wearing a silk cloak." It is impossible to make it rhyme in translation.

This relative was grandmother's uncle on Mother's side, a *fellah*[5] rooted in the soil who had not left his land for Anatolia. It is said that at the time of the famine he took to highway robbery, but he refuted the claim saying that he waylaid the bandits. "I was a travelling peddler," he maintained, "and would send my beast ahead of me while I followed at a distance... The robbers would appear, and throwing myself behind the first barricade I would shout at them, 'leave my load alone or I'll kill you. The bones of a viper aren't to be swallowed.' Some would resist so I would shoot... You can only die once. That's wisdom. In time, word about my wisdom got around the robbers; they learned who I was and avoided me. Thereafter, I found a new profession: an escort of travellers! I wasn't too hard on them. I didn't ask for a *piastre* or *millieme* from the women and children, but my profession prospered. I began to accept other businesses. People would come to me complaining: 'Uncle Ibrahim, we were robbed on the road; they stripped us of everything but our clothes!' The women and children would cry...some of them would fling themselves into my arms. My heart isn't made of stone... I would say, 'All right, where were you robbed?' When they named the spot I would nod my head. That would be so and so and his band. Every band had its spot. In time I became acquainted with the areas belonging to the different bandits. I also got a band. I would go to my beast, unfasten its tether... I didn't go empty-handed, exposing myself to danger...that wouldn't do. It wasn't from fear but it just isn't sensible. It is the basic rules of the game... I learned from the land. He who sows reaps. I used to put in the saddlebag a striped woolen cloak, a jug of *arrack*,[6] a pound of jerked meat and a handful of tobacco...and the donkey would set out in front of me. They would see me at a distance, and say, 'Barhum has come!' 'Yes, I've come...now then, give me the thing back!' 'You come alone and ask for the things to be returned?' they would laugh. 'Why not? I'm no stranger... I'm one of you and we are going to drink together. Take the saddlebag off the beast and let's have a feast.' They would take out the *arrack*, meat and presents...sit in a circle while I squatted on the ground hiding my gun in my bosom. The rules of the game...if one of them turned around behind me I would get up angrily and yell, 'No! The men

---

[5] A native peasant or laborer.
[6] A colorless liquid made from raisins.

25

face each other. I don't want any treachery.' 'Do you suspect us?' they would protest. 'God forbid! who would suspect a highway robber?' The feast would end and the negotiations begin... I would demand the things back and leave some things. I'm not stupid. They would send some men with me to carry the goods...upon their arrival I would honor them by giving them things from my house. Many times they refused to return their plunder. In that case the protector turned into a bandit. What was taken by force was retrieved by force... My band and I would ambush them...it wasn't easy. I was wounded more than once; some of my men were killed, the best of my men, but they were compelled to take me into account... They say I was a highway robber! God knows...what is important...I didn't leave my land... Here I was born and here I'll die!"

When my parents arrived at Uncle Ibrahim's house, he was away in the farthest field cutting down some trees. He was older now...in his later middle age. However, the land still lay close to his heart and he worked on it even on Sundays. "I'm enjoying myself," he would say. "As for the gun, it's been retired but so that it won't be eaten by rust I shoot in the air once in a while in response to a round of shots from a nearby field to let them know there is someone here, nothing else."

When his wife called him, he stopped his chopping, spat on his hands and rubbed them to soften them up. He would have liked to resume his work, but turning around he squatted on the ground among the trees to see who was there... "Some relatives have come to visit us," said his wife. So after straightening his trousers and dusting them off, he left his work... He arrived bending forward as if his hips were dislocated. Father introduced himself while Mother said, kissing his hand, "I am Miriam, Uncle!" Thinking for a while, he asked, "Rizgallah's sister?" "Rizgallah is dead, Uncle," replied Mother in tears, "I'm an orphan and forlorn!" "An orphan! My girl," he sobbed chokingly. "What has happened to you? Where have you been? Where is your sister?"

They went inside and Mother told him her story. He listened to her, his head bowed, from time to time striking his temple with his fist. Then he instructed his son to kill the big rooster. When Father put in a word to prevent this, he yelled at his son, "Kill it! Bring the wine jug. Are they eating us alive?" he added angrily. "You should have come to me, Miriam... I respect 'Basus al-Ameer'

26

but he doesn't always stick to the truth. He doesn't know who you are. Why did you forget me? It's my fault, people have forgotten me. I'm an old farmer... I don't have a silk cloak like him."

They drank coffee... He asked Father for his tobacco tin and stuffed it full for him, took the gun down, cocked it, calmly shoved two shells into it and, putting a few shells into the pocket of his trousers, said with a smile, "Who knows what will happen?"

After ordering the food to be prepared he arose. "Come with me," he said to my parents. "I'm the one to unravel this problem, not Basus or anyone else!" They left without another word. At the edge of the field he stopped and turned around. His oldest son, who was a married man, had slung his gun over his shoulder and followed him. "Go back to the house!" he yelled at him. The son refused. "Don't make me a laughing stock in my old age!" he growled. So the son set off in another direction...and he went on his way across the fields to Mother's land where the usurper's lay at the end of an orange grove.

He called to him from the outside, "Abu Abdu!" That person came out, welcoming him and inviting him to enter. He excused himself, saying, "I'd like to have a word with you." He squatted on the ground as usual, on the boundary line, pulled out his tin and was rolling a cigarette. When Abu Abdu arrived, he asked him, pointing to Mother, "Do you know this woman? She forgot to make herself acquainted to you... She didn't tell you that she was my sister's daughter." "My pleasure, Uncle Ibrahim," replied Abu Abdu courteously. "The one with right on his side gets his due. Basus is available and so is the government." "I understand, I know," Uncle said. "Come with us to pigheaded Basus...and fetch the papers that establish your ownership of the land or else give it up... If you're the rightful owner well and good. There'll be no need for the government... We are citizens of the same town and know each other. For shame! An orphan's property should not be encroached upon. You will give back the land or we'll shave our mustaches!"[7]

Saying that, he left without drinking coffee. "Don't delay," he added. "We'll settle the question so my niece can return home to her children." He went with our parents to Basus where a session immediately convened. When the usurper's attempt to establish his ownership of the stolen property failed, the bargaining over sell-

---

[7] This is a very serious oath. The moustache is a sign of virility.

ing to compensate began. Mother ceded the small piece of land in exchange for seven silver coins[8] that she collected from Basus on behalf of the usurper. She gave it to Father when they were on their way home.

However, after returning home, Father changed his mind about buying a gun to stave off the thieves. Instead he bought a donkey. "I don't want to sit in the house like a woman," he told Mother... "I'll be a travelling peddler. I'll trade needles and thread for wheat and *durra*..[9] We'll sell that and pay off the debt to this damned man, free ourselves from this yoke and get out of here."

---

[8] Worth twenty piastres each, i.e. one dollar each.
[9] A variety of sorghum.

Chapter 4

Father became a traveling peddler. He saddled the donkey with two wooden boxes, filled them with needles, thread, and matches along with all sorts of goods sold by a *sharshy*, as a traveling salesman was called.

He would be absent for a week, two weeks, and sometimes for a whole month. He would return walking behind his donkey with eggs, wheat, *durra*, barley and tobacco in the boxes...and a little money in his pocket. He would sell some of what he had brought back, buy new goods and be off again after a short respite during which we would have a taste of peace and happiness due to his presence.

We noticed from his dejection and Mother's anxiety that things weren't going as they should. As winter came on, Father's merchandise began to dwindle. I heard Mother saying to him, "You can't tell your profit from your capital." He scolded, threatening her with a beating. He began returning with half of what he had previously brought and leaving with half of what he had set out with. When he no longer replaced his goods, we did not realize that his enterprise was entering the liquidation stage.

He was absent during the winter for a long time. It was a hard winter. I remember it very well because of its harshness and due to it being our first winter in this field amidst other fields, encompassed by all these fearful apprehensions.

Rain, rain, rain, a grey atmosphere, with the sky as far as the eye could see a vast expanse of gloom as if there was no more sun or moon. Rain, nothing but rain. Rain coming down in sheets. A leaking sieve of infinite capacity. Bleak fields on all sides. And rain. And I, morning and late afternoon watching the rain, fixing my attention on how bubbles formed in the mire, floated on, disappeared. And something played a peculiar, monotonous, sad tune like a wailing melody, like distant church bells, like our evening prayers.

Rain, rain, rain. Nothing but rain. Mother, around the hearth telling stories about God and man. About Noah and his boat and the flood that came. "Forty days, forty nights, the rain continued. Noah entered the ark and saved himself and those with him from drowning. And the dove flew over the water and returned carrying an olive branch and on the horizon was a rainbow. But man, whom

God had saved from danger, went back to his sin. They hated each other, they blasphemed God. Floods are bound to come if they don't repent and give up their wrong-doing..."

So that there shouldn't be a flood, people must renounce their evil ways until the day arrives when "the lamb lies down with the wolf." Mother prayed humbly to her Lord seeking His mercy and forgiveness.

Ever since her stories about Noah, the ark and the flood, we imagined that, if the rain continued for forty days and forty nights, there most certainly would be a flood. We began counting the days. Every morning we got up to see how far up the water had risen. To us, Noah appeared to be an old man sawing wood and building the ark, and whenever we envisioned the dove, the olive branch and rainbow, we were reassured. But our apprehension would return and we would ask Mother, "If the rain goes on for forty days will there be a flood and will we all be drowned?" Sometimes she didn't answer, at other times she would deny it or confirm it. Father's absence increased our anxieties.

"Why is he so long in coming this time?" we asked her.

"The rain has stopped him... When the weather clears up he'll come."

"And if it doesn't clear up?"

"It will certainly clear up... This is the *lazma*.[1]

"When will it stop?"

"When the earth has drunk enough."

"When will the earth have enough?"

"I don't know!"

At times our questions would upset her. When that occurred she scolded us so we would shut up, or she might sigh, not wanting to talk anymore. In order to save kerosene she wouldn't light the lamp. The house was lit from the light of the fire on the clay hearth which filled it with smoke. The flames made the features of her young face look red and glowing. When she grew tired of talking she would silently press her lips together, twist her neck around like a branch turning towards the sun and stop throwing sticks into the fire. The flames would die down, making her cheeks look pale with black shadows dancing on them. Silence would en-

---

[1] The rain that continues, especially in the coastal area, for a week or more, uninterruptedly.

compass everything around us. The rain alone kept on playing its monotonous tune in the void.

We usually went to sleep around the hearth while she told us her stories during the first part of the night. So she was obliged to stay awake by herself listening to the barking of the dogs, the jackals, the wind and the rain. She did her best to make us stay awake, "Tonight I'll tell you about al-Shatir Hasan," she would say to entice us. We would have shut the door at nightfall and put a block of wood from a mulberry tree behind it. After we had eaten whatever we had on hand, Mother would seat herself on a mat in front of the hearth with us around her and start in on the rendition of her stories. We would promise her not to go to sleep...my sisters would try to do so... But despite the sound of the rain, the blaze of the fire, and the magical world of the tales, my sisters would start yawning, their eyelids would close, by the middle of the story we would be asleep, and she would find she was telling stories to herself. She would rouse us up, threatening to tell us nothing more after that night. We would open our eyes, take in one or two sentences, then a head would fall on a shoulder, then another and another until it was apparent again we had slept and she was telling stories to herself.

Our staying awake with her afforded her courage to face the fear stalking across the fields, roaring in the wind, coming down in the rain and darkness, creeping silently like some horror she instinctively sensed. She would rouse with a start, expecting at every moment to hear a digging in the wall or a knocking at the door.

A branch would snap, some timber would fall, a dog bark. At that, Mother, with the spontaneity of a hen that sees the shadow of a raven on the ground, would gather us in her arms as we slept.

Our house wasn't a house; it was more like a tent in a desert. The wind blew against it on all sides, packs of wolves raced towards it from every direction and thieves hovered around it. The mother and children were at the mercy of this nightmare. Screaming would be useless; there was no one to hear; fright and the wind would stifle the sound. When we slept, Mother became two frightened eyes, forever rotating around the walls, two listening ears and a bundle of frayed alert nerves. And the long night and rain.

The weather cleared at last. One evening at sunset we saw a rainbow in the sky and the rain stopped. In the morning Mother

31

went to the *mukhtar* to get a loan for some things we needed. He had intended sending a watchman to us to request her presence. She got ahead of him and went. When he saw her standing in front of the shop like a beggar he yelled at her, "You bitch! You'll not go back home today. They won't see your face. I'm going to shut you up here until your husband who fled from the grove returns."

When Mother tried to explain our situation to him, he took up his stick and came out at her. A man ran and grabbed the stick. Mother retreated as far as she could but the *mukhtar* kicked her in the stomach. She fell in the mud sobbing, imploring his aid, "Oh our *mukhtar*! Have mercy on us, our *mukhtar*!"

The stick fell. The chance blow struck her shoulder. The men ran quickly to surround the *mukhtar* and separate him from her. With some persuasion and effort, they got him back in the shop. Mother remained on the ground, under her mud, over her drizzle from an overcast sky. The wind blew her headkerchief off. With streaming eyes she bowed her head, wishing the earth would open up and swallow her. Perhaps it had pity on us her children, awaiting in the house lost among the fields... Mother got up staggering, her kerchief in her hand. She was crying and reproving God through her supplications, "God! Oh God! How often have I beseeched Thee that my head should not be uncovered and behold, have you uncovered it in order to try me? Your will be done. And as Job said, blessed be Your name and may Your eye that never sleeps watch over us and witness our low estate."

Her muddy shoes in one hand, the palm of the other resting over the place she was struck in the stomach, with thorns under her feet, wood on her back, surrounded by growling dogs...an outcast, she experienced a surge of both defeat and impotence. She sat down in the middle of the fields on a boundary line where no one passed by to recover herself and take stock of her position. There, secure from prying eyes, she could raise her head and examine what surrounded her on the outside, then examine her inward being, her past and present to convince herself that she was still a human being, still able to face people, to receive insults and bear them. She would endure much more for the sake of those left in the house lost among the fields. However, she had also to leave everything behind here; bury it in the ground as a sprout of defeat, a plant of hate, a kernel of anger until the time in the future when the little ones grew up and made a life of their own.

32

The rainbow that had adorned the horizon the previous evening was a disillusion. The earth had no need of the water but the water wanted to give it another washing. It was obliged to comply with an anonymous call to wash the earth again, to water the seeds buried in it so that the wealth stored inside them might spring forth.

Before noon clouds had completely spread the grey cover that they had expertly woven over the broken blue of the morning. The rain fell in torrents again, the bubbles of water formed and burst, drops dripped continuously from the bare branches. I was at the door watching the bubbles the rain made in the puddles of water when Mother came into view on the muddy track. She was wading through mire paying no attention to the rain as if she was oblivious to it or didn't care. Holding back her tears and hiding her pain, she was making a supreme effort to fool us. She claimed that she had fallen on the way and that the *mukhtar* hadn't been in his shop. She didn't take me in her arms...she avoided our eyes and due to her misery we avoided questioning her. She went to the other part of the house to change her wet clothes and there collapsed in a corner. My oldest sister kneeled down in front of her and they wept together silently. They cried like two grown virtuous women over the exposure and the torment of the pain and tears...

Since we had to have kerosene for the lamp and something to eat with our bread, Mother went straight away to our neighbors in their huts in these fields. She returned with her spirits renewed along with a young fair-complexioned fellow, the son of a female relative of Father's who had acted friendly towards us and had loaned us some of the things we needed. She sent her son to us. He was the first person to enter our house since Father had left on his journey.

His presence among us afforded us companionship and some reassurance. We were in greater need of him the following night. An incident took place in which no shots were fired nor screams heard. However, it increased Mother's fears.

Father's female relative came with her son. From her whispered conversation with Mother, I picked up some phrases that puzzled me for a long time. One of them was, "He rode her." She said it in a whisper.

She related in the most alarming manner how, "They assaulted," the woman in question. "Didn't she scream?" asked

33

Mother. "They gagged her mouth," replied the relative. "They drew daggers on her." Because of my conspicuous attentiveness to the conversation, Mother scolded me and asked me to go and play. I did so.

The news got around afterwards that the scoundrels had attacked the house of a woman in an adjacent field when her husband was absent. I had heard previously that thieves had broken through the wall and got into the house of that woman who had a cow. Now I was hearing that they had attacked another woman. I envisioned them coming down[2] through the roof... I began imagining that some night they would descend upon us through the roof also. I would stare at the roof listening to every movement up there. Immediately after an increase in the din on our plastered roof, my listening would intensify. It was now February and for some reason or the other the roof had become a theater for tumult within us. Mother would say, "Don't be afraid...that's cats!" In fact it was cats, sometimes we heard the meow and scratching as one dropped down onto a branch of the tree adjacent to the house or leaped from the roof to the ground. We would start up in fright, our hearts thumping. No one said that the thieves took a cow from the woman they attacked or stole any of her belongings. I couldn't find any explanations from our relative's words except that they rode on her back. In order to amuse me, Mother used to crawl on her hands and knees with me on her back... How I enjoyed that game and she too. There was nothing in it that led to fear or to get upset over. So why was this woman afraid of it? Our relatives said that they "rode her," not that they beat her... I fancied her sitting there when all of a sudden one of them dropped from the roof, ran behind her, put his hands around her neck and asked her to crawl like Mother did. Then he rode on her back like I did. So why was she so upset? Was it because he was heavy?

The first encounter I had with my young relative, I took the opportunity to say, "I know what a thief does to a woman when he attacks her house..."

Lowering his leg that I had been riding like a horse he turned to me, "You know! What does he do?"

"He rides her!"

---

[2] The word used in Arabic is *nazala; nazala ala* means attack or assault. The boy uses the form *nazala min*—meaning descent.

34

Laughing, he took my head in his hands and lifted me straight up in the air, "And who said so?"

"Your mother!"

When he told my mother what I had said she pulled my ear sharply and scolded me, threatening to beat me if I repeated those things or mentioned them in front of my sisters.

As for this woman, her husband drove her out of the house. In the summer I had the chance to play with her children. The youngest one would cry, asking for her mother. I couldn't get to the bottom of the reason for all that was going on... The one thing I regretted was that I couldn't talk about the wonderful game I was being deprived of.

One day the banished woman came to our field, sat in a row of pomegranate trees bordering it and dispatched someone to bring her children. She was disheveled and as wretched as a homeless beggar, or a madwoman who slept among the tombs... From her dusty feet in old tattered shoes, I could tell she had come a long distance and had wandered many paths.

Squatting down in front of her on the ridge, I glanced furtively at her as she sat there with her head bowed, distractedly playing with stalks of straw.

"Won't you go and fetch me a bowl of water?"

There was entreaty in her voice. She had put her hand in her breast pocket and taken out a paper wrapped around some candy and coated chick peas. She gave me a few, keeping the rest for her children. I hesitated before accepting them. If she had wanted to be friendly or kiss me, I would have fled. She had a strange appearance...not like Mother or our relative. Something that gave me the impression I should be on my guard and draw back from her. Possibly it was my feeling about her having been put out of her house. Or perhaps her sitting on the edge of the field and the look of her without a kerchief on her head both contributed to it. It seemed she met this same rejection wherever she went. It was reflected in her indifference, a kind of passive resistance of a woman stoned by everyone without having harmed anyone of them or having had any guilty share in the crime committed.

I left to fetch the water. Mother gave me a dish of food that my sister volunteered to take to her, but Mother prevented her. She wouldn't allow my sisters to go to the "tainted" woman... Mother also partook in the action of casting stones. I had never seen a con-

35

sumptive put out of the way and cut off from his acquaintances. When I encountered that situation after I was grown up, the consumptive met with sympathy and had some visitor in the isolated hut into which he had been put. But no one sympathized with this woman, no one came to see her. Her children did not come...their father would not allow them to see their mother. I went to her alone, and placed the cup of water and dish of food near her without uttering a word. The woman understood that Mother didn't want to receive her or come to her. She didn't say anything. She didn't eat. She lay down and slept...then she went on her way without us knowing when.

But on the ridge near the dish she left the paper with the candied nuts for her children.

Chapter 5

The cold rainy winter days followed one another... Sometimes the weather would clear up; a bitter cold east wind would blow, drying up the muddy roads and making it possible to walk.

On one of those cold sunny days we saw at the edge of the field a lame donkey with its front leg wrapped in a rag, winding its way toward the house followed by Father. Striking it on the rump with a twig whenever it stopped and pushing it with his other hand whenever it became stubborn, he drove it nervously toward the house with a look of defeat on his face.

We ran to him delighted to see him and the beast. How often we had dreamed we would have one of her kind. I wanted him to pick me up and put me on her back, but he didn't. Instead, I went up close to her, shaking a twig in my little hand, urging her on. My sister tried to take her by the halter. Mother ran to meet him, then, before long stopped in her tracks ashamed, confronted by the scene of having begged the Lord on the nights of rain and terror to spare her this. But as usual the Lord had forsaken her, leaving her to be afflicted like Job, whom the poor have taken as an example of patience in the face of misfortune.

There were eggs, walnuts, two hens, a turkey and some grain in the saddlebag... We were all very happy with these things except Mother who realized that her husband had again failed. According to Father the she-ass had fallen on a rock and her left foreleg was broken. That meant that, despite its being set there was no possibility of her recovering. She was as good as done for from now on.

Mother didn't question him right away about his long absence or what had happened to him on his travels. If she did so, he would revile her saying, "Make your objections to God's judgement," and hastily shut her up with a nervous anger she understood and dreaded. In the evening or the morning he would talk about the hardships he had faced, leaving to obscurity her suspicions. Her suspicions that spoke to her of his drinking, intoxication and sleeping places. We would learn, when we grew up, about these calamitous traits of a father who drank whenever he got the chance, got drunk and slept anywhere, even in the open country or the tavern, leaving himself and his belongings to the mercy of passersby, bums and drunks.

This good father who did not talk idly, did not ask for food or clothing and who traveled with death with no seeming sense of fear. He refused to accept injustice with the hotheadedness of one who did not take the outcome of his actions into account. When he was drunk he was despicable, waking up in the morning as limp as a cotton rag with a bottle of *arrack* beside him, weak, condemned by his appetite in the presence of a woman.

And whenever he went through such an experience he paid the price. He paid it with such extreme feelings of guilt that he would make those around him feel sorry for him without having asked for anyone's sympathy. His remorse was the kind that produced the same action out of which it grew. He repented, not over his feelings of responsibility, but because his remorse brought him back to the state of guilt he had been in. It tormented him, then he reveled in his torment as it made him long for the deed. He would then return to the same torment and same deed.

After a night of repentance and being wary of talking about what had happened, Father got up in the morning ready for any new enterprise. It always happened thus, making one imagine from the earnestness with which he pursued it that this enterprise would be his work forever.

It was futile for Mother to ask him how or why he had got into his former predicament. He would set out with every intention of returning as he had left, manifesting all his feelings of responsibility as a husband and father. However, with the same intent, or more properly speaking, laying it aside, he would forget it all as if he were neither husband nor father. He would live anywhere and everywhere, drink and sleep as if he were in his own home or just as if he were homeless, oblivious the whole time he was away of what had taken place before his absence. In some way or the other he would lose his memory, living with no sense of his responsibility just as he had previously lived with a sense of responsibility.

In the morning, with the signs of remorse still on his countenance, he turned his attention to cultivating the field watered by the rain so as to plant some green vegetables. My sisters and I went to have a look at the she-ass while she was eating. Her abdomen was somewhat swollen, giving rise to hope within Mother's breast that we would get a little donkey if we took good care of her.

However, the problem of fodder stood between us and that. The possibility of Father wanting to set out again made it such a weighty issue that Mother gave in to his desire to sell the donkey shortly after that.

He traded it for a goat and some silver coins. When they came one afternoon to take it away, our hearts were touched by grief as if she had been one of us. Before they took her out of the house Mother gave her a drink saying, "Go blessed one." We tied the goat up to the same trough. She was so thin and her ribs stuck out so prominently like the rib cages of the Indian fakirs, that Mother had misgivings about her withstanding the remainder of the cold winter and living until summer. Her presence became an added nutritional burden because she had to be fed, even in the spring, dry fodder that was difficult to get hold of.

As for the few silver coins, Father launched a new enterprise with them: work that would get him nowhere, but that he or the likes of him expected to get something from. The first few days of his return had scarcely gone by when his zeal for working the field flagged and symptoms of wanting to leave became evident. He announced that he was going to work as a shoemaker in the villages he had gone to as a peddler and returned from a failure. Mother now had to humbly beseech the Lord to grant him success, we had to crawl back into our snail shell of fearful apprehension; the darkness, the wind, the desolate field and all the ghosts of the long nights had to give up tormenting us; the thieves had to leave off raiding houses in the neighboring fields; and the *mukhtar* had to forget we were there in his field with his debt hanging like a yoke around our necks and not send his watchman to summon Mother as had happened before. However, that was absurd. Knowing it was inconceivable, Mother raised objections and wept, but her objections and tears did nothing for her.

Father bought shoemaker's tools and set out carrying them in a bag on his back. The direction he took would occupy our attention for a long time. Through the trees and over the boundary line we would see his face as he came towards the house. This alone would dissipate the gloom settling down upon us as we followed his disappearing back that the borderline ridges presently screened from our view.

The days rolled on with Father absent. Mother fancied he had run out on us; that he had moved to some faraway place leaving us

39

behind in the middle of a wasteland of fields; that he had abandoned us because he could do nothing for us. We were prisoners in a certain way. The *mukhtar's* debt was the bond, the mud hut the prison, and the silk harvest when we would raise the worms wouldn't come for months. Even if a miracle occurred and there was an outstanding harvest, it would not pay off the debt. Part of it would remain, we would be compelled to get a loan with interest. The debt would accumulate during the next winter leaving us again anticipating the silk harvest. A harvest that might be successful or unsuccessful as raising silkworms required a great deal of skill and luck. This is what had cheated Mother as a child, a young girl and a wife.

We, then, were prisoners. Not because that idea got stuck in Mother's mind and we learned from her, but because we actually were. After Father's departure we were placed under surveillance. The *mukhtar's* steward began roaming around our field like an inspector and the *mukhtar* would send for Mother to make sure we were still there. In order to justify the summons, he commissioned her to help his wife with the house work as long as the forced labor in the fields was not required in the winter.

The paranoic was one-eyed, an evil one-eyed man, stupid enough to show his hand. That showed Mother that she ought to flee, but how could she flee and to where?

"Has you husband fled?" He asked menacingly.

"He hasn't run off, *mukhtar*. He went to seek his living."

"Liar...your husband fled to eat up my money... You sons of bitches! I felt sorry for you and handed over the field and house. I opened up an account for you in the shop and in a few months your husband runs away leaving you! What can I do with you? Who is going to defray the debt? And what about the silk harvest? Listen! Do you know who I am? I am al-Lowshiya[1]... I can hold you in custody in this house. I can hang you on a mulberry tree like a stray dog...and if need be I'll sell your children..."

"What wrong have my children done, *mukhtar*? Don't revile me unjustly... We are good people; we aren't taking what belongs to you."

"No one can take what belongs to me..."

---

[1] The administrative office of the town where the governor of the district was located, also the policemen.

40

"Even if we could we wouldn't do so... My husband is a respectable man and I am a chaste woman."

"Your husband is a son of a bitch and you are a cheat...you are waiting for the summer to get away. I know your kind. I would imprison you with your children from now on but your duty is to work in the grove, to dig around the mulberry trees and produce the silk, so for that reason I'll leave you in your house...stay in it. But don't ask for a grain of salt or a drop of kerosene..."

"How are we going to live? The children are hungry, Mr. Elias."

"Go and bury yourselves," he roared, "you and your children. Die...and your runaway husband will come back... I know how I'll get him back... Now get into the house...don't parade yourself in front of the shop... I don't like looking at that expression on your face."

The sharecroppers, hearing about Mother's situation felt sorry for her but did not interfere. The *mukhtar's* meanness and cruelty were well- known and they were hirelings just like Father. Anyone of them was liable to be forced to flee or be imprisoned if things got too bad and it became an issue. When Mother heard about these problems she would say, "What a disaster, how will he ever face the Lord?" Perhaps others said the same and in the *mukhtar's* presence they would loudly repeat the saying: "Don't try to frighten me...it is a matter between him and me and we understand each other... I'll face him with the *zaitat*[2] and the priest's blessing."

The *mukhtar's* good wife was persecuted as much as the sharecroppers, so Mother found solace in her company. She helped her to bear her neglect and called her "mistress," but her mistress could not give her anything. On her way home from the *mukhtar's* house in the evening, Mother was obliged to pass by the shop to reassure the *mukhtar* that she hadn't stolen anything from the house.

Mother despaired of escaping before even thinking about it, just as she despaired of us ever being able to pay off the debt at harvest time or of the mercy of the severe winter that year or of Father's return. She said her heart told her that some evil was going to befall us. She may have fancied that father had run off leaving us as pawns or that he had been robbed and killed. On that basis we

---

[2] The oil used in the church for blessing people.

41

would be left orphans and stranded. Her staring at the path Father would return by became a morbid preoccupation, her feelings of longing for her lost sister became those of a person in crisis and, in turning her thoughts to our relatives in Latakiya she became like a forlorn alien turning to her family and her faraway country.

She talked increasingly of her sister during the winter nights. She drew us a picture of her with every conceivable word. Her talk about her brother Rizk was accompanied by copious tears and a remonstrance to Azrael, the angel of death. Then she would praise God, asking His forgiveness, and blame death in the person of Azrael who had taken her brother with no pity for her. The misfortune of this loss was doubled by Father's absence and the *mukhtar*'s baseness.

"If your uncle were alive he would come to us; if Rizk were at the other end of the world and heard that we were at the mercy of this tyrant, he would drop everything and come. He would know how to teach him a lesson. He would say to me, 'Go to the *mukhtar*'s shop and don't tell him I'm here... I'll come after you and make out I don't know you...stand in front of the shop and swear back at him. If he raises his hand he will have to reckon with me.'"

Our eyes would shine with a desire to witness such a scene. We had never seen the *mukhtar*. He was an evil, one-eyed man, as Mother described him. His other eye was made of glass. He was so terrifying he appeared to us in our dreams and if we had ever heard his voice we would have fled from him and cried. In contrast, it was our uncle whom we had never seen, our brown-skinned, cheerful, strong uncle that we loved with all our hearts. One day my oldest sister asked me as she fondled my hair: "You, when you grow up, will you be like him?"

"Like Rizk?" replied Mother, looking at me regretfully but hopefully. "I wish it could be so."

Then kindly rectifying it, she added, "Who knows...you look like him at any rate...but you, my little fellow, you are very skinny and we haven't any nourishing food to make you grow strong..."

My second sister got up and brought half a loaf, "I'll give him my share," she said.

No one objected, so I ate the half loaf hoping it would nourish me and make me strong like uncle who alone, if he were here, would protect us from the *mukhtar*.

42

Meanwhile, until I grew up and became like him, until we rejoiced at Father's return, until summer arrived bringing out the mulberry leaves and we raised the silkworms and reaped the silk harvest to pay off our debt and then set out again on our travels, we had to get through the rest of the winter days. Until then our young imaginations would sketch an image of evil and fear in the person of the *mukhtar*, and an image of goodness and safety in the person of our uncle. Until then we had to live on bread alone, bread made from *durra* and barley and baked on the *saj*[3] by Mother. When it became dry she sprinkled it with water to soften it so we were able to chew it.

In the late afternoon she used to sit on a mat in front of the door, her tongue wagging and her eye on the road. She would sit there until nightfall and hope was lost. In the darkness before lighting the candle and locking the door she sang her customary folk song.

> Evening has come and the heart turns to thoughts
> of you.
> The sun has set but none of you has returned.
> Where is the messenger of good tidings so I can
> ask him about you?
> Our home town is far away and I have no news of
> you.

Her voice would spread through the silence across the fields, soft, fine, tinged with sadness and pain. We would raise our heads to see if she were crying. The darkness shielded her from meeting our eyes until hope aroused within her or she contrived it for our sakes by singing:

> You who are going to Aleppo, my love went with
> you.
> You who are bearing grapes, and on top of the
> grapes, apples.
> Each has turned to his beloved, as for me my
> beloved has gone.
> Oh for a breath of wind, to bring my beloved back
> to me.

---

[3] A flat piece of tin on which flat loaves were baked over an open fire.

The wind never brought back Mother's loved one in response to her singing. Night would fall making us retreat inside and lock the door by sliding the bolt and putting some stones behind it. Then we would gather in the inner part of the house, light the firewood we had gathered during the day while Mother partitioned out morsels of bread and morsels of hope. That hope that set with the coming of night to return and rise with the morning star, with unflagging anticipation at the path along which Father would appear.

"Tomorrow," she would tell us every day, "your father will return and won't go away anymore. Spring will come, the leaves will come out and clothe the mulberry trees in green, we'll raise the silkworms and God will bless us with silk at harvest time. God is merciful, children. He never forsakes His own. We shall sell the cocoons, pay off the *mukhtar*'s debt and leave. We'll go back to your uncle's in Latakiya and live in a house built of stone where there will be people around us and you will all go to school."

One day she announced with joy that the *murbaa'niya*[4] was over and we were entering the *saad*. [5] She said that *al-saad* was in four parts: it began with "Saad of the slaughter" and ended with "Saad the hidden." She told us stories about it that we had heard before and remembered. We had committed them to memory because they were the calendar for reckoning the connection between the winter, the cold, and the coming harvest. In her stories she mentioned that "Saad of the slaughter" was called that because Saad was a shepherd who had been pasturing his flock on a very cold day. While he was in the wilderness, it snowed, cutting off his return home. His old mother, fearing for his safety, said, "If he slaughters he'll be safe, and if he doesn't slaughter he'll die of cold." Saad was a clever young fellow. He slew a camel and crawled inside it to warm himself, thus escaping from death. After this Saad, so Mother said, came "Saad the swallower." The amount of rain may have decreased, and the earth, being in need of water, would gulp down the rain when it came down in torrents...

---

[4] The hardest part of winter: the forty days from December 10 to January 20.

[5] *Al-saad* (good fortune or lucky star)—twelve and a half days.

Then it would be "Saad al-Saud," the lucky one, when the sap ran through the limbs, the buds sprouted on the branches, the leaves came out on the trees, and the earth was clothed in green. Lastly, at the beginning of spring would be the time of "Saad the hidden" when the young girls strutted about because the time of the cold had gone by...

Thus were the days of *khamasiniya*[6] divided, that followed the *marbaa'niya*. We began counting them along with her, day by day. Whenever it got colder we would ask, "Is Saad slaughtering today, Mama?"

"Perhaps...if this is the coldest day of the winter."

"But it is the coldest day...look...we are almost frozen stiff..."

"So he'll slaughter today and tomorrow it will be warmer..."

Saad slaughtered quite late that year. It was extremely cold and the cold continued into "Saad the swallower." When Saad al-Saud came around, we rushed into the field to see how the sap was running through the trees. In fact the branches had a slight translucent redness and were budded out. Upon the *mukhtar*'s request, we started digging rings around the roots so they would catch the rain that comes with the beginning of spring. And at the beginning of spring something happened in the family that caused us distress and tears.

---

[6] The fifty days between Whitsuntide and Easter.

Chapter 6

The *mukhtar* refused to give us any amount of the mixture of *durra* and barley from which to make the coarse dull grey loaves. By now Mother had sold every little bit of jewelry or trinket she owned in order to feed us. She had pawned some of the pots and pans so we had nothing left to sell or pawn. The *mukhtar* had finally closed his ledger in her face and her entreaties and explanations brought no results.

In all probability she secretly begged a handful of flour. We had seen her going across to a neighbor's house and returning with a small bundle tied up in the hem of her dress. We ran to meet her at the edge of the field, returned with her to the house, gathered around her, suffering the pangs of hunger, while she proceeded to make this handful of flour into dough, bake it, then portion it out to us.

In the bitter cold of the morning the *mukhtar*'s steward came, asking for her by orders from "the mistress." She left without raising objections, leaving us awaiting her return in restless hope. We told ourselves that "the mistress" might have persuaded her husband, the *mukhtar*, to give us flour until harvest time. But we feared that the *mukhtar* would raise objections and drive Mother away like he always did. Calamities had become a routine possibility: our absent father was a secret affliction, our wished-for uncle had gone on a journey from which he would not return.

My oldest sister was old only because of the difference between our ages. She was a child of ten years, but it was her destiny to mother us in the absence of Mother. At least those were my feelings, which my two other sisters shared. We would gather around her, cling to her and obey her because until the absent one returned, she was the person in whom we found protection from danger, reassurance for our fears and the answers to any question that came to our minds.

That day our dependence on her unconsciously increased. We didn't contradict her once. When she refused to give her sister a piece of bread before mealtime, the latter didn't stubbornly insist. We had come to understand the necessity of our mealtime being at noon, not before. If it were not at noon, it meant that we had no bread and must not persist in asking for it.

In order to keep us from thinking of Mother and her return, she took us out to the field, assigning a mulberry tree for each one to dig

46

a small trench around that would catch the rain water. She excused me from the work, but I insisted on doing the same as they did. In fact, hankering to assert myself, I started in digging with obstinant persistence. Having achieved very little, I put forth every effort. Then my zeal waned, I sat down on the ground, leaned against a mulberry trunk and slept.

I woke up inside the house, lying on the mat. The door was closed and there was no one near me. I reckoned that Mother, having returned, was with my sisters in the field, so when I opened the door and did not find her, I cried. Something may have given me a shock or my failure in digging and going to sleep may have embarrassed me. I could also have been subconsciously offended because I had not found anyone near me. Consequently, when I behaved so stupidly I grew more ashamed of myself and cried all the harder. My oldest sister's efforts to calm me succeeded only after great difficulty.

When we asked her if we could eat, she went to see where the shadow of the house lay just like Mother did. She asked us to wait until it reached the fixed mark so we went out to watch the shadow of the house with longing eyes and empty stomachs. Our sister was most likely as impatient as the rest of us, but she had taken on the role of the mother and all its duties. She refused to feed us before the shadow reached the mark. Then pity for us made her indulgent. After sprinkling the bread with water and covering it until it was soft, she divided the loaf into quarters and we ate.

Afterwards we sang, we danced, we played, we went out to sit on the bench built onto the side of the house looking in the direction Mother customarily returned from... The sun's rays weakened, it declined and set. If she had been with us she would have sung her folk song, "Evening has come and the heart turns to thoughts of you." We had learned it by heart. We may all have had the idea of singing it, but no one sang. Feeling the need to stick together, we had sat down side by side, tight together as if we were afraid of being snatched away in the darkness or that by clinging together we would draw courage and warmth from the mass of little bodies, with their hearts throbbing with grief at the absence of parents, and fright at the darkness of night creeping up to inundate them.

A gust of wind in the tree, an animal moving in the undergrowth, a commotion or sound nearby. When something like that happened it was like a needle piercing the fragile outer skin of our endurance, making our hearts thump in alarm. My youngest sister cried and I may have cried too. We ran together in terror inside the house. We locked the door and in the darkness of the locked house we all wept together. Our sister tried to quiet us down but for some reason she broke into tears with us as she searched in the darkness for a match to light the lamp.

Our weeping grieved our mother upon her return. She told us that we were no longer little and must not be afraid, that the neighbor's children, the same age as we, went out at night to the *mukhtar*'s shop. No one was going to assault little ones. Thieves didn't kill them, in fact they sometimes gave them things to eat. Thieves stole, and what did children have for them to steal?

Her tender encouraging words made us ashamed. Our thoughts turned to the neighbor children who were not afraid to go out at night. My sister said they did that because they had a dog to accompany them. Mother said we could have a dog, too, after the silk harvest when we would have food for it. But we pleaded with her to get us a puppy saying we'd give him part of our food. After a little reflection, she agreed to get us a puppy when the neighbor's dog whelped.

That evening she treated us more gently than usual. She did her best to appear calm and content in front of us. She gazed lovingly at our oldest sister for a long time, stroked her hair, listened to us as we tried to outdo each other telling her about our work in the field and how we had dug those trenches around the mulberry trees. When Sister said that I had dug a whole trench, I didn't say anything about this lie that pleased me and for which I received a kiss and a seat in my mother's lap. I made up my mind to work harder the next day. However, we didn't work in the field in the morning because a visit from the *mukhtar*'s steward in the forenoon terrified us even before we realized what lay behind it.

Mother had hidden from us what had happened to her in the *mukhtar*'s house. After many years she would relate it with the selfsame, sad feelings. However, that evening she concealed it, bearing her agony and grief alone. She feigned sleep until we slept, then kept her vigil, recalling the sight of the *mukhtar*'s evil face as he ordered her to bring our eldest sister to be a servant in his house.

She didn't fail to understand that the *mukhtar* wanted Sister as a servant and a hostage; that the little child who dreamed of going to school must go live far from us, a stranger, wretched in the service of a man who knew no mercy; that she would remain a prisoner prevented from seeing her brother and sisters until the debt was paid enabling us to leave the cursed field and the town that never showed us a smiling face. Mother had unhesitatingly refused the *mukhtar*'s order.

"My daughter is young. She isn't suitable to work for people," she boldly exclaimed to his face.

"We aren't like other people...the *mukhtar* is different from other people."

"We respect the *mukhtar* but my daughter is young."

"You bitch...are you barking in my face? I told you to fetch your daughter to work for us and you refuse? I'll break that haughty nose. I'll bring you and your children with you here. You'll all work for us..."

"We are working in the field, we don't work in the houses..."

"You eat up my money and run away...Where has your damn husband gone? Just you wait... I'll teach you how to answer."

Mother wasn't frightened. She said she wasn't afraid. She said that the *mukhtar* had come out of the shop, beat her, and taking hold of her had pulled her into the cattle shed where he locked the door on her. She screamed, beating her fist on her chest. When those who heard her came running trying to rescue, her he threatened to shoot them, declaring he was going to hand her over to the authorities.

It was quite possible for the *mukhtar* to accuse her of theft, or to inflict any sort of punishment on her. He wasn't merely a *mukhtar*, he was a landowner also. He was the government, as he had declared. What could this young mother do against the government but knock on the door from the inside, call for help, wail, then fall at the *mukhtar*'s feet begging to be released to return to us. That was all that remained for her to do. She did not arrive at that point for nothing.

A prison inmate eats but she didn't eat; a prisoner drinks but she didn't drink. What did hunger or thirst matter to her? She had no appetite for food or thirst for water. She was afraid for us, and as evening drew on, her fears increased. So when the sun went down she lost control of herself and started pounding on the wooden door with her fists and screaming in tears. She could have died or gone mad imagining us in that lonely mud house as little bits of soft human flesh, young birds on the edge of the nest in a white poplar tree cheeping for their mother who had gone to bring them some seeds. She knew we weren't cheeping but crying. She could envision us crying in the dark room, in the dark field in an even darker world. She could see nothing but darkness as she gave up on everything. Concern means blame. Whom could she blame? Whom did she have? Who remained? Her brother? Her sister? Her husband? Those over there in our distant city for whom "The sun has set and we have no news of them." No news will come from them, nor will they hear her in the prison. Don't call for anyone.

"Ah, Son," she told me after I had grown up, "I never thought that anyone would hear me, neither in heaven nor on earth. I didn't cry for anyone in heaven or earth. I cried for all of you, and for you. In my mind I heard you screaming, 'Mama!' And I screamed inside myself, 'Oh my darling!' Then I tried to force the door, to smash it, to tear it off. When I found it too much for me, I pounded on it with the palms of my hands, with my fists, with my head too... Don't feel bad son. I'm not telling you this to upset you nor to let you know how much I suffered because of that love, nor just for your sake to make you feel sorry for me. I'm just telling so you will know it, remember it, then forget it after you remember it."

"Good, Mother. I have remembered it and forgotten it and I shall go on remembering it and forgetting it, remembering and forgetting. I have lived it, still am, and shall go on living it forever."

"No, son, you never lived it. You aren't a mother. You will never have a mother's heart. I don't wish it. You are a man so you must have a man's heart, a heart like your uncle whom you never saw.

"It was Rizk alone," she went on, "upon whom I called in my imprisonment in the *mukhtar*'s house. I knew he was dead and couldn't answer but in his death he was closer to me than the living... May you live as long, my dear, as he did and a hundred years more.

"I couldn't imagine you would spend the night in that hut without me," she said. "You would go out, overwhelmed by fear for yourselves and me, wandering through the field and the paths of the neighboring fields, weeping and calling for me. You might get lost or fall into a ditch or watercourse or be eaten by some wild beast.

"Oh that heart of a mother! Oh, the heart of the poor mother bird when she sees danger lurking around her chicks whose wings have not grown and who have never left the nest. I have seen her in our field. I was like her in my struggle to feed you, in my effort to make your feathers grow and in my fear for you before those feathers sprouted and afterwards.

"I started screaming, crying and pounding the door until it was opened. I found myself in the arms of the *mukhtar*'s wife who was also weeping. She was a mother too. She had children. She understood a mother's heart. Having defied her husband, she let me out telling me, 'Go to your children, you poor thing, but in the morning the *mukhtar* will send someone to fetch you and he won't give you anything to eat if your daughter doesn't come to our house... I don't want her to come to our house. Other sharecroppers are willing to have their daughters work for us. It is better than working in the field. They earn money for it. But the *mukhtar* wants your daughter most probably to be sure that you won't take your children and run away just like your husband did.'

"She took me a distance from the shop and then said, 'I would like to give you something for the little ones but I don't dare. You poor woman, you haven't eaten since the morning. Come and I'll give you a little something to eat.' I didn't eat, son, I only drank and thanked her."

The *mukhtar*'s wife persuaded Mother to send our sister to her. She may have promised the *mukhtar* that she would convince her, and Mother's release from the cattle shed depended on an agreement she had made with him. Besides, the shed could not be used as a prison since the cows had to be kept in there at night.

The *mukhtar*'s wife, who had gained Mother's confidence, advised her to accept the idea of our sister working in her house, assuring Mother that she would treat her as her own daughter and that no harm would come to her. She would not allow anyone to beat her. She would live inside the house with her and whenever that could not be guaranteed and our sister became upset, she, the *mukhtar*'s wife, would contrive to smuggle her back to us. The wages for her services would induce the *mukhtar* to give us food to eat until harvest time and her wages would also reduce our debt enabling us to leave if we wished.

It was difficult for Mother to give her consent. She had worked as a servant in people's houses. But she had been an orphan and it had been at the time of the *Safar Barr*, when children didn't attend school. Likewise, it was equally difficult for Mother to see us hungry. The heart suffers hellfire and more when it is obliged to sacrifice one part of it for another part. It is a heart and the heart cannot be partitioned off. Mother was given the task of dividing her heart, of surrendering a living piece of it to torment in order to avert suffering from the other living piece of it.

The night she gave up our sister she was as wretched as if she were damned. Mother didn't wash Sister's feet like Christ did his disciples. She knew she was going to be parted from her, but she didn't wash her feet; she gently stroked her forehead, nothing more. And she didn't kiss her as Judas Iscariot had done. Our mother wasn't a Judas. However, she dreaded her tears would betray her. As a mother she felt within herself that she was betraying her child's trust in her. But it was fate that was the traitor. Taking the sin upon herself in its place, she did not kiss Sister. She only patted her head and went to bed early, pretending to be asleep until we slept. She spent the night awake in penitence for a sin that circumstances, not she, had committed. She took the place of those circumstances in bearing the burden of the sin.

If the night would only tarry, the morning would hesitate to appear. If there were no night or morning. If only a miracle would happen between night and morning... If the absent one returned and the bearer of good tidings whom she asked for in her song passed by, bringing her news of those there in that distant city. So far away that neither she nor we knew the distance separating us from it, although in fact it was quite near us. If the wolf, in answer to divine decree, changed into a lamb and the *mukhtar* gave up his determination to take the child as a servant and pawn. If...if...what a string of delusive wishes; what a spider's web spun by mothers' hearts. You, yourself, in a web of misery and reality, are the cord that will be fastened around the neck of the son sentenced to defeat, the daughter sentenced to separation from her mother, her brother and sister and her childhood to go live without a mother, brother, sisters and a childhood.

My mother didn't sell my sister for thirty pieces of silver. However, she got in exchange for her what was more precious to us than silver. She got barley and *durra*. We were hungry. Sister was the ransom for hunger. The mother had resigned herself to let the child go to work in the *mukhtar*'s house. Darkness veiled the faces of the seller and the sold, the faces of the mother and the child. The night concealed within itself the sea of grief with its debris. It was merciful to all of us. The child slept while the mother remained sleepless thinking of how she was going to face her daughter in the morning, of what words she would use to tell her, "Go, my little one, work so we can eat our bread from your services."

The absent one did not return: the bearer of good tidings did not knock on the door; the wolf did not change into a lamb; only the morning, unconcerned about anyone bringing happiness or misery, came at last.

Little one, child, may your eyelids be heavy with sleep in the morning, invite sleep in the morning. From this day forward you will have no more childhood, you won't be able to listen to the sto-

ries mothers tell. You will be awakened with the dawn by some-
one's feet kicking you. In the evening before you are allowed to go
lie on your worn-out mattress you will be overcome by sleep as you
stand against the wall awaiting your master's commands.
Weariness having made you succumb to sleep, you may collapse in a
corner abandoning yourself to sweet slumber that a commanding
voice or a smart slap will presently disrupt. Sleep, little one, your
mother is keeping vigil. It has been decreed from time immemorial
and forever that children should sleep and mothers keep watch.
You are as carefree as it is possible for the poor and children to be.
You are confident that tomorrow will be the same as yesterday,
that you will play in the house with your brother and sisters, sit up
at night with your mother around the fire and go to sleep in your
same bed.

Mother didn't wake her up early. She left her sleeping until
the steward arrived demanding that the mother take her daughter
to the *mukhtar*. It was at that moment that Mother cried. She told
us she cried so much that the hardhearted steward turned away so
as not to see her tears. He went out claiming he was going to take a
turn around the field. After drying her eyes, Mother awakened us
one by one. She told us she was going to take sister with her to the
mukhtar's house because the mistress wanted to give her clothes
and sweets... Calling her to hurry to get dressed without saying
anything that would reveal her suppressed sorrow or unleash her
held-back tears, she set off with sister behind the steward. We
stood, my two remaining sisters and I, gazing at them, from our
place on the outside bench, until the paths, trees, and ridges dividing the fields hid them from our eyes.

Mother returned alone at noon, broken and forlorn. She told us
that sister had stayed at the *mukhtar*'s to play with his children
and that she would come home the next day... She then hurried us
outside into the field asking to be left alone until she rested and
her headache let up, after which time she would join us.

Going into the field in obedience to her request, we tried digging around the trees without working up any enthusiasm. We tried
playing but had no energy or zeal for it. Something was missing.
We were the young ones, our sister was the older one, our leader.
Our sense of the empty place among us filled us with gloomy list-
lessness. Perhaps because the field was dark and dull that day, we
banded together and stayed under a nearby tree wrapped up in our
melancholy and lassitude.

I went back to the house in violation of Mother's wishes. It was my longing for my sister and my searching for her warmth and affection that influenced me to do it. That day we were in need of Mother, to be near her, to seek shelter, like chicks, under her wings.

Mother was crying, singing and crying. That day I heard songs I would often hear after that, songs that would be farewell songs for my sisters who would leave one after the other on their lonely paths of separation to service in the houses of the rich.

The singer was speaking as the sister was saying: "Mother, oh Mother, the departure time has arrived. I bade you farewell, Mother, and the time will be long."

What did the little ones know about the length of time? We believed that our sister would return the following day. But it was a distant tomorrow, just like Father's return and seeing our relatives and our departure from the accursed town and the bleak field.

Twenty years or more would have gone by when, one morning, Mother and I saw as we were walking through one of the wealthy quarters of Beirut, a *fellah* from the Latakiya countryside giving up his young daughter as a servant in one of those houses. He was on the point of leaving her as she clung to him in tears yelling, "I don't want to stay here, I don't want... Take me with you. I'm kissing your hand. Take me, Father, take me with you."

Mother stopped in her tracks, faced with this scene. It was with great difficulty that she resumed her walking in silence, with her head dejectedly bowed... When I asked her "What's the matter, Mother?" she sighed, shaking her head.

"Nothing son," she said, masking the former grief in her breast whose wounds had been laid bare. "I don't know the *fellah* or his daughter, but that sight saddened me... Your oldest sister cried like that when I left her as a child to work in the *mukhtar*'s house. She clung to my dress just like this child to her father's trousers. She too yelled, 'I don't want to stay here. Take me with you, Mother. I'm kissing your hand. Take me with you!'"

Mother was silent for some steps then went on, "Oh, what a pity, son, I didn't take her as she begged... Like this *fellah* I couldn't take her as she asked..."

Bowing her head in silence, she did not speak the rest of the way.

Chapter 7

Saad al-Saud arrived, sending the sap through the trees... The mulberry trees budded and put forth leaves. The field was clothed in green. The grass sprouted on the boundary lines and, under the trees, the red lilies grew up tall between the beans that Mother had planted with the help of our relative and her son.

In the morning, the dew wet our bare feet as we ran through the trees chasing butterflies or picking lilies. Mother had sent us to gather narcissus that grew on the borderline ridges. We would pick bunches which she made into a large bouquet to take to the *mukhtar*'s wife when she went to see our sister and to fetch some of the necessities from the shop.

In the open country, that species of white flower she used to call the "spring flower" grew there as well. And in a damp area beside the house, red, white and wine-colored carnations bloomed. Mother said that the carnation was the most beautiful of the spring flowers; indeed it was the essence of spring. She sang:

> Freely, freely given,
> Flower of carnation
> You are our spring.

At this time Mother was much more serene and more inclined toward optimism. Father had come home one day with a canvas bag on his back, containing his tools, and a basket of eggs hanging over his arms. He had also collected some grain, but Mother, who was happy at his safe return, was not long in becoming alarmed at his failure after this long absence.

As usual, following his return, he appeared to be broken and repentant, cursing the circumstances that had victimized him and the sickness that had disabled him. Mother said nothing. She knew there was no use talking, but that in his irresponsibility and drunkenness he forgot that he had a wife and children.

What hurt Mother more was his lack of decency even in showing sorrow at Sister's absence and her becoming a servant in the *mukhtar*'s house. Although Mother was incapable of hatred and found it advisable, from a woman's standpoint, to be obedient and patient in front of her husband, she could not, despite her goodness, love him outside of her wifely duties. The greatest achievement of true love is that it be a genuine interaction with the person, that it does not bow to the views of tradition and duty, indeed it cannot do so.

She had come to understand at an early age that manhood lay more in a man's good qualities than in the size of a man's body or wealth. I heard Mother scolding Father when she was fed up with him; I saw her pushing his hand away from her saying, "If you were a father like other fathers we wouldn't have to put up with the *mukhtar*'s abuse nor would you be content to have your daughter working as a servant for people. I assumed that you would be angry and wouldn't sleep before going to bring her back."

Not only did he fail to get her, he did not even go to see her. It was neither a matter of urgency nor desire with him. My sisters' work as a servant for others was a door that had been opened for him and remained open.

True to pattern, when he returned after a long absence his heart throbbing with remorse, he arose early in the morning to go to work in the field. At noon he said that the silk harvest[1] alone would ensure our liberation and departure and that he would never have gone away if there had been work for him to do. Summer had now arrived so he would work in the field day and night, and if we would help him everything would be just fine. We would pay off the *mukhtar*'s debt and have enough left over to enable us to move away from here.

The news of Father's return must have reached the *mukhtar* for he sent his steward to summon him. Mother advised him to go, not to fly off the handle nor be rude to him lest he get angry and ruin the harvest for us. Slinging his jacket over his shoulder, Father left with the steward, quite unconcerned. His irresponsibility had now been transformed into belligerency, both of them welling up from the same pit: a lack of concern for the outcome.

When Father returned, he told us we were to raise two boxes of silkworm eggs, and that he had come to an agreement with the *mukhtar* about everything. The reality, according to what the steward said, was that the understanding was a necessity on the *mukhtar*'s part: Father had threatened to clear out without paying

---

[1] Cocoons of silkworms. The harvest alluded to here is the raising of these worms.

him one *dirham* of the debt. Addressing him in a loud voice and pounding with his fist on the wooden door of the shop with fiery impatience, he had shouted, "You have reviled me and my family, you infidel, and accused me of running away... I don't run away secretly; I leave openly. I'll go where your hand can't reach me..."

Confronted by Father's nerve, the *mukhtar* adopted a more flexible manner. Our relative said he did so out of fear, but Mother said that the *mukhtar*'s fears were for the harvest and the debt. He wasn't afraid of us leaving because we wouldn't do so as long as our daughter was his hostage.

At any rate, Father obtained two boxes of eggs. The boxes were shaped like the boxes of cheese with the trade mark *La Vache qui Rit*, imported from Europe and guarded by the *mukhtar* with the utmost care. Contrary to all the landowners, the *mukhtar* did not hand over the boxes of eggs to the sharecroppers before incubating them in a small heated room in his house prepared for this purpose. The quality of the silkworms depended upon the quality of the incubation. And the cocoons and harvest depended upon this. The village lived the whole year on this harvest. Its lands and fields were set aside for mulberry trees, not for planting wheat or fruit. The *mukhtar* would distribute the worm eggs according to the number of these trees each *fellah* had in his field. If he had too many he would sell to whomever had need, or if he lacked he would steal from his neighbor's field. To decrease the stealing and the quarrels, the landowners would distribute the eggs in amounts estimated by their stewards. Some of the sharecroppers would be swindled by chance or on purpose according to the steward's accuracy or the bribe paid or the promise of one at least.

April had made a showing in the leaves of the watered and cultivated mulberry groves. The desolate wilderness was transformed into a flourishing place of habitation. The forests of bare brown branches, extending as far as the eye could see, became forests of triumphant lead-colored green with a blue sheen, glittering under the rays of the morning sun with beads of dew.

Putting a basket into each of our hands, Mother dispatched us to gather cow dung from the fields and the roads. During the winter we had gathered dung to make *julla*[2] used as fuel. Now we were

---

[2] Dry dung.

assigned to gather it from the fields to make *karany*[3] on which the silkworms are placed after they hatch. Because of great demand, it had become precious, so Mother would set out with us early, covering long distances to obtain it. We would wait behind the cows as they pastured until they dropped dung, then hurriedly scoop up the dung with our hands. In the house Mother would set about with the skill handed down to her, forming the flat cakes of cow dung into bigger rounds, the size of confectioner's trays. She would leave them sitting on smooth, fine earth until they were sufficiently dry to move into the house.

To add to the long, thin pole of white poplar and reed mats left to us by the former sharecroppers, we went with our parents to cut down poplars at the far end of the field and to gather reeds from the edges of nearby swamps. In this flood of activity and amusement, we forgot our fears and thoughts about our sister in the *mukhtar*'s house. Every evening Mother would pray with the two boxes of eggs on the shelf in front of her in the place of icons, ending her prayer with a petition we would repeat after her: that God would bless the eggs that were in them and make them healthy silkworms.

During those days Father showed himself to be upright, diligent and sensible. He only left at night. Night after night he would be absent, returning in the middle of it when we had succumbed to sleep after the day's hard work. He had carefully dug his private "tunnels" through which he would crawl to houses in the neighboring fields to drink and to make love. It became public knowledge afterwards that a widow woman in the neighborhood was his mistress and that he had fought with a fellow villager over her. They came to blows one night in the field and the wounds on his face were a result of that, not from the fall he claimed he had had in the ditch at one of the boundary lines.

I imagine that Mother knew what was going on and quarreled with him over it, but was forbearing so that he would not go off at the peak of the harvest when we were most in need of him. The *mukhtar*, having heard of the affair, sent his steward for Father, who refused to go see him. "The *mukhtar* has no business with me until harvest time," he said to the steward. "If he refuses to give us what we need to keep us going, I'll sell the whole harvest on the

---

[3] The singular is karna. It is shaped in the form of a tray with a brim.

first night we have no light. And if you or he or any of his crowd raises a hand against me, I'll either kill him or cut down the mulberry trees and ruin him." The *mukhtar*, being thoroughly acquainted with Father's hotheadedness, impetuosity, irascibility and indifference to outcomes, turned a deaf ear to his refusal and resigned himself. He left him to his own devices in the matter of women, especially since he, the *mukhtar*, was neither enamored of them nor of drinking. The harvest was more important to him than the bosom of that beautiful widow over whom men fought, as Mother described her to us later.

In the middle of April, Father prayed. It was at sunset that we saw his stance in front of the two boxes of eggs. Mother stood behind him with us standing reverently around her just like the saints she had so often told us about, while he closed his eyes muttering under his breath. He prayed silently in contrast to Mother who prayed aloud. Most likely he was not repeating the same prayer, and his mutterings being words he had gleaned from here and there, he preferred to say them to himself. Then, becoming quickly exasperated, he ended his prayer, turned to Mother who usually went on a long time, cleared his throat in order to stop her and in a tone of reprimand said, "Amen." Catching on to him she quickly responded, "Amen." Thereupon, he took down the two boxes of eggs, and after kissing them, handed them to Mother who also kissed them. We all did as they had done, then carried them to the other part of the house set aside for the nonexistent animals, where the firewood, dried cow dung and the hearth were.

Then Father set in motion the operation we had been anticipating for so long. Opening the boxes, he placed the tiny eggs resembling ant eggs on two cloth rags, covered them and lit a fire. After closing the door behind him, he sat down among us with the dignified bearing of one who has just performed a good deed, to the straw tray in the first part of the house, from which he partook of his supper. After that we slept, but he stayed up, declaring to Mother that he wasn't sleepy and was going to look around the field. But he didn't return... They brought him back to us in the middle of the night dead drunk. Mother feared that our silkworms wouldn't hatch after Father had resisted the *mukhtar*'s instructions to let him incubate them, so as to save the fee for that. She resorted to entreating the Lord not to forsake her, and to bless our harvest this year.

And behold! the Lord had pity on us and did not forsake Mother this time. He may have granted Father's prayer that he recited to himself and made the hatching successful.

After some days, when the two rags were full of the hatched worms, Mother rushed in to see the sight that filled her with joy. They were tiny worms just like the ones in flour, crawling over each other. Gazing at them in delight, she called them the "blessed ones" and instructed us to say this to them whenever our eyes fell upon them so they would multiply and grow.

Our parents held a ritual celebration on this occasion. They carried the cow-dung trays close to the hatchlings. Mother then stripped the leaves from a branch in one stroke while repeating a special invocation with the first deposit of succulent mulberry leaves. Placing an overflowing handful of these leaves on the tobacco shredder, Father shredded them until they were green threads just like short thin pieces of paper that are interwoven and sealed in a circle to be used for decorations. He strewed them over the bottoms of the cow-dung tray; then lifting up the first cloth with the hatched out silkworms, he dumped its contents carefully on top of the mulberry leaves, then did the same with the second cloth. When he was finished with that, Father lit a small fire, asked us to leave the place, closed the door, his face radiant and exultantly said to Mother, "Rejoice...perhaps we shall reap a good harvest."

The next day, he cut some mulberry branches and stripped them; then peeling off the bast, he twisted it. Driving two equal stakes into the ground at some distance from one another, he tied cords of mulberry bast to both of them, thus commencing the fabrication of that reed mat called a *batur*. After shredding the mulberry leaves just like he had done the first time, Father strewed them over the worms in the cow-dung trays as we followed him with our eyes, relishing the revelation of something new everywhere in this strange industry of raising silkworms. It occupied the whole village, became its only topic of conversation in houses and gatherings and the cause of its conflicts until the end of the harvest.

Several days later, he said that the worms had held their first fast. In fact the worms had remained without food for two days after which Father resumed shredding greater and greater quantities of mulberry leaves. He spread these over them in anticipation of their second fast after which they would be moved to the *samadiyyat*,[4] where unshredded mulberry leaves would be strewn over them to nourish them and make them grow.

With Mother's help, Father set up a long, wide scaffold that was the framework for the rectangular tiers of reed mats placed one above the other like the bunks of a ship's crew.

The supports were four long, round, strong, white poplar poles upon which the tiers of woven reed mats were raised. We covered them with mulberry leaves, and upon these green floors we emptied the cow dung trays. The silkworms that had finished their second fast spread themselves over them. We strewed more leaves on top of them. We watched them crawling, crushing and gnawing the leaves, then raising themselves on top of them, clinging to the edges—lively, healthy, pampered and surrounded by prayer.

"Now the real work begins," exclaimed Father. "Raising real silkworms begins after this stage. We must feed them well and be careful of the mulberry leaves so that none go to waste. Then he explained what was expected of us in the following manner: after the sun rose and the dew had dried off the leaves, he would start chopping off the mulberry branches. Our business was to carry them to the house without letting them touch the ground or get any dust on them. Silkworms were so particular that they had an aversion to dirty, coarse leaves. In the house we were to strip the leaves off the branches onto a clean mat, then throw the branches out in the sun to dry for winter fuel. The leaves had to be strewn over the tiers of worms twice daily, shortly before noon and before sunset. Father called the noon meal "lunch" and evening meal "supper." He would say when he was sitting in the shade "Come on, let's give the worms their lunch," or, "Let's give them their supper."

As soon as we would throw the mulberry leaves on the reed mats where the worms were scattered, that beautiful, soft music resembling the burble of sluggish water falling over a smooth rock would begin along with a faint rumbling whisper. This music would start like a creeping sound, then spread and rise when the worms scattered over the green leaves by boring through them or crawling on top of them, forming each leaf into a work of art by their marvelous lacework. Now that Mother was convinced that the worms

---

[4] The singular form is *samadiyya*—the bench raised up off the ground upon which a bride sits. This word applies to any raised area.

were doing well and that they were eating with a good appetite, her eyes were filled with sweet exuberance. "Eat blessed ones, eat!" she would say, watching them with all the hope and tenderness she possessed. Pulling me by the hand, she would order my two sisters to go out, shut the door and go to do the housework or prepare the food with the zeal of a busy bee. Her hope was not limited to a future of vague plans but one animated by the coming departure and an anticipated new life.

Day after day the worms grew larger, longer, thicker, rounder and took on more luster. They had a yellow luster. One day Mother shouted in glee, "The worms are ready for *sheeh*."[5] She kept asking Father when it would be time to put in the *sheeh*, rushing him so much that he scolded her. "Don't get in a hurry!" he said, "Don't be so impatient." However, early in the morning he prepared the *sheeh* we had pulled up out in the open countryside, then watched the movement of the "blessed ones," biding his time relying upon his experience in this regard.

After a few more days, the worms were as thick as a finger, as yellow as a sun-ripened peach, glowing like honey in a translucent container. They were pregnant with the golden fluid they would discharge as amber threads upon the *sheeh* that they would resort to when they stopped eating their food, to fabricate the precious, cherished cocoons that would be both their gift and their grave.

When Mother opened the door at the conclusion of these days, she let out a scream of fear and slapped her sides in dismay when she saw the worms straying in disorder off the mats, crawling on the posts supporting the tiers and their edges. At the sound of her voice, Father came running from the field. When he saw what she had seen, he realized that he was a little late. However, calming her fears he yelled at us, "Bring the *sheeh*." Climbing up the *samadiyyat*, he tied some *sheeh* to the top of each post, in the middle of it, and on the edges of the crossbeams so the wandering worms could find their twig of *sheeh*. Then he put *sheeh* on the reed mats with avid skill. "Set your mind at rest," he assured Mother, "we won't lose one worm." As a further precautionary measure, he placed a reed mat on the floor, strewed it with mulberry leaves so that if a worm fell for some reason or the other it would

---

5 An oriental variety of wormwood.

land safely and could be put back in its place without coming to any harm.

"We mustn't cut off their fodder," he told mother in a commanding voice. "The worms don't go to the *sheeh* in one fell swoop. It is necessary that we neither cut off the fodder nor increase it. The worms that have had enough and are spinning their cocoon will climb up on the *sheeh* and those whose time has not yet come will find food until they are satisfied."

Throughout the stages of raising the silkworms, Father issued instructions we were bound to obey and follow. We kept an eye on the worms as they dangled from the *sheeh* to spin their cocoons on it. We found Father intelligent and wise in those days. We ignored his drinking and going out at night to meet the widow. He did this at night, but during the day he was with us. He didn't travel like he used to and this in itself was a longed-for happiness.

Little by little we learned the meaning of the cocoons being spun on the *sheeh*. The matter of going to school had not yet crossed my mind. I did nor know what it was nor where it was to be found. Mother's hope of us attending school when we left the village was the hope of a draft drawn on the future, a hope that would be dashed with the coming days. It would be dashed with respect to my sisters and almost in my case too. But Mother would withstand the frustrations with her spunk, her tears, and her vigilance, and succeed in enrolling me in school to learn to read and write. Later, I read in the city of Iskenderun the *qaseeda* of Abu al-Ala al-Maarry[6] containing the following line:

It was the worm that gave the silk its texture
And its texture may be brocade.

The teacher set out to explain its meaning by telling us about the silkworm, and he would catch me absentmindedly wandering into another far-off world, colored with rain, sunshine, and greenery, adorned with cocoons, *sheeh*, mulberry trees and visions that trig-

---

[6] Abu al-Ala al-Maarry (973-1057)—a late representative of the renaissance in poetry in northern Syria, or the period of great Arab poetry. He was called the philosopher of poets and poet of philosophers. He took reason for his guide and pessimistic skepticism for his philosophy. His quatrains have been partly done in English and are said to have influenced Dante's *Divine Comedy*.

gered a burst of memory. He would rap his ruler on the edge of the table and say, addressing me: "You! What are you thinking about? Repeat what I have just said!"

I would stand up dazed by the great shock of suddenly returning from the past of my childhood to the present of my youth. I was about to explain the meaning of his line to him, but the word "brocade" had fouled me up and incapacitated me. It was as confounding as it was astonishing. The pupils' laughter made me shake so with embarrassment and sensitivity that the teacher took pity on me.

"What were you thinking about?" he asked kindly.

"About silkworms..."

"What worms are those? The ones in the poem?"

"No...the ones that were in our house..."

"In your house?"

"Yes, I really saw them... I saw how they hatched, how they ate, and how they spun their cocoons. But in our village they were called raw silkworms, not brocade worms!"

"Brocade is not a name for worms," he replied in amusement. "Brocade means silk; it is a classical word used in school, my little teacher. Do you understand?"

I nodded my head affirmatively but I secretly cursed "the brocade," preferring our village word, "raw silk!"

Chapter 8

The weather turned hot in May, and all the silkworms finished spinning their cocoons. The tiers of shelves were dotted with a jungle of *sheeh* upon which the blessed worms had woven cocoons around themselves. They no longer needed to be fed, and all we had to do was harvest the raw silk, stuff it into bags and take it to the village *mukhtar*. After weighing it, he would put aside for us one out of every four bags we turned in. He would subtract one of ours to be counted against our debt to him, and the rest was ours. If none remained, the *mukhtar* would began another debt page for us in the ledger for the new year.

The house was a glorious sight; it was gratifying to behold the shelves with their twigs of *sheeh* transformed into a thick, wide, oblong tree decorated with resplendent silk cocoons that sprang out like little fingers, looking like a complete tree with part of the stem visible. The cocoons were so intricately woven that any loose threads fluttering in the wind would wrap themselves around the cocoon to form a single mass of silk. Each individual cocoon, however, was totally independent of the rest. Each maintained its own shape and its own place on each beautiful sprig. It was all so well arranged, nothing haphazard, no crowding and no sign of aggression. It was as though each silkworm had carefully estimated the amount of space it needed, then settled to spin its cocoon, leaving just enough space for the other silkworms to weave theirs.

So many times, while holding one of those sprigs of *sheeh* laden with golden yellow cocoons, Father would proudly exclaim, "I'd win a prize if there was one! In fact I'd even get first place. I doubt whether any of the other sharecroppers have a better harvest this season. None of their *sheeh* are as laden with silk as mine. If I weren't modest I'd take one of my sprigs of *sheeh* and show it off in town."

One day, accompanied by his deputy, the *mukhtar* appeared for an inspection tour of the sharecropper's homes. As usual, the visit was unannounced, and was made to assess the harvest, so that none of the sharecroppers would be able to hide or smuggle out any of the crop. The *mukhtar* always overestimated the harvest, and then accused the sharecroppers of theft whenever there were discrepancies at the scales. And discrepancies were inevitable, just as were the problems that were to follow.

The *mukhtar* circled our tiers of shelves and then climbed up, examining every sprig with his one good eye, while his face remained as rigid as his other eye which was made of glass. He never seemed to have a nice word for Father. We children, watched from a distance. We usually hid because we were so frightened of the *mukhtar*. Mother had told us so many bad stories about him that we had a frightening image of him in our minds. We prayed that he would leave quickly and not harm our parents.

But this day I noticed that Mother was smiling at the *mukhtar*. I thought maybe that was her way of deterring any evil that might emanate from him. She was pretending to forget all the harm she had received from him, about which she had told Father nothing. Perhaps it was the good harvest that had wiped away all bad memories.

Father invited the *mukhtar* to sit with us on the stone bench. He refused. Instead, he walked away to inspect the mulberry grove and the summer vegetable garden.

"Enjoy, eat and enjoy!" he said, in an envious, resentful tone. "The land is mine but it's you who enjoys the fruits."

"Oh, but the land, the fruits and everything is all yours, sir,"replied Father. "Yet men are never satisfied until they get a hold of a handful of earth."

"Don't be insolent!" the *mukhtar* said. "Is this the way a sharecropper talks to his master?"

"When the master is like you, sir, the sharecropper will be like me!" retorted Father. "Or do you think we are your slaves? You're mistaken, *mukhtar*..."

"You're a fool, at any rate," answered the *mukhtar*... "You with your sour disposition! Sweeten up a bit. How is the candy these days?"

"Very good, sir. Yesterday the vendor passed by here so we bought some with a pound of raw silk. The harvest floor is more generous than its owner."

"You do it...you go ahead and buy sweets and other things beside..."

"I'll buy whatever I want to...*arrack* first of all."

"Don't try to get smart with me," the *mukhtar* was really roused up at Father. "If you lay a hand on any of the raw silk, I'll cut your hand off!"

"I haven't touched any of it yet...but I'll do it after today...and if you are too genteel to do it I'll cut it off."

"Okay! I have estimated your harvest. When you deliver it we shall settle the account."

"We'll settle it the way you want..."

He turned from him without saying anything. He went away angry. He was a mean, sordid person, so he left angry. In his obstinacy, Father yelled after him, "We'll settle the account if I deliver the harvest... I'm going to sell it and buy sweets and *arrack*. You can go butt your head against the mulberry trees."

The *mukhtar* did not reply. He may not have heard or may have refused to lose his dignity in front of his steward since Father's contempt for everything, as the *mukhtar* knew very well, would bring him to the point where he could do anything.

No sooner had the *mukhtar* left than Father got a small turban, stripped off enough cocoons to fill it, carried it off somewhere and brought us back some fluffy candy. The kind that the hawkers bring around to the fields to trade for raw silk when it is being harvested.

He didn't do it again, not because Mother objected, but by this offense he had defied the *mukhtar* who, intending to make peace with him, sent us some fluffy candy and a bottle of *arrack* with one of his cronies. He asked Father to pass by whenever he found the time as he had another bottle of *arrack* for him and he told him he wasn't to go without anything he wanted. "Mr. Elias is displaying his benevolence these days," said Father, "and after the harvest is handed over he'll bare his teeth, the sly fox. Does he take me for a fool?"

"You be civil and polite to him too," said Mother... "No one refuses pearls."

To give expressions to this civility, Father took him a large sprig of *sheeh* laden with cocoons, beautiful and soft, like a cotton bush heavily laden with open bolls resembling snow-white stars. Holding *sheeha* by its stem, he lifted it up high, saying to Mother, "Glory be, it will weigh two pounds." Delighted and amazed at Father's skill, we looked at its creamy silk sparkling just like the stone pine tree did at Christmas when decorated with gold liras.

Like farmers, silkworm growers used to compete. True, there were no prizes to win, but the best grower earned fame. Father had a good reputation among the growers and that year he won a bottle of *arrack* from the *mukhtar*'s own vintage. And he came back home, ready to start with God's blessing picking the cocoons and stuffing them into bags.

So we began the harvest, picking the cocoons one by one, each member of the family working on his own *sheeh*. We would throw them onto a sheet that Mother had spread inside the room. The cocoons rustled down softly onto the sheet and a strong scent of raw silk filled the house. The cocoons were like peanuts in their shells, only much bigger; the pile got higher and higher.

Father was full of praise to God while he scooped up the cocoons from the sheet with both hands and put them into the bags that mother held open for him. We were all overcome with the pride of success. We did not talk about our good feelings, but we experienced them. We sensed them deep in our hearts that year when we sat down to eat and drink. The entire house became as bright as though there were a different and more intense sunlight inside. Father and Mother spoke to each other in sweeter, more tender tones. There was no more fear, no more separation from Father. Father was with us and we felt like we owned the world.

Ours was the joy of harvest, the same as if it had been a mound of corn ears or a pile of grain. It is true that we were not farmers, but we sowed and reaped like them, and here we were filling the bags with our crops while Mother sang and we followed her. When Father took a drink, we sat around him exchanging glances of joy, hope and happiness.

"Persevere and win," said Father.

"We've persevered through many bad times, haven't we?" Mother said.

"Yes, yes," repeated Father. "Don't remind me, please. You don't know how much I suffered... A man doesn't tell his wife everything. But the important thing is that our blessed worms have given us a good harvest this season. Life has become as pleasant as a summer breeze. We'll move away. I don't stay even if they fill my hands with gold. God's world is vast."

Mother closed her eyes with a satisfaction she had never known since we had come to that village. She went back to her work, praying and rejoicing over the prospect of paying back debts and regaining her daughter who worked as a servant for the *mukhtar*.

But the good summer breeze quickly changed. The delightful days of honey and hope were transformed into a time of gloomy depression, a steadily increasing drying-up of the smiles and laughter on peoples faces and on ours. Especially on the faces of our parents, whose joy was slowly replaced by despair. For the news from the town was bad. The silk dealers who usually flocked into town and lined up to buy the silk crop did not come. Only a handful showed up. Even those who had paid in advance for the raw silk were slow to claim their share; the landlords who owned the mulberry groves took their portion of the crop reluctantly, and refused to buy the sharecroppers part. At the same time, they refused to allow the sharecroppers to sell as they pleased. This meant that no debts were paid and no new loans were available.

Early in the mornings, the men would set out for town, or go to see the landlords or shopkeepers. They would remain in town for long periods of time but always came back empty-handed. Even the transient peddlers were now few and far between. Those who did come by refused to take raw silk in exchange for their pastries and other items as was customary.

Father filled a small bag with cocoons and took it around to all the nearby shops. If he had been caught by the *mukhtar*'s deputy, he could have been thrown in jail on a charge of theft. He could even have gotten killed if he had tried to resist. In any case no one took his silk in exchange for the flour, oil and kerosene that we wanted. He was forced to take the lowest price so he would not have to carry his load back home.

"Oh, God," Mother lamented, with tears in her eyes. "What is happening to us? Why have You turned Your face from us?"

"Because you've given him a headache with all your pleas, that's why," Father shouted back. "Be quiet now! We're not alone. Whatever has happened to us has happened to other people."

"But we're not from here, we're strangers," she insisted. "We say we intend to move on, but how can we when our daughter is still in the *mukhtar*'s custody. I simply cannot leave her here as his hostage and servant."

"Go ahead and work it out," said Father. "Go to the *mukhtar* and tell him what you just said or go to the town and persuade the merchants to buy the harvest."

"I'm a woman and that's a man's work."

"I'm not a man...I'm a woman like you."

"You've been that all your life."

"All my life I've been a woman? Oh you bitch... Did I become a woman by living with you? Take that then..."

He gave her a resounding, cowardly slap on the cheek. Mother broke into loud wails, and we rushed in terror towards her. This was the first time I had seen her struck. I never imagined that she would be struck or that Father would beat her. Clinging to her to protect her and show her my love, the love she had won by all the suffering she had born and tears she had shed, I cowered in front of Father. I was filled with feelings of terror and hate towards him.

The men gathered from all over the area. They came together because they shared the same plight and because they had nothing to do. They talked and cursed as they poked the ground with small, dry sticks. They squatted on the floor in a circle, muttering and brooding over their troubles. Whenever we heard them say something that we did not quite understand, we asked mother to explain. Nevertheless, we learned it by heart from hearing it repeated so often.

"Indian silk has destroyed us!"

"You mean Chinese silk."

"No, it's Indian silk."

"The silk be damned anyway! We haven't seen it. They say it's lousy—an artificial silk. Yet it's sold everywhere abroad. What can we do? The dealers are only go-betweens. They buy and sell, and if customers from abroad turn them down, they'll turn us down."

"Don't you believe any of that nonsense! Ours is natural silk. It's strong. People can't do without it. This is just a nasty trick to lower prices. As soon as we sell, prices will go back to where they were before. We'll be the only ones who lose."

"So?"

"So—those who have money can wait. But those who don't? What will they do? Eat dirt?"

"You can't eat dirt. The children are hungry. If only the bastards would buy, we'd sell at any price."

"Let's hold on a little longer. They'll buy. The prices will go up."

"We have to hand in the crop, and the one quarter that we get to keep won't even be enough to pay back our debts."

"Let's keep the whole crop," suggested father. "Let's not turn in one single cocoon before the *mukhtar* actually buys our shares."

"What about the government authorities?"

"They can all go to hell!"

"What are we going to eat?"

"We can sell a small amount for any price, but we could keep the rest until the prices go up."

"You're putting your life in danger, you don't know landlords and their stewards!"

"Oh, yes, I do, I know them well. I've dealt with them. They can shoot me if they like. But the children must have food."

The word "shoot" scared Mother. She was afraid of all firearms even when empty. She would say, "The devil will load it!" These days recurring news of crimes, robberies and problems over fields in nearby villages spread rumors of a landowner killing his sharecropper, of sharecroppers refusing to hand over the raw silk, killing the steward and fleeing.

It was an opportune time for believing every story and rumor and opportune for outbursts of threats and carrying them out. Father meant what he said. At least the others owned something. They had flour to make bread. Having become sharecroppers before us, they had saved some wheat and barley, and had provisions stored up, some of which remained. Whereas we were starving, and to keep us from dying of hunger, Father was liable to commit any foolhardy crime, even stealing or killing.

It appeared that the *mukhtar*, having made inquiries about Father's threat, was on his guard. He requested some police from the town. His steward and the guard slung their guns over their shoulders. They circled the fields in pairs, making their headquarters at the widow's, stirring up a fuss that infuriated Father. He had now stopped going out at night, but, taking advantage of the policeman's siesta at the widow's, he carried off some cocoons and traded them for wheat and barley. He did this expecting to be released from suffering, the delay of which angered people so much that they were on the point of exploding. Soon evidence of doubts of this release appeared on their faces. The catastrophe was at hand, the sharecroppers, their wives and children groping about in confused misery, teetering like penguins squawking over a coming gale without knowing how to ward off the approaching danger.

What could the men accomplish? Even if they defiantly refused to turn in the raw silk, what would happen? There, in the
village, summer begins in May, and at that time every year, raw
silk cocoons are bagged in burlap sacks and taken to the landlords
and dealers. Then, a process to choke worms in their cocoons begins.
Otherwise, they burst the cocoons open and the little butterflies fly
out. The raw silk is spoiled and loses its value completely.

In May, people used to say, the wheel of the year has turned
full circle. They meant that silk season had begun, that the cocoons
were ready to be opened. After the cocoons are opened, the silk is
ready to be spun. But not everyone had spinning wheels! Most were
owned by landlords. Sharecroppers made their own small wheels
to spin some of their silk which they wove at home for their own
clothing. The dealers, however, took their raw silk to the city,
with the cocoons still unopened.

But the spinning and weaving activity came after the
"choking" process, an elaborate, technical operation. First, the
bags of silk cocoons are put into a pit-like room. A fire is lit in a corner, and when smoke fills the room, the worms choke and die inside
their cocoons. But it has to be done quickly. This is why everyone
rushes to turn in their crop and the landlords are also in a mad rush
to either sell their harvest or begin this choking process. After
that the spinning wheels begin to turn, the air is filled with smoke
and the looms begin to roar.

The town bustles with activity in the Main Square and in the
harbor. There, the purchased goods are loaded onto barges and
shipped away. The share croppers, who have waited all year to
receive one quarter of the crop, pay their debts and buy food and
clothing, return to their fields to plough and plant vegetables.
They pick the figs and dry them for winter. They press the grapes
and olives, either working for themselves or for others in return for
wages. In the fall, they gather firewood and cattle droppings and
save as much as they can for fuel. That is the season for celebrating
weddings and other happy occasions. In the winter, they hibernate
in their mud houses scattered across the fields.

Mother knew all about it. She had experienced it all as a young
girl and remembered stories her folks had told her when she was a
child. Through her discussions with Father and with the neighbor-
women, we could always tell what was going to happen in summer,
fall and winter. Her only concern became that of a deliverance con-

centrated upon selling our share of cocoons, paying off our debt, retrieving our sister and leaving.

However, that year the predictable work cycle was disrupted. Everything came to a full stop and was set backwards. The silk season used to be like a river that carried in its flow the boats and barges of our little town. But suddenly it struck a treacherous dam and everything was hurled backwards in a raging murky tumult. Scared and threatened creatures were strewn in the middle, their barges near collapse and they themselves near drowning.

For the dealers never came to buy the crop that year and the very few who did arrive waited until they could impose the lowest prices. The greedy landlords hoped to acquire the sharecroppers' shares for an insignificant price. But some of the sharecroppers refused to sell. Father refused to turn in any of his crop. Everyone held their boats in the river's current. But just before the waters struck the treacherous dam, everyone suddenly surrendered and unloaded their barges into the wild flood to escape from drowning.

On the last possible day, Father ran home to get one of the cocoon-filled bags to take to the *mukhtar*. The latter would not let him use one of his animals to transport the bags of raw silk. Father tried to rent a mule but could not find one. That day, all the village folk were busy carrying their cocoons to the landlords or to the choking rooms, hoping to prevent the final catastrophe.

But the heat had already been intense that season and the cocoons that had not yet been choked burst open and let out tiny butterflies. The butterflies filled the house, flew out to the fields, and across to neighboring houses like a wave of invading locusts. The fear wasn't for the bit of produce in the fields nor the bare mulberry trees but for the cocoons whose weight was decreased and whose silk was ruined.

What a terrifying catastrophe it was! What sorrow befell Mother as she cried over our bad luck that day! Father kept shouting for help at the top of his lungs. He wanted us to grab as much as we could and follow him to the *mukhtar*'s house, where there were long lines of people waiting to use the "choking" rooms. He picked up a large double sack, Mother carried a single bag on her back and a full basket in her hand. My two sisters carried a basket each. I was the only one with empty hands.

The road was long and rugged. Even empty handed I could hardly walk so I was told to stay and guard the house until they got back. I wept and caught up with them but Mother begged me to return and stay at home. She scolded and threatened me, then ran along behind father, with both my sisters following her. I tried to run and catch up with them, but I fell and did not feel like getting up again. I was expecting Mother or my sister to come back to pick me up or stay with me, and for this I cried and rolled in the dirt. But they didn't. I cried stubbornly until I was weak and fell asleep there, lying in the dirt under the hot sun.

On the way back, they picked me up. Night had fallen and it was dark inside our house. Mother and Father only spoke a few words. They simply sat there on the stone bench in front of the door, enveloped in silent despair.

Chapter 9

That year's harvest was the last silk harvest in the village. The last one because synthetic silk would put an end to natural silk. If there was anyone left who still raised silk worms in the coming years it was only because it was a challenge or foolhardiness, or it was for the local manufacture of clothing. Our parents spoke a great deal to us about this, stirring up that which over the length of the years lay sleeping in our memories. It fills in the data about things that happened in the past and are told these days. They always agree that the Indian silk ruined people, the sharecroppers first, then the landowners, finally the whole village.

"This business is dead," Father said to Mother one day. "The blessed worms have died; we too have died. May God have mercy on us!"

"But unfortunately we are still alive!" answered Mother. "Where is death?"

"Alive? Is this life?" he asked, looking at her in scornful anger.

He went on to tell this story: "There was a poor man in our village; not a bite of bread to eat nor clothes for his back. One evening as he was sitting in a gathering he started talking. 'Today when I was in the wilderness a lion suddenly attacked me,' he said.

"The listeners were astounded. 'A lion?' they asked.

"'Yes a lion.'

"'What did you do?'

"'When I saw him I fled. I ran and he ran after me. I screamed and he roared. I hid in a thicket but he pounced on me. I climbed a tree but he lay in wait under it until my strength gave out and I fell.'

"'And after that?' exclaimed those present.

"'He ate me!'

"'But you're still alive...'

"'Alive?' he asked with a grin. 'Do you call this a living?'"

"Don't scare the children," chided Mother. "There aren't any lions in the wilderness."

"The man didn't mean a real lion...," replied Father. "A lion is a compassionate wild beast. He meant poverty..."

"At any rate, it is enough that we didn't die," said Mother.

Father didn't reply. He was really suffering. The blessed worms had died and in his opinion the people had died with them. He saw this with his own eyes. We saw it too, but, as a man, he felt it more profoundly. The image of the catastrophe remained indelibly imprinted on his mind. He would relate it to us and to others at length, mentioning how he had carried sacks of cocoons on his back to the *mukhtar*'s house to where sharecroppers from all the fields also moved their sacks of cocoons on their backs or on the backs of their animals. The *mukhtar* was there, halfheartedly receiving his sharecroppers' harvest, gloomy of face, cursing them because they were late, the cocoons had begun to take to the wing, the price was going down and everything pointed to ruin.

The sharecroppers turned over their harvest and returned downcast. The *mukhtar*'s ledger was closed; not one new piastre on account. His shop was closed; not one grain of *durra* or barley, not one drop of oil or kerosene. The paths from the fields to the landowner's houses and from them to the fields swarmed with men, women and children. They were covered with dust, disheveled, barefoot and worst of all, hopeless.

"Go if you want to," the owners of the fields said to them. "Even if we can dispose of the harvest at any price, it is the last one. We can't guarantee anything... We may flee the village just like you... The worms are dead. Raising raw silk has come to an end. Indian silk had put an end to both us and you."

"We are the ones who have come to an end," said Father. "As for them—that one-eyed swindler and the rest!"

"Don't say the one-eyed," remonstrated Mother. "God created him. No man is to blame for his handicap."

"Shut up, you... God knew the snake's subtlety, so he put his legs in his belly."

"Nevertheless, it is not right to be sacreligious."

He shot her a look of burning anger. He was broke; no *arrack* and no tobacco. In the house there was nothing but dry bread and a little of the *durra* and barley mixture. The widow had no time for him, being occupied with the general disaster, with repelling the boorish policemen and night watchmen and in arranging her affairs in some particular way. Thus his association with her had come to an end for some reason or other.

He was in such a turmoil that Mother's fears of his leaving us increased. Not because he had no work or that he showed any inclination of leaving, like the silk worms who had shown signs of fasting before they spun their cocoons, but because he was desperate. And in this hopeless state he was liable to resort to any action, to leave and never return.

Mother appealed for aid to the widow, about whose attachment to Father she had heard in some way or the other. She went to visit her. As Father would say, Mother didn't cry easily but she was overly sensitive and in our predicament didn't know what to do to prevent him from leaving.

She took me with her on this visit. She washed my face, dressed me in a gown she had made by hand and tattered sandals that fell off my feet on the road. So she carried them and carried me part of the way. Before we arrived, she put me down to fasten them on my feet, telling me to keep them on no matter what, as it was improper for me to be barefoot. Not only because I was her son, but because we were from the city and city children were different from country children, even different from the children of the woman to whose house we were going.

When we got near the house I was beset with feelings of shyness and fear. Mother was embarrassed and scared also. The woman's reception was restrained. She was beautiful but bold and of ill-repute. Probably reckoning that Mother had come to censure her or blame her, she was prepared for a quarrel. However, after shaking hands with her, Mother complained to her about our circumstances just as if the widow were her sister. The widow, on her part, treated her with indulgent sympathy. Her facial expression changed; she looked distressed. She was transformed into another woman, hospitable and compassionate, a real human being. Her femininity flowed from genuine feelings and her abundant generosity, and from this store she showered upon Mother. She gave to Mother an expression of love and compensation for the gossip about her wickedness. I loved her, and submitted to her hugs and kisses just as I would love the other woman Zanuba, who would appear by a marvellous coincidence in days to come.

The widow used to tuck up the hem of her gown in her waistband, thus revealing her plump shapely legs. It was said that she always did that to excite men. But she let her dress down in deference to our mother. Seating her on a chair with a wooden seat, she lifted me up and sat me down beside her. Then Mother dismissed me to go play with the widow's children after which the two started in on a long conversation.

On our way home Mother extoled her very highly, describing her as being as good as a saint. I understood that the woman had promised Mother she would convince Father not to leave and would assist us in settling up our affairs so we could go back to the city. As we were leaving her house, she gave us some things... I don't remember now what they were. But they were in a basket that was too heavy for me to carry.

"You carry it, young fellow," she said encouraging me. "It isn't as heavy as you think...it's light...here, oh.. Or are you naughty like your father?" she laughingly added.

Mother smiled at the joke. She wanted me to be naughty but not like Father. She was such a sincere soul that she found it difficult to doubt or hate, so didn't take the woman's joke as an offense. As she didn't believe she was bad, she was now more convinced that she was blameless. The widow, having yielded to Mother's request that she carry the basket instead of me, kissed her when we parted.

Mother told everything to Father in detail. I assume that she disguised the purpose of the visit, but informed him that the neighbor woman wanted him to go visit her and take me to play with her children.

"I won't go...," replied Father slyly. "What does this police-men's customer want with me?"

However, one forenoon not long after, he became quite affec-tionate towards Mother, affectionate to the point of suspicion. After shaving and dressing he said, "Put on the little fellow's gown... I'm going to see what that damned woman wants with me."

"Did you like our neighbor's children?" he asked me as we crossed the field. "Today I'm going to let you play with them for a long time... Go to the field with them... Don't get lonesome and cry. You're a smart boy, aren't you? The children play in the field, not inside the house. When I'm finished with my business I'll call you and we'll go home... Do you hear?"

He was carrying me on his shoulder when he said that; he had been carrying me ever since we had gotten beyond our field, walking with quick long strides, joking and talking to me as he went along.

At that time I didn't have those special feelings of affinity toward my father; I had a feeling he was doing something forbidden for me to see; something arousing excitement, evoking jealousy and secret animosity; something that went on at night causing fights, whose ultimate goal was a woman. This feeling emerged later when I was awakened one night by a struggle whose ultimate source was Mother, who was neither screaming nor crying. But she was not talking like she did in the daytime; she was whispering. I could hear her whispers as I lay beside her in the same bed, but I did not dare ask her because I sensed that it would not be proper to ask her about it, as it wasn't something that happened during the daytime. I had never seen it happen during the day.

Therefore my feelings towards my father were quite natural. I accepted what he said willingly. I did not understand what I saw even if it was stored in my memory. Then, when a similar incident occurred, the veil was lifted bringing all the ends together with a sudden shock-like clarity. The man in this case was the master of the house I was working in after I had grown into a youth.

This widow was different the day she greeted Mother than when she received Father. She said something that upset him. She didn't swear at him but it roused him. He took me by the hand and was on the point of returning to where he came from, when the widow pulled me away from him saying, "Go on, you, and leave the little chap."

I wavered between the two of them. I wouldn't stay if Father left. If he did so I would cry. I was so embarrassed by the situation that I hated the woman whom I had loved on the former visit. Carrying me in her arms, she called from inside the door, "Come in. Or do you want a special invitation?" she added with a smile.

I don't recall what he replied or how long he stayed outside. Taking me to the back part of the house, she filled my pockets with raisins, and when I came out Father was there. He had entered. He had just entered but angrily. There he stood, brown-skinned and young, confronted by the fair-skinned young woman. Both of them were pretending to censure the other, but underneath this thin crust lay desire. I was the obstacle preventing the realization of this desire. When the woman sat me down on a chair and returned to the back part of the house, he followed her. I heard a commotion and then some words I couldn't make out. Silence reigned, then whispers... She was the one whispering, there was a small outcry followed by suppressed laughter. She came back to me radiant. After a short while, Father reappeared and his scowl had vanished.

My happiness at seeing them in this state banished my fears of a fight breaking out between them. However, the embarrasment of my presence still existed. I saw them winking at each other without understanding a thing. What significance was there in a male and female being alone in a house? What harm would it do them if I stayed with them or went outside to play with the widow's children? These questions never occurred to me at the time. I was pleased with Father when he asked me in a friendly manner to go play with the widow's children and pleased with the widow when she was quick to take his advice, ordering her children, who were in the field, to come and take me to play with them.

I went and played with them.

In a short time the door of the house was closed.

The door of the house stayed closed for a long time.

Chapter 10

Had someone persuaded Father to stay? Who? We, the sister held as hostage, or the widow?

Probably no one. He was the kind of person who lived his present completely separate from his past; who lived his past without it having any effect on his present. He wasn't just a passionate lover; he was a lecher. His small head, his peach-colored, full lower lip, the skin on the palms of his hands with their long, thick fingers all exuded a blind animal lust. When it was quenched, it was over, when it hungered it slavered until it ate and was satisfied. Apart from that, nothing mattered; no love affair lasted; he was impervious to it so it never got the better of him.

Neither Mother, my sister, nor our neighbor, the widow, not one of them, had anything to do with his remaining. Nevertheless he stayed. It may have been due to the fact that the *mukhtar* didn't tell him to stay! If the *mukhtar* had done so, Father would have gone, driven by a latent tendency to contrariness within him.

The *mukhtar* didn't tell his sharecroppers to stay or leave. The landowners took the same course. Those who wanted to stay, could... The fields would come to no harm if they left; there was nothing to worry about if they stayed... The shops and ledgers were closed. Those who had money and grain were secure. This is your Safar Barr was an idea that cropped up in people's minds: mouths finished off the scant provisions; famine showed up like symptoms of the plague. People sold some of their belongings; some sold all; others took out loans; some ate weeds and begged. By the end of autumn there were no more weeds, loans or handouts for beggars. We, in our barren field, received some donations: a large bowl of flour, a handful of bulgur,[1] a dish of oil, fistfuls of dried figs. The widow was in the vanguard of donors, possibly due to her compassion for us and her fear of our dying of hunger or, maybe because she loved Father. There was something about him other than his brown skin that attracted women to him. It could have been his irresponsibility. Magnanimity also played a role. He possessed that quality that lured feminine solicitude.

---

[1] Cooked, parched and crushed wheat.

However, even if the donations continued, they would not have been enough to sustain us. How could they, since whenever they were cut off my sisters and I would go around drooling hungrily, screaming for food.

It drove Mother to tears. Father wandered around the house in dismay, on edge, blaspheming God in his hunger. He resolved to depart at nightfall, hesitating to leave in the morning, roaming about the fields searching for food, or carrying off whatever household goods we had left to sell. If he failed to sell them or failed to obtain something to satisfy our hunger he would return discouraged, entreating Mother with abject looks which she understood. She would then go crying to the neighbors to beg for something for us to eat.

One day she returned empty-handed. For two days, Father's attempts had been fruitless and now Mother's efforts had produced nothing. By evening we were as wilted as tree branches cut at midday. No longer having the strength to scream, we let up. We had arrived at the stage of dizziness that awaits the starving.

Carrying me on her back with Father dragging my two sisters and finally carrying one of them, by nightfall we were in front of the *mukhtar*'s house. Mother rapped on the door while Father, fleeing to the field to escape the horror of the situation, watched us from a distance. Fortunately, it was the *mukhtar*'s wife who opened the door, somewhat terrified at the sight of us. We two were clutching Mother's skirt while our other sister shyly hid behind her. In the evening darkness, we presented a tableau of a beggar with children in the abased stance of pleading, expressed by tearful eyes in emaciated faces. This was a picture drawn by tragic misery; a picture depicting motherhood in two contrasting positions: one of asking for charity in the splendor of sacrifice and the other giving it, in the magnificence of pity.

The *mukhtar*'s wife kissed Mother and she cried on the woman's breast. Then they cried together. They were weeping for us hungry children on this cold night, and over such wretchedness as this that embraced not only us but all children in every famine and disaster: all the little ones clinging to the skirts of mothers, pleading at the doors for a crust of bread.

After taking us in, she shut the door. Mother didn't mention Father's presence outside. She couldn't bear to have him in the same situation we were in; it isn't uncommon for a man to beg but if he does so in front of his wife or a wife does so in front of her husband, how can the hot blood in the veins continue flowing in private? How can they look each other in the face when they feel the contempt of menial servants? No, there is no pleasure in shattered pride. Mother wasn't thinking like that, but she wanted to spare Father from being in a cruelly ignominious position for a man. Wanting to keep him out of the way by keeping him out of the tableau, she took upon herself all the misery in the tableau.

The *mukhtar*'s wife gave us food to eat; she also gave us the privilege of seeing our sister. Mother kissed her. We were confused, happy and confused. Here was our sister after so long being away from us. We could hear her, see her and touch her. She could touch us too. She came to us. Came close to look in our eyes. Taking me by the hand, she smiled at us but that was all. We were not in our own house. She was a servant in her master's house. Therefore there was awe, strangeness and sadness. We stopped eating. Were we embarrassed by our sister?

The brother, Joseph, was eaten by the wolves. Joseph was in the well. They were the ones who threw him in the well. We didn't throw our sister in the well. We didn't take her blood-stained shirt to Father. But in our encounter with her, we were just like Joseph's brothers were with Joseph. The only difference was that we and our sister were equally scared and embarrassed. We were equal components of the tableau. She wasn't the keeper of the granaries we had come to buy.

We ate until we were satisfied. Mother didn't eat until we were full. Probably so that we could fill ourselves. She had the capacity to go hungry so we could be satisfied. The *mukhtar*'s wife noticed. "Eat, Sister," she said. Mother ate a bite from the dish of other people. The dish was inside the threshold, but it belonged to others. What difference would it make if it were on the outside? Some are merciful enough to invite the beggar inside. We were inside; Mother dipped her bread in the dish shamefacedly, her head bowed, her eyes brimming with tears, her thoughts on the outside: *If the mukhtar's wife had only allowed me to take a dish home with me, I would have shared it with the one who stayed behind hungry and ashamed in the mulberry grove.*

The *mukhtar* was in his room with the door closed; closed not because of his phobia, but because of his anxiety. He was going over his accounts, useless accounts to go over. He was doing it out of habit. No one was paying up. During the year, his ledger had been filled with numbers that he hoped would be changed into money at the end of the harvest; he hoped he would be able to cross out the numbers and collect the money. Just like the sharecroppers, he had not known that he would be buffeted by the winds of adversity.

The French Mandate after the Turkish occupation: we were free of the Turks. The *Safar Barr* is remembered but will not recur. The French are better; they are civilized, white people, blue-eyed. The *mukhtar* heard about the uprisings against the French. Where? In the Damascus area. Before that, in Aleppo, the Latakiya mountains, the Qusayr, in the district of Antioch. The whisperings were over now. The *mukhtar* had told people that revolutionaries were criminals. He refused to give any financial support. For a whole year he refused to go to Antioch and was delighted when the French were victorious. He went with the big wigs to welcome the high commissioner in the town. For years he raked in profits from raising silkworms and its trade. After that he took himself to Aleppo to have his glass eye inserted.

"Their liras are lovely... they ring better than the *Rashadiya*,"[2] he would boast.

He bought new properties in an unbelievable manner. They were purchased, at any rate, not extorted, and were registered in the bureau of landed property. There he was in his room checking his records with the door closed, not out of fear of what was in the records, but out of apprehension. The French had been human beings until they brought in the Indian silk.

"Why did those sons of bitches bring in the Indian silk?"

"Ask the merchants..."

"Those sons of bitches outnumber the French..."

"They're shareholders..."

"Neither shareholders nor... they are ruined same as us."

"Cry for yourselves... the bigwigs, and merchants are in good shape."

"Why don't they give us food to eat? After serving them all these years here, they are closing their doors in our faces."

"They no longer need us."

"What is there to do?"

"Leave..."

---

[2] An Ottoman coin.

"To where?"

"Who knows?"

"But we originated here... We don't know anything except raising silkworms."

"Raising silkworms is done with..."

The *mukhtar* was in his room behind the closed door. We were on the threshold of the house eating from a straw tray. Outside, the night was cold... winter was early that year. Our sister was crying; she wanted to go home with us. But Mother, out of love for her, did not want her to go home with us... We no longer had a home; we had become beggars; the people had become beggars. Tomorrow or the next day we would leave. We couldn't stay here until we died of hunger... We must leave.

What the *mukhtar*'s wife put on the tray in front of us disappeared. Mother thanked her. Bending over her hand she kissed it, wetting it with her tears and kisses. Realizing our circumstances, our sister cried with her. She didn't insist on coming with us. The *mukhtar*'s wife, a mother like our mother and by nature generous, took advantage of her husband's crouching in his room to fill a sack full of provisions for us and a bottle of oil. Opening the door for us she said to Mother,

"Come back often... don't be ashamed..."

We returned to the house in the darkness... Father was waiting for us at a short distance. He carried the sack and me in his arms. Dragging my two sisters along the rough path, Mother followed us across the fields. She carried them on her back in turns, her voice encouragingly repeating,

"We're almost there!"

We walked but we didn't arrive.

When one of the girls cried, Father yelled at her to shut up. At that point I buried my head in his breast and the rocking motion of the walking put me to sleep. When I awoke the next morning, there was no father in the house.

He had gone...

Chapter 11

This was a house belonging to a feudal lord whose home was in the city of Iskenderun. In order that he might manage his lands directly he had a dwelling in the village of Qara Aghash where his estates lay.

I don't know how Father became acquainted with this feudal lord nor who led him to him. However, the tribulations the family would live through, the situation we would find ourselves in, and likewise from recollections and words spoken, I would learn that Father had concluded a bad bargain with him. The consequences of this bargain made us his servants, and the sister who had gone on ahead was the vanguard and the hostage whose wages paid our moving expenses to the village.

The fragments of memories would come and go as my awareness of things increased with age. Memories whose images are almost complete now may still have some gaps in them, and imagination may turn for help to some of the influential members of the family to verify finishing off the fringes of one story or another. But things come to light, raised with effort from the lowest level of an old dark well, in the memory where events were deeply rooted, in spite of childhood. It was as if these cruel events had been carved in by a knife of continuous misfortune. The family had been buffeted by whirlwinds on all sides as it revolved in the vortex of the storm like a sailboat that had lost its mooring, broken its rudder, and was being tossed about in the stormy waves. It was without a helmsman or with one and with a captain not qualified to be captain or too irresponsible to be one because he lacked the qualities necessary for good management. Basically he did not sense that he bore responsibility for the family.

I don't mean to imply that it was our family's boat alone that experienced this buffeting in the relentless sea of great poverty. But it, due to the irresponsibility of its captain, was in a worse state of disarray in the struggle against the tempest and more quickly lost in the tumult. It was actually lost... and, when it would be decreed for it to make the shore, it would have lost some of its members despite the fact that it was still in the first phase of its trackless wanderings through the uncharted areas it lived in.

It was Father who concluded this contract and handed over our sister to be crucified on the cross of service. He returned to us in our bare forsaken field bearing brass, not silver, and payment for the debt from another debt. He had to surrender himself and us to crucifixion on crosses similar to the one our sister had been crucified on.

Nevertheless, it was good fortune—in spite of its misfortune—that brought him back to us with that very low price in his pocket for our coming servitude. It's a wonder he didn't drink it up or depart for the devil's lair that lured him with a call that in his stupidity and lust he gladly responded to, or that on his way back he did not turn aside to indulge in the irrational behavior that was a driving force in him from one absence to another. This time he kept his wits and his will to return to us, in order to take us with him to reunite us in servitude to one family after our having been in the servitude of two separate families.

Therefore, around the date he had set for his return he came back to us without delay, bringing a rich loaf of white bread from Antioch. He cut two pieces of it for my sister and me with his sharp knife and ordered us to go to the other part of the house near the great hearth. We obeyed him.

We obeyed him not because hunger had taught us great respect for bread, this all-sufficient means of livelihood that we used to request in our prayers morning and evening as our dearest wish. And not because Mother would kiss the loaf whenever we got hold of one and raise it to her forehead before she divided and distributed it amongst us. It was because it was white bread, the kind we had dreamed of, that had now become a reality.

My sister's pointing out to me the importance of what we were eating raised my consciousness about its significance. I put my cupped left hand under the piece of bread that I put into my mouth with my right hand for fear that the white crumbs might fall on the floor and be dirtied in the dust.

It was customary duty at any rate, an exercise between carefulness and habit and thus training in stinginess. I am really surprised that it did not develop into stinginess just as life's cruelty to us did not develop into a hatred for life around us. Quickly devouring the pieces of bread, we returned to our parents who had been discussing our sister who had gone on ahead of us. I heard Father telling Mother that our departure would rescue us from this village and this wilderness where owls screeched. We would work for the new

87

master whose wife was good and kind. We would live in comfort not to be compared to our wretched state here. Mother was listening in fear and bewilderment, agreeing to the journey but not willing to sell the household goods as Father was suggesting, insisting that moving these articles would be difficult and moreover we needed their price.

I suppose we sold some of them. According to Father, selling was always accompanied by a promise of buying. "Tomorrow," he would say, "we'll make up for it. God will provide us with the means to buy better things." Mother would object, knowing that what was sold would not be replaced and that the ease of selling was only countered by the difficulty of buying. This resistance infuriated Father, making him scold her and beat her. Then he would take the stuff and sell it openly or secretly. He often did it secretly, leaving Mother with no resource but tears when the loss of some article came to light or whenever Father denied having seen or sold it.

So we bundled up the belongings we had left, and our parents went to inform the *mukhtar* that we were leaving.

We could have left covertly at night or in the early morning without our departure arousing anyone's attention or interest. The surrounding houses were empty, the mulberry groves were being cut down and burned or their trunks gathered for wood. The paths were filled with columns of travelers on the backs of animals or in carts drawn by donkeys or cows. The fathers who lacked these means carried their things on their backs, dragging their children along, fleeing from hunger, fear, and thieves, traveling together to be safe from highway robbers who lay in wait for them in the valleys and the foothills of the mountains.

It was possible for us, in this state of collective emigration, this mutual dissolution of contracts to forsake our mud hut and the mulberry grove, empty except for the whistling wind, and flee the whole village without letting anyone know and without anyone asking about us. But our oldest sister was with the *mukhtar*. Considering her to be payment for the debt, he had tightened his watch over her since learning that Father had returned and that we were on the point of leaving since it had become impossible for us to stay on.

Father's lengthy beseeching diatribe, Mother's tearful entreaties, and requests from those who were acquainted with our cir-

88

cumstances and sympathized with us, were of no avail. The *mukhtar* spurned them all. He would not give us anything to eat and could not cope with us remaining hungry. We were of no use to him as *fellahin*. So he made it known that we were free to leave, but as far as our sister was concerned, he would keep her until we payed our debt.

"You're free to do as you like!" said the *mukhtar*. The landowners had said that before him, and he had said it to other *fellahin* beside us. The sweet word "freedom" had become frightening, meaning no money, no food and no concern for the unpredictable destiny of the families who had lived on raising silkworms. The arrival of artificial silk was finishing off them and the silkworms together.

Therefore the word "free" became an odious term to the *fellahin*, who came from their fields seeking aid from the owners of the fields. As a consequence, they rejected this term, bringing up the matter of their servitude being in exchange for certain conditions, among which was the stipulation that they should be sustained until winter was over and the growing season arrived.

Father did not bring up the matter of our contract, and the *mukhtar* who held it no longer had any need for it. He shut his door in the face of Father's anger after he had threatened to shoot him, charging his watchman to drive Father away and if he returned to arrest him.

What could our parents do? Antioch was far away, heaven was far away and there was no one to give ear to their pleas. If they had taken the chance and gone off to Antioch to lodge a complaint, they would only have been exposing themselves to harm. Even if they reached it, they would have to spend the night there, and how could they leave two small children alone? Even if they left us in the widow's charge and went, where would they make their complaint? How would they take legal action against the *mukhtar*? When would the case end? Would they win it?

Father, who did not view Sister's remaining with the *mukhtar* in the same light as Mother, said, "There's no use in suing him! Whoever enters the door of the court never leaves. The *mukhtar* has influence and the administrative officer will be on his side. It would be better for us not to oppose him."

"What are you going to do?"

"I don't know."

"And the girl?"

"We'll leave her with the *mukhtar.* "

"Leave her with the *mukhtar,* you hardhearted wretch!" screamed Mother in a panic.

Father was speechless. He may have underestimated what Mother's reaction would be. Perceiving now that he had been remiss in even apperaring to have the incumbent fatherly bonds that bound him to his little daughter, he realized that Mother would never leave without her.

She was afraid that if she were separated from her she would never meet up with her again. If she didn't take her with her, who'd bring her to her? She would stay, accept the hunger, endure the damage, work as a servant, beg, just so she would not have to forsake and leave. Her nightmare about fleeing was like a nightmare in a dream, where she was gathering up the seeds that had slipped between her fingers. Every time she bent down to pick up a grain another one fell. In the terror of the nightmare she was, with her own defenseless hands, warding off the wild beasts that would carry off her children. They had sought protection with her in the boat whose timbers were breaking asunder and whose bottom was pierced, leaving it a wreck tossed about in the raging sea, not understanding how she came to be there.

"If we don't leave this one, we'll leave the other one," said Father, having suppressed his outburst of anger. "You are no more tenderhearted than I."

"You have no heart," she exclaimed. "I don't want to hear what you have to say."

Coming to a halt, he looked at her askance, giving her to understand that the blows were coming. She payed no attention. She went on leaving him sputtering out the curses that were on the tip of his tongue. She heard but did not answer. Nothing was going to dissuade her from her purpose. However, her intention was mixed with anxiety. Father's words were torturing her. "If we don't leave this one we'll leave the other one." It tortured her because, despite its cruelty, it was a truth that there was no way of getting around. She realized that if she went, she was leaving her daughter behind to be lost to the family or to live as a stranger, denied motherly love and the joys of childhood. And if she remained here, the sister who had preceded us to Iskenderun would be exposed to the same fate.

What was she to do? Which of the two solutions should she choose when neither was a solution? To whom could she take her complaint since the *mukhtar* had closed his door and Antioch was so far away? Give up? Giving up all hope meant coming up against a stone wall and surrendering. Mother even in her hopelessness did not want to give in. She didn't even imagine that to be an alternative or a possibility she was capable of accepting. Her little family must stay with her so that her wings could keep on sheltering her chicks. But what means could she use to ensure that?

"We have no choice," said Father, suppressing his exasperation in an endeavor to convince her. "This one is our daughter and so is the other... We'll inevitably get out of this predicament if we have patience... We'll leave now; then when I can borrow the money I'll come back and fetch her."

"I'll never leave my daughter with the *mukhtar*!"

"And our daughter in Iskenderun?"

They argued back and forth, searching for a solution but not coming up with one. Whenever Mother stuck to the idea of remaining, Father reminded her that staying was the same as leaving and that she must in either case be separated from one of her daughters.

That night Mother did not sleep. She told us she had not slept, that she cried and Father scolded her, threatened her, then caressed her, trying to make the matter easy for her. But she remained sleepless, crouching there on the bed with us sleeping around her.

She left the house in the morning before sunrise without telling us her purpose or destination. We weren't aware of her absence until after she was gone. Father searched and called out to her. My youngest sister and I went out to look for her in the field. We prayed humbly to God but did not find a trace of her.

Father ordered us back into the house while he went to ask about her at the widow's. Afterwards he went to the *mukhtar* and also enquired at the neighbors. When he returned without her, we started crying for her. He tried to comfort and reassure us, but he was just as upset and sad as we were.

She returned in the afternoon, satisfied, accompanied by an old lame man with white hair. There was a gun slung over his shoulder and a bundle in his hand. Mother was carrying a sack. In the bundle and sack was food: figs, oranges, flour and a bottle of oil. Provisions for days, but in circumstances like ours, provisions for life.

"Your uncle! Kiss his hand. Pray that he may have a long life."

I kissed his hand with all my heart. Like a puppy I wanted to lick his hands, his shoulder, his body. After shaking hands with Father, he kissed me and my sister, then squatted down holding me in his lap along with the gun. I was scared of the gun I had heard about. Our house lacked this weapon that the thieves feared. Father was unable to buy one like it. In the stories of robberies it had become, in my mind, as highly esteemed as Uncle. Now this person whom Mother called "Uncle" had returned to us and with a gun too. What joy! What reassurance! What a miracle took place in our house that day!

"You're leaving then?" said the uncle to Father.

"It's our lot!" answered Father, offering him his tin of tobacco and pulling my hand to get me off his knee.

"Leave him," said the uncle. "This is little Rizkallah."

"If Rizkallah were alive, we would never have reached this state," sobbed Mother.

"God rest his soul, Mariam! Don't cry, Niece... You should have remembered your uncle and come to him."

Mother burst into tears. "I was ashamed. I didn't have the face to do it in the condition I'm in. Fate has brought us low, Uncle!"

"Why are you crying?" Father scolded. "Aren't you satisfied?"

"Let her be," interrupted Uncle quietly. "The poor thing has had too much to bear. Tears will bring her relief... And this bastard *mukhtar*! O.K... don't fear."

Mother stopped crying, and got up to fetch a knife to peel oranges. I stuck out my finger and touched the gun. The barrel was cold. I wanted to touch it again but the uncle pushed me towards Mother saying, "Give him an orange."

We ate, feeling that something in our life had suddenly changed. Despite the traces of her tears, Mother was happy and Father was both delighted and embarrassed by the uncle whom I secretly hoped would not leave; that he and his gun would spend the night with us; that he would even stay until we departed so the *mukhtar* would no longer have any power over us.

Father rolled a cigarette for him. The uncle smoked with relish, the smoke coming from his nostrils rising and permeating his white hair while silence reigned. Mother was regarding him with a look of hopeful entreaty, wanting him to say something about what he had in mind about saving us. But the uncle was lost in cigarette smoke. After dragging on it several times in succession and tossing the butt away, he suddenly rose as if recalling what he had come for.

"Come on!" he said to Father. "Take me to the *mukhtar's* house and don't you speak..."

"And I?" asked Mother.

"You stay with the little ones."

"And the girl?"

"We'll see," the uncle cut her short.

"Oh my Lord! The *mukhtar* is a bastard and I'm afraid."

"Are you afraid for me or for the girl, Mariam?"

Mother didn't reply. He was confident and awe-inspiring, despite the fact that his outward appearance did not at first sight give a good impression. He had a friendly face with small sharp eyes. His left leg was slightly lame. When he got up, he set out right away without looking back or saying a word.

He preceded Father, the gun over his shoulder and a stick in his hand. His torso was bent at the top of his spine, the legacy of a natural curve due to old age and working in the earth.

We settled down to wait, but Mother was ravaged by anxiety. She beseeched God not to let anything happen so that the uncle would be successful in fetching back Sister. She kept going in and out of the house and to the edge of the garden and back. If we asked questions, her answer came in disjointed words of vexation. She was bent on setting out to join the uncle and Father at the mukhtar's house but I clung to her and Sister told her we were afraid to stay in the house alone after nightfall. Mother turned back inside but was unable to sit with us around the hearth. Despite the cold, she kept on going out to the field, the whole while listening closely.

Our sister came back to us that night. Mother heard their voices from the edge of the field. When Mother heard Father talking, she shouted his name. When he answered back, she asked about our sister. From inside the house we heard Sister's voice.

"Mother!"

Mother rushed towards the source of the words shouting with joy: "My precious darling! My dear one!"

We lost no time in running after her. However, the darkness hid those approaching, preventing us from venturing to catch up with Mother in the field. We rubbed our hands together in joy. Sister said afterwards that I clapped. But I did not kiss our returning sister. I cowered before her like a stranger, seeing her for the first time.

After supper Father talked to us about our departure on the morrow. His tale of what had taken place at the *mukhtar's* and the uncle's part in rescuing Sister magnified the uncle so in our eyes that he became as great as the other uncle who was dead. Mother said she would never forget the kindness and compassion of this one, who was called a highway robber. He had demanded the land from Basus and the girl from the *mukhtar* and got them both. He had brought us food to eat and tomorrow he would return to accompany us to the town.

"Yes, his good deeds will never be forgotten," confirmed Father. "We may meet again some day," he added. "The mountains don't move but people meet up with one another... I've seen many men but the like of him, his geniality, simplicity, wisdom, courage, I've never seen before... Believe me I've never seen the like."

"Just imagine that the *mukhtar*," Father said to Mother in great admiration, "with all his cruel tyranny was afraid of him, even if he did not curse or strike him. He did not raise his voice in the beginning. He was so calm I feared the *mukhtar* would think him of no consequence. He didn't knock on the *mukhtar's* door. He was too proud. He squatted in the courtyard with the gun in his lap, just as he did the day we went about the land, slowly rolled a cigarette, then said gently to the watchman, 'Give my greetings to Mr. Elias and tell him that we have come to redeem the girl. So he can bring out his ledger for us to sign.'

"Having seen him, the *mukhtar*, beseeching God's protection, did not come out. Hiding in the house, he sent his son to ask for the payment of the debt. 'Bring out your father, son,' said the uncle. 'We are responsible men like he is. Tell him to have the kindness to come so we can settle the account.'

"The *mukhtar* refused to come out to us. At that the uncle raised his voice, 'Mr. Elias! The little one is my niece's daughter. I am her legal guardian. Let her go with her calmly and take me hostage in her place.'

"When he didn't hear any answer he got up and went to a cow tethered in the courtyard, saying to me in a voice he intended the *mukhtar* to hear, 'Loosen this cow and take it. If the girl doesn't arrive tonight we'll slaughter it.' When I hesitated to untie the cow, he yelled angrily, 'To whom am I talking? Are you scared when I'm with you? I told you to untie this cow... Loosen her or I'll slaughter her on the spot.'

"At that moment the door burst open and a man from inside said, 'Take your hands off the cow, Barhum!' Uncle jumped behind a tree, took his gun off his shoulder and said, 'I won't take my hands off the cow until you take yours off the girl. If there is a man among you, let him stop us.'

"The *mukhtar* talked from behind the door, 'What about the debt, Barhum?' 'What about the girl's labor, *mukhtar*?' retorted uncle. 'And the family's labor? Doesn't it count for anything? We aren't running away from the truth... Have the goodness to come so we can settle our accounts... But we shall take the cow before we settle up. You have the girl; we have the cow. We are ready to settle up. Please just come out of the house.'

"The *mukhtar* didn't come out. He didn't answer. He disappeared inside. In a short while the girl came out. When we were on our way home, Uncle said, 'Travel tomorrow and I'll take care of the rest of the account with this son of a bitch. I'll teach him how men do business.'"

Our parents had talked for a long time after that. Mother was proud of her uncle. That was the last night we spent in the village... In the morning we bundled up our few belongings, Uncle arrived with his donkey and I don't know where Father got hold of another donkey. After loading our stuff on them, they set me on top of one of the loads and we left the field for the town. There we hired a Ford car with fenders to take us to Iskenderun. This was the finest car I remember riding in.

Before leaving, Mother kissed Uncle's hand, telling us to do the same. But she didn't cry in the town as she had done when we left our hut in the field. The widow and some of the neighbors had flocked in to bid us farewell. At the moment of departure they exchanged some words. Mother asked the widow to take our cat. She kissed her warmly and the widow kissed Mother and gave us provisions for the journey.

"Good bye," said those present.

"Pardon us for leaving," said Mother.

They did so and we left.

That was the last time we ever saw our village.

Chapter 12

We got out of the car at night in the village of Qara Aghash. We slept in a mud house attached to the house of the landowner for whom our sister worked. Before sleeping we ate bread and yogurt. For some reason the yogurt sticks in my mind. It was good. I may have never tasted anything better before, or I may have been so hungry that I found it so delicious.

"There are plenty of good things here," Father told us cheerfully.

That night we dreamed of those good things and of seeing this new world we had come to. As we threw ourselves down on the only two beds we had brought with us, Father said, "Here we won't want for anything, the mistress will give us whatever we need."

In the morning, Father accompanied Mother to the new master's house. His name was Christou. He lived on the top floor in one of the large courtyards belonging to the landowners who lived on their farms. We had never seen master's houses with two stories. The white-walled stone buildings were objects of our admiration.

Upon awakening and not finding Mother, we went into the courtyard. Then I went wandering around the field with my sisters. We climbed a sand bank to discover on the other side of it a wide expanse of blue water with a large thing traveling on top of it. We had never seen anything so big before. That evening, when we asked Father about the blue water and the huge thing going along on top of it, he told us that it was the sea and what was traveling on it was a steamship. It had several decks with quarters for the crew, bedrooms, beds and everything travelers might need.

The blueness and the expanse of the sea enthralled me, and the sight of the boat delighted me. I began going to the sand bank to wait for the steamships to go by. When one came into view, I would clap and hurry to the house to call my sisters to view the spectacle.

The discovery of something new around us everyday thrilled us. The fields here differed from those in al-Suwaydiya. We saw towering trees with green fonds, and very long slender trunks. We were told they were date palms. We also saw geese, ducks, rabbits and the red glow of the sun setting in the ocean. However, our circumstances did not change; in fact conditions at the new landlord's rapidly deteriorated. I heard mother saying, "We have jumped from the frying pan into the fire."

"I didn't think he was such a bastard as this..." said Father. "He deceived me."

"I don't know why but they always deceive you..." retorted mother. "Life was better there in al-Suwaydiya. At least we were free; we weren't hired servants and we had a house to ourselves. If it just hadn't been for the Indian silk..."

"Have you gone back to your wailing?" chided Father. "What use is that now? Don't make life miserable for me!"

It was Father who said, "Don't make life miserable for me!" Mother realized that, without her saying anything, life always besieged him on all sides. It had been so before and as a matter of course he may have wanted it to be that way, so he could be justified in leaving. Having got us all here, he now would depart. This was what she dreaded. He had placed us here as hostages just as he had done in that field, and would take off. Realizing this, Mother now showed no signs of disappointment. She had hoped to live in the city so she could send us to school and enjoy with us an easier and better life...all these hopes were quickly being dashed.

Iskenderun was at a distance. We never saw it. Qara Aghas was a village on the outskirts, dusty, muddy, full of prickly cactus hedges, fig orchards and ignorant dirty *fellahin* with eye inflammations ravaging both the old and young. The devil had inspired Mr. Christou to live in it, to personally oversee his land. He thought that Father would be useful in cultivating and managing and more especially in guarding the properties to prevent the *fellahin* from stealing. Father's uselessness very quickly becoming apparent; he began to treat him harshly, reproaching and cursing continually.

Christou was a disgustingly obese skinflint. He was not an original landowner but had inherited it, and the *fellahin* who labored in it, from relatives. He was arrogant: wearing suit pants, and a hat, and carrying a whip, he followed the *fellahin* from morning until evening with curses. Having often been frightened by him, as soon as we heard his voice, we would run and hide. His clothes made him conspicuous, since he was the only one who wore suit pants and we had seen nothing except gowns or Turkish trousers.

Immediately after our arrival, Mother was shifted to work as a servant in his house along with our oldest sister who had worked for the *mukhtar*. My youngest sister and I were left in the house. With the passing days we got used to the place and made friends with the children of the *fellahin*. Like them, we went out tramping about the fields barefoot, catching opthalmia and other diseases. We were submerged in all this filth: dust, mire, manure. We were not allowed to go up to the master's house on the second floor nor play with his children. We would see the mistress on the balcony; from time to time mother would talk about her and we would hear her voice when she yelled at us to get away from the residence. She would throw water on us if we played in the shade of the balcony during the siesta.

I used to wonder what it was like on the top floor. How did those up there live? Why had all the rich fair skin like the master's wife? How nice for a person to be fair like them!

I would see her reading the paper or writing, amazed at how she could understand what was written, how she could distinguish one word from another when they all looked the same and how she could memorize them all and not forget them!

The dusty main road passed in front of the master's courtyard which was enclosed by mud walls on the side next to the road. Between this fence and the back walls of the master's house, was a narrow lane about two or three meters wide where the mistress threw her papers, newspapers, magazines and books she was finished with or did not want. Upon discovering this place one day, I frequented it without anyone's knowledge.

I gathered a lot of pictures from there. Sneaking my mother's scissors, I cut out some that I showed to my sister. She was so pleased with them that she went with me to the alley to look for more pictures. I would pick up a piece of paper or a newspaper and look at it in astonishment, telling myself sadly, *If I could only read what's in it I could read all these papers!* I would return to the house with the same question in my mind, *What's in all these papers?*

There was another place that drew me without leaving me with any remorse. It gave me sweet gentle delight in exchange for the constraint of the courtyard and the bewilderment of the alley. I would escape to it in the mornings and late afternoons to sit in the sand on top of the bank watching the ships going and coming. I would follow them from the time they came into view until they disappeared, observing the last trails of smoke dispersing small clouds from the funnels.

The sound of the ship's sirens cheered me as they moved off in the direction of the line that joins the blue of the sea with the blue of the sky.

At first I was afraid to go down the bank; then driven by the desire to see the ships from close up, I ventured. One day someone in a row boat waved to me. He passed along the shore so I waved back at him. After that, I waved at all who passed in front of me on the sea, but no one else noticed me or responded. I ran along the shore after the ships and boats, waving and shouting at the top of my voice. When I received neither a greeting nor a response, I was filled with a sense of shame that scattered my joy. I went back up the bank to sit on the sand, waiting for a ship to go by. I went to sleep, awakening at the sound of Mother's voice as she shook me in her arms.

They had searched for me a long time, in the courtyard, the field and the main road. My sister led them to the alley where the papers and the pictures were. Father got angry, swearing he would punish me. But Mother protected me in her arms, taking in my place most of the painful blows from the pomegranate stick he rained down on me. She ordered me never to go to the sand bank alone and never to go to sleep on it, because there were lots of scorpions and snakes there. They were poisonous and there was no antidote for their sting.

I had seen some of those snakes. Father said it was of the variety *Uqdat al-Joz* and that the most dangerous adders were the yellow ones, the ones with variegated colors that lived in the sand banks. Just before our arrival one of them had bitten a *fellah* who died immediately. Having heard of this danger, Mother feared for me. Every morning, she would exhort me and plead with me not to go to the field or the sand bank, saying that she would allow me to do that when she bought me shoes. Ever since our arrival, she had been dreaming of going to the city to buy me shoes, and urging Father to ask the master for a sum from our account. But the master, who had concluded the bargain under whose terms we became hired servants in his house and field, asserted that our work was not worth our food, claiming that he had been duped by us, and threatened to dismiss us all at the end of the coming harvest.

One evening, Mother returned from the master's house crying. The mistress had cursed her and beaten her in front of my two sisters who worked as servants in her house too, making her realize that she was also considered a servant. She had, previously, believed she was only going to help the mistress.

Seeing Mother crying in humiliation moved me to feel that our life here, as it had been before, was bad and wrong, that the world was full of evil and misery, that the *fellahin* around us were happier than we. They were more content, they planned their lives without thought of affairs like shoes or clothes.

"I don't want shoes," I said to Mother. "I'll go barefoot like the others and never go to the sand bank again."

Fondling my head, she silently ruffled my long hair with the palm of her hand. The pain of her subjugation was more than words. Her defeat stemmed from her loss of hope and her struggle to improve her lot above that of the ordinary *fellaha.* It also sprung from her suffering due to the fact that she was neither *fellahin* nor the mistress of a house and thus had not become accustomed, nor did she desire to become accustomed, to the life of a hired servant to which she found herself descending.

Breaking my promise, I went secretly to the sand bank. I got bored with the house, the courtyard and the alley. There were no new pictures in the papers piled up behind the residence, and we didn't have a field of our own as had been the case in al-Suwaydiya. Mother didn't stay in the house to tell us her fascinating stories. Playing in the dust with the *fellahin* children irritated my inflamed eyes, in addition to my sense of being a stranger among them with a desire to be by myself to recover the environment that colored my imagination.

My longing for the sea challenged me, making me forget my duty to obey despite my great love for my mother and my endeavor not to trouble her nor make her cry. I would go there driven by feelings of pleasure akin to those a child experiences when participating in a new game. The sea's wide expanse relaxed and soothed me; the birds, circling above it and washing so carefree in the water that I had never bathed in although I could feel it on my body, kept me company. When a ship came into view on its surface my delight knew no bounds. Despite my feelings of wrongdoing, my fear of snakes and of being found out by Father and punished, I would steal out to go to that sand bank, determined not to go past it to the shore or to stay too long. But no sooner would I reach it and see that beloved blue spread out before me, than I would forget myself, my fears would leave me, and I would advance one step at a time toward the soft, smooth sand so enticing to play in and to run on, leaving faint traces of drizzle behind and before me.

One day as I was returning home, what Mother had warned me against happened. A snake coiled up in the shade of a rock on the sand burning under the sun's rays. It was the same color as the sand. Its head stretched out at the end of a neck raised above that cake like a circle was staring at me with terrifying eyes as I came running towards it. I had taken it by surprise just as it had me. It glided along, its round circle loosening coil by coil as it stretched out, flicking its tongue menacingly, etching a trail in the sand.

I screamed, frozen with fear, and when I set out running I fancied the snake was following me. Hearing a rattle behind me, I dared not turn around or stop. I ran faster, screaming, until I stumbled and fell on the sand. Sensing then that it had caught up with me and that it was about to strike me with its fangs, I rolled around in the sand emitting sharp, sobbing sounds that were heard by a *fellah* who ran to pick me up. When I calmed down, in his arms, he was able to take me home with tears streaming down my sand-covered face.

Father did not beat me. Running to me with the *tasit al-raba*[1] Mother made me drink three times, splashed the rest of the water on my face, then lay down with me as I shivered in her arms. She told me afterwards that I was sick for a few days and that a *sheikh* came to recite incantations over me. He wrote an amulet for me, which mother hung around my neck. I never went back to the sand bank, not out of fear alone but due to the family moving from Qara Aghash to the village of al-Akbar in the district of Arsuz after my two sisters succeeded each other in becoming servants for two families in the city.

I remember that Father hired two carts, each drawn by a horse. Putting our household goods in one, we rode in the other with Father sitting beside the driver. As the cart jolted and swayed along the rough road, we held on to the sides or clutched each other in the advancing darkness. We were under a dome of darkness and space, going we knew not where.

---

[1]Literally the cup of fear or bowl.

We were traveling along in the late evening, when the full moon came up. The dampness was high that night, so, stretching out in the cart, Mother covered us with a thick quilt while she sat there awake, sad, broken and resigned, contemplating the shining moon, the tranquil night, the shadows cast by the trees and bushes, and the unknown future she was going to. The driver's voice was raised in a folk poem as if it had been called forth by the occasion:

Laden camels, with their bells tinkling
And I am thinking of the days gone by.
I carried my goods and returned whence I came from
As I am a stranger, and no one bought from me.

Chapter 13

In the morning, the two carts landed us in a filthy dusty square in the village of al-Akbar. Cows, sheep, donkeys and all sorts of animals were gathered there on their way to pasture.

Along the sides of the square were ridges and a ditch in which muddy water flowed, with ducks swimming in it while hens clucked along its banks and under fig trees whose leaves were thick with the dust that rose from the square.

Some men collected around us while we drew together, awaiting Father who had gone to arrange housing for us. The carts had unloaded their contents and departed. I had heard one of the drivers tell Mother as he was unloading our belongings, "Your husband is crazy...what has brought you to this estate?"

"I don't know," answered Mother. "Fate!"

"He's mad," said the driver sympathetically. "You should have refused."

"And go where?"

"To the city."

"It's our fate!"

"Madness!"

After shaking his head regretfully over our madness and looking perplexed, he urged his beast on. The cart rattled forward, its wheels creaking. Turning in his seat behind the reins he said, "If things don't go right and you come back to our district, I'll take you to the city in my cart... It's a shame for you to stay here... For the children's sake don't stay here... You will perish!"

"But God is with us," answered Mother with broken resignation. "What is there to do? It is the result of the times..."

"But you are going to perish... That is not right," added the driver.

The other driver yelled, "That's enough talk... You've scared them."

But he persisted, "Yes, you will be lost!" he asserted as he disappeared around a bend in the road behind a cloud of dust that the wind wafted towards us.

Mother said no more. Her lips were dry. The sight of us had attracted passersby, who began stopping and turning around to look at us questioningly, either silently or speaking to Mother. Children pushed and shoved towards us; in the forenoon the sun became like a furnace; the dust was thick.

An old *fellah* suggested, "Go over there...under the trees. What are you waiting for?"

"We are waiting for my husband," replied Mother. "We can't leave our belongings here."

"No one will touch them...and we'll help you to move them if you wish."

"Thank you...we are going to move into a house directly."

"Where is your house?" asked the old man. "Who are you going to live with?"

"We don't know yet. My husband knows. He'll be back presently."

"Let the children go to the shade then. The sun is very strong."

Mother ordered us, my sister and me, to go to the shade of the trees on the edge of the square, but we refused. When the old man tried to pull me by the hand, I hung on to her dress. At that he said to her, "Put something on his head." I refused that too. I was embarrassed at our situation, miserable at being under the open sky among strangers. Mother got some bread out for us from a cloth bundle. They brought us water in a gourd and after drinking we sat on our possessions awaiting Father's return, which was long in coming. The people clustered around us pitying our state.

That day our destruction that lasted three years began. That driver's prophecy came true. He wasn't a fortune teller. He didn't need to be. When we see clouds, it will rain... He saw the clouds. A family exposed to storms; a tree plucked from its earth, its roots exposed to the midday heat, dried up. A place away from home is not a homeland; the willow will not grow in the desert. We were a willow in the red desert dust, victims of the whirlwind and burning sun. A mother, two children, and a father who was a flop in a poor rural area. Poor to the degree that hunger, disease and superstition on one side of the scale was balanced by the tyranny of a feudal system on the other. Every *fellah* crept around under the burden of the two weights, carrying them each one on the end of a yoke on the nape of his ulcerated neck just like a Chinese serf, awaiting release in death where his master can no longer order him to stand up, to work, or flog him and torture him with starvation.

In this poverty-stricken countryside where the inhabitants were as lean as an old maid with a wooden breast, we found ourselves that morning. And, unfortunately, we only added to its poverty. By some means or the other, those who lived in it had found shelter for themselves. They had a master, work, houses and graves. We had none of these things.

Some man in this village had duped Father, ever ready to be misled, for the sake of moving on. He declared to Mother that a man had said something to him that enticed him to move here with us, seeking his livelihood. Where was the man? Where was the house? Where was the land? He was silent...the remorse! His face was contorted with failure! His face blamed himself more than you ever could. In this state, he, more than you, deserved sympathy. Have pity on him, on yourself, on those around you and on this world of yours to which you have committed; this world you cannot repudiate or leave because in it you are responsible for those you have worked to bring into it and have grown up upon its ground and are linked to your fate!

Oh Mother, our mother, do not say anything to our father. Here he is returning, as he always does, preceded by failure. Share his failure with him. He is your husband, so you and we too must stand by him, not against him. It isn't what he wanted but he was forced into it. He isn't alone in his misfortune since this is a fate shared by all who, like him, stumble about in the mire of a disintegrating life.

We transferred our few belongings underneath the ancient fig tree on the edge of the road. We did it together silently in mutual defeat. After arranging our goods, Mother took a bedsheet that Father hung on the tree to screen us from the eyes of passersby. It was humiliating to sleep in the open on the roadside. I do not know if the *fellahin* offered to let us move in to one of their houses. I don't remember why or how we stayed under the fig tree behind this curtain on the side of the road. It could be that in our first days in that rural area we were putting into practice sentiments that time would eventually force us to abandon: feelings that we were urbanites and that our life, even that in al-Suwaydiya, had not entirely been that of rural people. That when it came to a matter of cleanliness our tolerance had its limits. In Mother's view living in one room with another family was unacceptable. Possibly in al-Akbar there wasn't more than one *fellah* family that had a house with more than one room. Therefore we were forced to remain in that place waiting to move into a house or to return to the city.

The fear that Mother lived with, keeping her in a state of continual alarm, now became a twofold fear. It was that father would go off leaving us under that tree, under the open sky, strangers, poverty-stricken to the point of a degradation that, even if we accepted it, was useless. No one in this place owned anything to be given, even had we asked. The *fellahin* had showed us all human generosity. At first they had brought us yogurt mixed with water and loaves of bread, and we had gathered dry branches from the fields for a fire to cook over. But our condition worsened after that due to the fact that sleeping under a fig tree brought on disease, and we sickened. The *fellahin* said that the air under the fig was so foul that it would be better to stay under a mulberry or walnut tree. But there was no mulberry or walnut, so illness was added to the eye infection. Mother fell subject to a malady no one knew a cure for that confined her to bed until she was at the point of death.

Near us was a small irrigation canal that formed a pool in which geese and ducks swam. Beyond the pond, the irrigation canal again took up its flow in a grassy ditch along whose sides frogs croaked in chorus in the evenings. Mosquitos flew about in spherical layers above the pond, lengthening out when buffeted by the wind, then becoming ball-shaped, then thrown into disorder only to return to cluster again. The fig tree with its milky ooze, dust, thick leaves and low branches was an alluring hideout for hordes of these insects. It became more enticing when we were under it, our blood becoming their plunder. Our faces were spotted with their bites. The *fellahin*'s friendly advice about lighting a fire of green branches so the mosquitos would be driven away proved useless. Our bodies were succulent, our skin tender. We were in the open without mosquito nets. In vain, we tried burying our faces in the pillows under the covers. The payoff wasn't long in appearing: malaria! It announced itself in a befitting manner: ague! In the forenoon, I would crawl to sit in the hot sun shaking with cold despite its heat, until the chill was followed by a fever. Then I would crawl again towards my sick mother to creep beside her in the bed under the fig tree behind the curtain that shielded us from public view.

I suppose that my sister suffered as I did. We often squatted together in the sun and crawled to our sick mother for shelter under her covers. We would stay there in that condition, asking for nothing but water until the fever left us and we would get up to enjoy a day of release followed by a day of sickness, subject to recurring bouts of intermittent cold and fever.

Our bouts of malaria were to last for years. We were left with devastating chronic illnesses resulting in dysentery that we contacted from living near the stagnant pool. We would later resort to boiling quinine leaves and drinking the tea. But, in this village, we didn't discover any quinine medicine, nor was their a tree anywhere. The treatment the *fellahin* used and we used also was urine. We drank our urine. Yes, I'm sorry to say! That happened. We drank our urine! I would urinate into a glass then put it out in the open to let it sit overnight. Then, in the morning, I would drink it. It was loathsome and burned my tongue. I would cry and refuse, but Mother would plead with me and overcome me with her entreaties. A *fellah* advised us to let it sit over night in a hollowed watermelon. He gave us one, and we did so but neither the taste nor the benefit derived changed.

We treated the eye infection with a powder resembling soft coal dust. Father got it for us from a *sheikh*, a folk doctor. Our eyes had swollen. The white had grown as red as blood, the eyelids puffed up so that we could not open them in the morning before washing them with warm water. In the evening, they would burn so much we would cry. To quiet us down, they erected a rope swing for us with a sacking bag on it in which they would put me and swing me until I slept. If I woke up in the night, Father would pick me up and walk around with me under the trees. One night he spanked me to shut up. Mother cried. Although it was very painful, I shut up so I wouldn't have to see my sick mother crying over me.

An elderly *fellaha* came forward with a wonderful natural remedy: that we boil an egg, cut it in half and put a half on each eye to absorb the fever heat. She said that a roasted onion would do in place of the egg. As this was easier to obtain, we roasted one. They would select a small onion, bury it in the ashes, take it out hot, wrap it in a white rag and bandage it to my eyes. At first I would jump up and down or roll in the dirt from the heat and pain. Then, when the onion cooled off and my eyes also, I would doze off in the swing for hours on end, sometimes until morning. When the onion failed to cure the inflamed eye, the sincere old lady advised us that the reason was that the bandage on the eyes was white. So, Mother changed it to a black one, but that didn't help either. The eye inflammation didn't clear up until the coming of autumn, when the heavy rains began to lay the dust and we moved into a mud hut in a small field belonging to one of the landowners.

Before that we remained three months under the fig tree on the open roadside, dirt under us, dust over us, in the village square. In the morning it was the gathering point for the village flocks from whence they moved off grazing behind the shepherds, stirring up clouds of red dust in the face of the rising sun. If the flocks passed by on the paths opposite the fig tree and the cows and bulls started chasing each other or the shepherds chopped off leaves for the goats and sheep who then dashed off shoving and pushing each other, it was like billows of smoke blown by the devil towards us. It stuck to the leaves of the tree, and the horrid dust sifted down on us covering the bed, and Mother lying on it, with a layer resembling powdered brick.

Father tried to work as a cobbler. He constructed legs for a wooden crate to convert it into a shoemaker's box and sat under a tree awaiting what would turn up. At that time, I believed that Father was a cobbler and that he would earn something; that the village would bring their shoes to him to mend as he did ours. Every time a man or a woman came, I expected to see something in their hands. But all my expectations were disappointed, not because the villagers failed to bring their shoes to be fixed, but because they did not have shoes. They were barefoot. It was summer, they were barefoot, and in the winter this state of affairs did not change very much. It only changed for the men and some of the women. As for the children of my age, they were without shoes in all seasons. Being without shoes made life pleasurable for me, and I had to do without shoes for three years.

While Mother was confined to her bed under that damned fig tree, she would send my sister and me to see how Father was getting along, if he was doing anything. We would go to find him sitting idle, and brooding. We would stay beside him a short while. Presently, he would order us to go back to our sick mother who might need us.

He finally mended a shoe. Was it out of pity? Possibly! Or it may have been that some of them had to go to the city. They brought some old shoes that had to be fixed. We were happy that day; Mother muttered her thanks to God saying that she had not been afraid of starving as much as she had of Father leaving if that *fellah* had not brought his shoe to be mended.

Where had he learned this trade? Had he learned it? Had he ever learned a trade and mastered it? With the exception of clearing out and drinking, the answer is negative, and even when he left it was as a vagabond and his drinking was an addiction not for pleasure or sport. I doubt that he knew how to drink wine or talk about it knowledgeably. He never mentioned it. He sipped it on the spot, when he was walking along, and, when he sat, he drank it quickly. No ritual! No distinction between good or bad wine. The appetizers were anything that was on hand: a pinch of salt if there was nothing else. He drank. He repented. He drank. Denial when sober or no talk about drinking. He would take an oath. Who would believe him? He would swear an oath with the bottle in his pocket and the smell on his breath. He would go out in the cold in the open air to drink his bottle. He understood that Mother knew. He would take an oath, curse and beat her, then be wretched. Mother hated him, pitied him. He deserved the kind of pity afforded to one who never mastered anything, neither virtue nor vice.

He mended the *fellah's* shoe, repaired a *fellaha's* shoe and was summoned to the *mukhtar's* house. He returned with a pair of old shoes that he mended. We had something to eat. Above all else he was working. The *fellah* gave him something from his house. But, as for money, it was a rarity. He only got it from the *mukhtar*. The *fellahin* didn't hold him responsible for skilled workmanship any more than he held them responsible to pay him. Both sides took circumstances into account and were tolerant towards each other. As far as father was concerned, he wanted to do something no matter what the return or even without any, because work in itself kept his mind and ours from dwelling on the terrible reality of our condition that we had no means of escaping or at least improving.

However, the dividends of mending shoes, even in this intermittent, miserable manner, came to an end in the middle of the summer. Cursing his luck, Father said, "If it were only winter!" Mother looked at him from her bed, smudged with particles of brick red dust that rose in clouds on the path and wind that blew in our direction, but did not say anything. Not having the strength to speak, she closed her eyes, groaning in pain, then grew quiet succumbing to her illness.

Chapter 14

The hot July days followed one another with us in the open, under the blazing sun in the daytime and the dew at night. It being difficult for mother to move like us into the shade, we tried shielding her from the sun by hanging extra sheets from the branches of the fig tree that had become our shelter.

She would gaze at us silently with an expression of wary resignation frozen in the depths of her eyes. The sky was no longer, as in the days of her youth, a band[1] of blue in an enchanted world. It now was a band of dusty somber clouds settling and pressing against her chest. The dusty scorching earth rose from the ground narrowing the empty space around her, enclosing her within two layers like a green leaf pressed between the leaves of a thick book, drying up and slowly dying of suffocation.

Mother withered, became emaciated and sallow, her cheek bones stood out, and her neck grew thin. She lay there a complete human skeleton just like a dry branch thrown to the edge of the field. She no longer spoke. She saw but said nothing. She was silent. Her silence was a protest, an anguish, a sorrow that we could not fathom. The look in her eyes remained veiled, distressed and distracted, for a moment anxiety over us flaring up in them, then becoming diffused with tears that made us cry when we noticed them. In childish fear, we tried to do something by bringing her water. That was all we had at hand. We helped her to drink. My sister would raise her head while I bought the water jar near her lips.

It wasn't very long before Father struck out, leaving us to the mercy of heaven. After borrowing a few piasters for the journey, he entrusted us to the care of some of our *fellahin* neighbors who became like our family. They did not lead us along the path of their hardship but taught us how to live in harmony with life in the center of this wretchedness. They taught us how to do as they did to obtain our bread so we wouldn't die of hunger. They let us share the

---

[1] The arabic word is *wishah*, meaning an ornamented belt worn by women (in older times a double band worn sashlike over the shoulder).

joys and sorrows of their miserable area in a village owned by a man whom they never saw but they feared nevertheless.

The gifts they brought us did not take on the form of charity, but we received them as such. Mother told us to take the things and thank them. It became customary when the flocks were passing through the square near us for one of the shepherds to call to us. We would hurry out with a vessel into which he would milk some goat's or sheep's milk for us. A *fellaha* would come bearing an earthenware pot with curdled milk in it and some loaves baked in a clay-lined pit oven. Or a *fellah* would come with a small basket of vegetables or figs. Their children would come in the mornings or evenings to play with us while the fathers and mothers visited with Mother in the late evenings comforting and encouraging her by prescribing certain herbs and amulets their *sheikh* wrote. They would charge my sister and me to do this thing or that for her. We would listen carefully...do as they said. This gave us a sense of confidence and of belonging just as if we had been borne in the village or were not strangers in it.

In Father's absence, the prophecy of the driver that we would perish in this rural world he had brought us to in his cart was fulfilled. Here there was no Mother's uncle nor relatives of any kind, no owner of a field like the *mukhtar*, whom we knew, despite his cruelty, was responsible for us as long as we lived in his field. Mother could go to ask him or entreat him with tears to sell to her on credit against the coming harvest.

Here, there was neither harvest nor field, not even a house whose door we could close to protect us from fear or to give us privacy. Behind it, we had awaited release from suffering in the summer, and amused ourselves by listening to Mother's stories, warmed by the mutual affection of the family that had not yet broken up. Two sisters were now servants for two different families in the city and we knew nothing about them. Mother had fallen ill, and we were incapable of managing to obtain a house to shelter us. Father had left us under this cursed fig tree on the roadside. Fear had expanded and become so linked with humiliation that as soon as the sun set we fled to Mother's bed where we slipped in on either side of her, succumbing to feelings of torment expressed by her feeble arms trying to enfold us.

She lay on her back the whole time, her former anxiety in our village, al-Suwaydiya, having now changed to withdrawal. Had

111

her unrest subsided? Had fear vanished? Had indifference taken its place? Perhaps it was the sickness. The mental breakdown that now appeared was total. Let the end come at least. In the meantime, while waiting for the passage to the other side, the gradual disassociation of the one about to leave the shore she lives on becomes an inevitable reality. It was now all the same if Father left or returned, if she ate or remained hungry, if she moved to a house or remained in the open. It seemed from her surrender to her illness that nothing mattered any longer.

Despite our ignorance of the danger threatening Mother, we were afraid for her; we were silent and melancholy too. When the weight of these feelings grew too heavy for us, we would rush to her for protection. Looking at us sadly as if she had recalled herself from her wanderings, she would beckon with her hand and we would come close, sit around her and ask her what the matter was, hoping she would answer and we would hear her voice. She would try to say something reassuring or amusing, but soon growing weary, she would revert to her wanderings and we would revert to our melancholy.

I was terrified one day by some children talking about death. An older girl told us that her mother had died. She had been sick and died. When she had kissed her dead mother, she found her as cold as stone and she never spoke again.

Leaving the children, I ran to Mother, kissed her hand, then her forehead. She looked at me, smiling. She kissed me too, asking me to go back and play with the children, but I refused. I was afraid she would become silent, never to speak again, that her body would become cold as happened to that girl's mother. My chief concern was that Mother's body would not grow cold. In order to make sure, I would kiss her. Taking hold of her hand I would rub it, talk to her, give her a drink or some food and from time to time ask her, "Are you getting cold, mother?"

"No, son."

"Let me touch it."

"Take it."

She would hold out her hand for me to take: it was warm! Thank God she was warm... My mother wasn't going to die; she wasn't going to lapse into silence and never speak again. I wasn't going to let her be silent and never speak again. I was going to keep her warm. If she became cold, I would light a fire to make her

112

warm again. For that, I gathered fire wood, thinking that if that girl had gathered fire wood and lit a fire to warm her mother's hand, she would have remained warm and continued speaking. Mother noticed what I was doing and understood. Holding me to her breast, she kissed me saying, "I'm not going to die...believe me... I couldn't die and leave you. God will help me to get better... God loves the little ones, He loves them dearly so He won't allow them to remain orphans in..."

She didn't finish her sentence; overwhelmed by her emotions she drew my head towards her, sniffed at my neck, kissed me.

"You will go now and play, won't you," she requested. "Go on... I'm all right... Let me sleep a little, don't be afraid for me, my darling, my little one, don't be afraid for me..."

I went to play for her sake. I was prepared to do anything for her. In the evening her changed behavior sent waves of reassurance through us. Bracing herself, she sat up, asked for water and washed her face. She said she was feeling better, that Father would return, that heaven was looking down upon us, knew about us and would help us. When I lay down beside her in the darkness of the night, I stared up into the heavens to see how they were looking down on us and seeing us. During these summer evenings, the sky was lit up by the stars. It was clear, beautiful, far away, shimmering. I fancied that it had real eyes and that those who dwelt there observed us; that they, like us here on earth, lit their lanterns hung in their windows in front of their doors. I wished I could distinguish the lantern of my uncle who had gone to heaven so I could call upon him, entreating him to come and take us. I started counting the lanterns in the sky. I became absorbed and happy in the counting. Then I woke up.

The sun was shining and the dew and red dust lay on our covers. The shepherd who passed by on the road had milked one of his sheep, brought the pot and placed it near the fig tree. A *fellaha* was talking to Mother, pointing in a certain direction, urging Mother to send us with her. I heard Mother saying: "Oh Lord...they're still little...they aren't accustomed to it...how will they act? What will they say?"

"It's nothing...nothing," said the *fellaha*. "Let them come with me, that's all... This is a blessing... It's a fulfillment of a vow. They'll give to them before they give to others... Strangers take before those of the estate. I'll tell them that you are sick and they will give them more because you are sick. Listen to me."

They discussed it, Mother and the *fellaha*. Our state of poverty forced Mother to agree. She wanted us to eat meat so we could get some proper nourishment. But she also realized what it would mean for us to go with this woman to the shrine asking for the *hareesa*.[2] But she consented to it so we could eat meat after such a long deprivation, hoping we would regain our lost vitality and enjoy ourselves like the children of the estate on such an occasion.

It was difficult for us to do that. I realize now that it was difficult. It was beggary. And for her to send us, she who had suffered so long that this might not come to beggary, the price was tears that she shed in our absence. She cried the whole time we were away. She may have wanted us to be absent so she could cry alone. She confessed as much to us, saying that she had refused to let us go to *al-khayriya*[3] many times. Then discovering that it would be better that we do so, she convinced herself that it was not begging: it took place in the city too, and the things were consecrated and distributed. She herself had taken vows and distributed what she had pledged, and advised us to do as she had done.

Outside the estate in a small wooded area, there was a large white tomb. Our neighbor told us it was the shrine of the saint. She enumerated his miracles. We didn't question her even if we didn't understand her. Had she left us alone, we would have preferred to stay with Mother. It was truly embarrassing to carry two dishes and walk barefoot at the heels of the woman to that shrine where the *khayriya* was held. Contrary to how we accepted people's charity under our fig tree, here our feelings were hurt. We were strangers, barefoot, each holding a dish in the hand. It was a long way, the sun was hot and my sister walked in front. I intended her to be in front with me behind so I could hide behind her to avoid the eyes that stared at us and the questions that were rained down upon the woman because of us.

---

[2] A dish of meat cooked with husked wheat.

[3] The vow or votive offering, where the animal is slaughtered and the *hareesa* cooked at the shrine of a saint.

There was a large crowd, men and some women. The fire was lit under a black cauldron huge enough to hold a camel. The woman told us they had slaughtered an ox, cut it up and put it in this pot. They were now waiting for it to be well-cooked so they could distribute the meat. The *hareesa* that we would eat would be stewed on what was left of it, and we would take some to our sick mother.

We stood side by side in the shadow of a tree, each holding a dish, with our eyes fixed on the cauldron and the fire under it. We tried keeping our heads bowed to avoid the eyes directed at us in curiosity and sought to distract ourselves by looking in other directions. We withdrew within ourselves, clinging to each other. I don't know why but we refused to talk to or play with the children. We were embarrassed by this unaccustomed humiliating situation that we would learn to become accustomed to with the passing days. We began furtively watching what was taking place around us, wishing we would be given something, anything, so we could take it and go to Mother.

The woman who had accompanied us left us for the crows. We could see her from where we were, talking about us in a whisper. She was answering questions about us, telling our story to those present. She may have been doing that voluntarily, prompted by a desire that we be among the first to be fed; that we should get our share of the meat that was on the fire and be given a portion for our sick mother under the fig tree. Thereupon, she came back to us, urging us to go play with the children. She told us that the food would be delayed until noon, so there wouldn't be any objection to us putting our dishes on the wall of the shrine where there were dozens of earthenware dishes in which the *hareesa* was to be distributed. They were called *ghadarat* and, as we learned afterward, the single form was the word *ghadara*.

But we chose to stay where we were. We stuck tenaciously to our place close to the wall, hanging on to our dishes. Had there been a way of escape I'd have done so. I loathed the thought of eating the *hareesa* and I no longer had any appetite for the meat despite my hunger and deprivation. To return to Mother, to seek refuge in her bosom became more desirable than all the gustatory delights. I suppose that the distance and the fear of bandits when alone restrained my movements, so I put myself under my sister's protection. We squatted at the base of the wall, and it wasn't long before I fell asleep. Sleep was a merciful relief from the grimness of the situation that had filled my eyes with tears many times.

My sister woke me up around the middle of the afternoon. The crowd had thickened now. Some *shuyukh* had arrived and those present had formed a circle around the caldron, preventing us from seeing what was going on. However, the woman asked us to get up and step forward. She requested that those in front of us make way for us a little but no one listened to her... Therefore, she pushed us before her and I caught the sight of a large copper cooking pot with flies flying above the boiled meat in it. A man had commenced dishing meat into the open hands greedily held out, one over the other, accompanied by prayer's and pleas for God's mercy. Whenever a piece of meat landed in a hand, the owner hastened to hide it in the pocket of his cloak, then withdrew carrying his earthenware dish to take his portion of the *hareesa* with a gleam of triumph and joy in his eyes.

I drew my sister's attention to a man putting the meat in the waistband of his underdrawers. The man stretched out the edge of his drawers and shoved the piece of meat into it, then pushed his drawers back in. My sister scolded me about this action of mine as he had seen her and was staring at us, so that I bowed my head in fear of him... The woman had succeeded in getting close to the cooking pot. Pointing at us, she said to the one responsible for the distributing: "The children the *sheik* recommended to you."

"The *sheikh* ordered me to distribute the charity to everyone."

"But they are strangers...from another village."

"From what village."

"I told you from another village."

"Another village could be anywhere."

"From the direction of the sea," said a man.

"You mean from the city."

"I don't know," said the woman. "Their mother is sick."

"I swear to it on my honor and religion," protested another man.

"On my honor I'm more ritually clean than you are."

His hand was on the meat remaining in the pot. He appeared to be snatching what he considered was his right and was prepared to fight for the sake of it. Others followed his example. They thrust their hands into the pot searching for pieces of meat among the bones. Those in the rear started pushing and shoving.

The one responsible for distribution yelled, "Oh, *sheikh*, they're plundering."

I heard a maniacal laugh from the edge of the shrine, "Oh beloved Khidr!"[4]

Those with him started running together. They understood that the turn of the notables was over and that the meat left in the pot with the bones had run out and that there was going to be a fight. On such occasions, this was bound to take place in the final stages. One of them got ahead and, lifting the pot up in his hands, ran off with it among the trees while the others, those who had not received anything, the idiots, and the young boys, chased him, cursing or calling upon God for aid. Those who had eaten and received their share of the meat laughed as if they had been expecting this and wanted it.

A middle-aged man of good intentions placed his hands on my shoulder, then taking hold of my sister's hand led us out of the crowd. He calmed our fears, telling the woman that our portion had been laid aside and we should give him our dishes so he could fill them with *hareesa* for us to eat. Then he would give us Mother's portion and some of the meat. We did as he asked, but we did not eat what he dished out for us. The sight of the people eating, holding onto bones and tearing off the meat with their teeth, or hiding it in their cloaks and pockets, and scooping out the *hareesa* with their hands with long dirty fingernails, or with wooden spoons, was repugnant as far as we were concerned.

The wrangling and snarling around us, the actions of the idiots, the insane and all manner of tramps and beggars who had heard of the charity and rushed to it, was upsetting and frightening as much as it was disgusting since we weren't used to that sort of thing. We were indeed strangers. When we told Mother all about it, she called upon God to protect us from ever getting into this situation again. However, we went back into the same situation... We got into the fray like the rest, for the sake of a piece of meat and a ladleful of *hareesa*. It became a natural part of our life here in this poverty-stricken village.

---

[4]*Al-Khidr* is the name of a well-known legendary figure.

Chapter 15

Father was not absent for long on his journey to Iskenderun. He did not work there; he had not gone to look for work. As Mother suspected, he borrowed something of our servant-girl sisters' wages and returned. Borrowing eats up the servant's life just like interest eats up the price of something mortgaged. Our two sisters' childhood was being squeezed out like a lemon, burned up like a cigarette and turned into ashes. It was a prison without bars, a verdant prison where the servant lives in the square stone rooms of the rectangle in the wooded area of the garden. Imprisoned for no offense, without trial and with no chance of appeal. In these cases, the law is an invisible thread. Necessity, poverty, orphanhood, are subjects not dealt with in law books, but when it comes to the application, they derive their strength from the money paid as wages and they demand their pound of flesh.

In the beginning, my father sold a year of my oldest sister's childhood. After that, a year of my second sister's childhood and when my youngest sister grew older he would sell a year of her childhood also. I ask myself: Why did he not sell my childhood? Was it because I am a boy? What is a boy able to do? No one will hire him. He won't do for carrying around the master's children or washing their hands and feet. And the mistress doesn't want him because he can't bring her a cup of coffee in bed; it isn't proper for him to do so as the mistress is naked or half-naked in bed. And, primarily, he isn't taught to sweep, wash and cook.

It wasn't because of my being a boy but because I was of no use. No one would have been willing to hire me as a servant, so Father did not sell my childhood. There was no buyer. My sisters' childhoods were sold for a year. Then Father borrowed against the coming year, and before it was finished he borrowed against the following one. I didn't realize that I was the one with the hungry mouth; that I was being nourished from my sisters' bodies, from their childhood, from their freedom; that I learned to read and write in the elementary grades from their ignorance. I assume they will never read these words, as they are illiterate and no one will ever volunteer to read them to them.

Father went to the city to borrow from my sisters' wages. He obtained a loan, drank, slept and forgot that we were there in the open under the fig tree. He forgot that my sister and I had begged, at that almsgiving, *hareesa* and meat to take to our mother who cried before stretching forth her hand to eat. We were in the same kind of area and rectangle of the verdant prison that our sisters were in. Our prison was an empty domain devoid of vegetation, and, just like a person in a prison cell lying sick on the cement floor, mother lay sick on an earthen floor, covered with dust, exposed, her emaciated form stretched out lifelessly but hanging onto life for our sakes.

When Father returned one evening, he carried a sack containing his things. It was too dark for me, I his child happy at his return, to see what was in the sack. I had the same dreams all children do at their father's return from a journey. Taking advantage of his inattention, I slipped my hand inside the bag and struck against something in it. It was round. Knowing that a cake is round, it seemed like a cake to me. For a few minutes, I fondled it, with excited dreams. In my impatience to discover what was in it and in my joy at the imagined cake inside it, the sack became like a hidden treasure a poor person stumbles upon and feels without having the courage to open it.

Alas! There was nothing in the sack but a lamp with a mirror, the kind that hangs on a wall. My hand had been fingering the round metallic frame of the mirror. Father emptied out the sack's contents in the darkness of the night. I was fascinated to see some flat circular disks the color of jujubes that appeared to be tomatoes. At any rate I went to sleep feeling happy at having obtained a few chick peas coated with sugar. The next morning we learned that Father had used the money he borrowed from my two servant sisters to buy some red leather, he called Moroccan, and half a car tire to make Aleppo leather shoes. He had decided, without calculating the risks, to promote himself from cobbler to shoemaker without having any knowledge about the making of shoes.

The curved rubber of the tire would become curved soles of shoes that could not be worn. The foot measurements could not be determined merely by some of the wooden lasts he brought for that purpose. The *fellahin* who risked following Father's suggestion to have shoes or red leather slippers made were very put out. Squabbles broke out, the shoes were rejected, the merchandise was unsalable, threats were made. We watched it all from a distance, from under the fig tree. What was going on in Father's workshop on the side of the road was tragic. We were grieved, fearing that the quarreling might lead to his being injured, but he was able by some means or the other to convince the *fellahin* that the fault was in their feet, not the shoes.

"What does the hairdresser do with the bald bridegroom? Look at your feet that no last can fit because they aren't used to shoes. Have patience, all new shoes pinch and scrape the feet."

His ready-made prescription for a *fellah* who returned his shoes was to mold them again. This operation was carried out by soaking the shoes in water and placing them on a larger last. Thus, this operation became molding the *fellahin* feet to the size of the shoes, not molding the shoes to the size of their feet. Disputes and fights erupted causing the *mukhtar* and notables of the village to intervene. They advised Father to return to his former trade of cobbler. He left off making shoes whose owners refused to finish paying for suffering a loss. That took with it the money he had borrowed from our sisters' wages.

From her dusty resting place under the fig tree, Mother saw and suffered. The tragedy of the indebtedness being repeated. We were all pawns this time. The shop owner in the village had agreed to give us some of the necessities of life ever since Father had commenced making new shoes. The debt piled up and the shopkeeper stopped giving us provisions, warning us, accordingly, to pay what we owed him before any thought of taking off. Thus the noose was tightened around our necks: no shelter, no money, no food, no work. The croak of the frogs in the brackish pond still reminded us of summer, but the yellowed leaves on the white poplar began falling. The fig season was at hand, signifying the change over to the months of rain and cold. The beginning of the melancholy autumn brought a new concern to the thirsty, wandering caravan stymied in this pit of impotency.

In the evenings when the kerosene lamp, whose mirror I once thought was a cake, dangled from a branch of the fig tree, Mother's eyes would be fixed on the wick, swinging in the same continuous circular motion. How her silence tortured me. She lay there gaunt, her eyes glazed, her mind straying, now here with us, then far away. She was my mother, something more precious than a mother. Not merely the mother who gave me existence, but survival too. I did not understand how to separate my existence from my survival. She was the reliable reassurance, gainsaying the terrible fear in my breast born of a thousand justifiable reasons, despite the paralyzed posture of the body stretched out before me. Before I knew the meaning of death, the apprehensive fear of dying overcame me and stayed with me for a long time. If my fears were realized and she died, I intended to cling to her, refusing to let anyone take her wherever the dead were taken. Her illness and the anxiety it left in me may have induced me to think at an early age about the destiny of those who die. A childish hope grew in my breast that my mother would not die; that she would not be buried if she did die; that I would stay beside her no matter what.

In the light of the kerosene lamp, some of the neighboring *fellahs* would come to spend the evening with us. They would talk, generally, about their daily life: poverty, hardships, the cruelty of the feudal lord and his behavior. Father would reminisce a great deal about things that had happened in his life. He was a brilliant raconteur with such an enticing way of relating things it was almost bewitching. He could change bygone events or news he had heard into a novelty, into an incident or story that would fascinate you and take you into his world of fantasy. As long as he was talking, he would make you forget the reality around you and the things that had been occupying you before you began listening to him. How often the *fellahin* sat with open mouths, their eyes fixed on the worlds he described in his real life or in his fabricated stories. But his tales contained no moral: virtue and vice, the oppressor and the oppressed were all the same to him. He would often make evil look good and disparage goodness, magnify the importance of overlords and men of religion, ascribing to them moral excellence and miracles. He would fasten tragedy like a necklace around the neck of luck that in his view was the only thing responsible for it.

Ever since those early years it has appeared to me that Father understood much about things: he had seen many cities, mountains and seas, and he had associated closely with all sorts of people. He always preferred fair people. Whenever he wanted to praise a woman highly, he would say she was fair with a round face and a breast that stirred the imagination. His favorite hero was al-Zir Salim,[1] his most worthy saint always an ascetic who subsisted

---

[1] A mythical figure in Arab folklore.

daily on a few raisin seeds. The only subject he kept silent on was wine, although he searched for it and managed to get it in some way or the other when we were not able to lay our hands on a loaf of bread.

Therefore, he was liked by the *fellahin* in this remote village, steeped in its ignorance, its acquiescence and its insularity. Those people who were good to us enabling us generously to live among them showed us the best way to get used to functioning like them, to beg like them, to dress like them, eat what they ate and also to believe in all the superstitions they believed in.

An amulet against eye infections hung around my neck and another against ague. Mother placed in the folds of her *al-asba*,[2] which she had wound around her head, papers that the sheikhs of this village and the neighboring ones had written. We also soaked the papers and drank the water from them. We burned sticks of incense. But none of these things succeeded in removing the sickness that afflicted her and which in the autumn showed up as twinges in her waist.

The *fellahin* suggested to Father that they shoot the twinges out of Mother's waist and he agreed. One day in the afternoon the ceremony took place. A sheikh with a full beard and a long index finger arrived accompanied by *fellahin* who lifted Mother up to a sitting position in the bed. One of them rode a stalk of sugarcane around her bed, whinnying like a horse. Over his shoulder, was slung a hunting gun loaded with gun powder only. They had put the short-legged table that we ate from on Mother's middle. The man shot at the table that was tantamount to the target. Then we boiled a young chicken and gave her the broth to drink. She went to sleep and sweated, her sweat being the sign of the success of the operation, and we looked forward to her recovery.

A few days after that, Mother's health improved. The pain lessened and she was on the way to recovery. Father claimed it was due to shooting at the twinges, and Mother believed him. But I was assailed by doubts about the twinging having been actually shot out and done away with, wondering where it had been hidden, and how he had hit and destroyed it. However, Mother did not leave her bed for another month when it grew cooler and Father took up a

---

[2]A black headcloth with a red or yellow border.

new profession: making *mushabak* that he sold in the village and the neighboring ones. Then he was able to provide her and us with some nourishment, and hope manifest itself by our moving to a house on the other edge of the village. It was nothing more than a mud hut in a garden of mulberry trees adjacent to a large, oblong storehouse, the granary where the grain belonging to the feudal lord, the master of the village, was piled. From it, the seed for the coming season was distributed.

Mother was delighted at the move to this shelter. From her happiness, we realized what it meant for a person to have a home; for the house to have a door that could be closed at night to shield its dwellers from public view, give them privacy in their affairs and protect them from the danger of thieves, wild animals and creeping things.

One day, a man appeared wearing a small pith helmet, white suit, riding a saddled horse and carrying a riding whip in his hand. Hurrying to hear from him, Father took hold of the horse's rain, spoke with him quickly and returned to us saying, "The *Bey* has come." Then, picking up a wooden chair, he covered it with a white cushion and carried it to the storehouse courtyard. The Bey sat down, gave the keys to some *fellahin* who had not been long in showing up, and some of them set about moving grain sacks into the courtyard. It was said that carts would arrive in the afternoon to transport the sacks of grain to the city.

However, another man also riding a horse suddenly appeared in the courtyard. Dismantling angrily, he yelled at the *fellahin* to stop bringing the sacks out and to put back those they had already brought out. After that, turning to the man who had arrived first, he slapped his face. This one was, quite clearly, his brother. He stood facing him, his arms folded behind his back, taking his older brother's cuffing without retaliating or changing the position of his arms. The striker then mounted his horse and rode away. The one who had been struck started pacing up and down the long courtyard in front of the storehouse, keeping it up until nightfall amidst the *fellahin's* silent astonishment and fear of directing a single word to him.

He was a young man, wearing boots, with a beautiful head of hair in contrast to the bald man who had struck him. And, according to Father's description, he definitely was fair-complexioned since he was one of the overlords. He most certainly won the astonishment and sympathy of those present, not because he did not return his older brother's slaps, but because he had been treated unjustly. The fact that he had been struck like them made him close to the *fellahin*, who were often beaten up by the police and landowners and sometimes by the *mukhtar*.

Mother took a packet out of the box containing a paper folded around a black powder that she said was coffee. Father took it to the older man on a tray. When he got close to him, we watched him from inside the house, excited by this dramatic spectacle that was ruffling the sluggish life of our village. It was accordingly a silent challenge to the older, more powerful man who had the ability to slap and shoot, but was unable to compel the one slapped to bow to him or unclench his hands behind his back.

The birds flying from the oblong grassy courtyard to the red-tiled roof of the storehouse found the scattered grain to be excellent food. They were permanent residents of the area with plenty of nests, who flew about incessantly in the evenings, chirping together as if their chirping were a thicket of intertwined voices. In the tense silence pervading the courtyard it was a soothing melodious choir. He was listening to them and probably everyone gathered in the courtyard was listening also, for they were the only sounds heard during the calm of that autumnal sunset that had witnessed the splendor of his event.

Father went up to the boss, raising his hand to his head in salute. Bowing respectfully, he offered him the cup of coffee. The other one, taken by surprise, stopped his pacing and stared into Father's face before asking where he was from, why he was in the village and if he had been present in the courtyard in the late afternoon.

"I wasn't in the courtyard," replied Father. He explained that to us later in the following terms, "It's better that he doesn't know he was slapped in front of us. We're from the city after all and are going back to it and we'll tell what we saw."

"Did he believe you?" asked Mother.

"I don't know. I alleged that I had gone to work and that you were all in the house. He took the coffee without making any comments. He feigned ignorance of the incident and I did too. The *fellahin* withdrew one by one leaving him there alone. I moved off until he called me to inquire about our situation. So I explained everything that happened to us quite frankly."

Our house, that I have forgotten how we managed to get hold of, was to the right of the storehouse, on a small rise in relation to the dusty road a short distance from it. Our mulberry field was a long narrow ribbon of approximately a hundred meters in depth, parallel to the road. Our only neighbors were two women, one an old lady living in a hut behind our house who crept over to us in the hope of getting something to eat. As soon as she reached our doorstep she told us that she was alone and poor; that she had had seven children who had died either when they were little or grown up; and that now, being destitute, she lived on charity. Mother, grieving for her, gave her a piece of bread soaked in water to satisfy her hunger. Since she was our neighbor, every day we would break a piece off a loaf for her the same as we would for anyone of us.

The second woman's name was Zanuba, a middle-aged woman whom we came to know shortly after we settled in this house, following an exciting incident that occurred one night in a surprising manner.

Zanuba lived on the opposite side of the road. Her house was locked up so Mother permitted us to cross the road to play in the woman's garden. She may have been away somewhere during that time or our parents may have become acquainted with her by some means. However, my sister and I were not aware of her existence and we had not sensed her physical proximity, until that rainy night when screams arose from the road and we heard obscene oaths, a commotion, clamor, men's voices and foul swearing, coming from it.

Father picked up the glass lantern and went out. Mother had entreated him not to do so; in fact, taking hold of him and chiding him, she had blocked the door, saying that since we were strangers we should put the wooden bolt on the door instead of opening it. However, scolding her, he pushed her aside roughly from the doorstep, telling her he was not a woman, so he must demonstrate that fact to those mean cowards who were committing adultery so close to our house; otherwise they might venture to come and start brawling with us.

He was in the right: he understood the rules of the squalid game due to his frequent vagrancy when he left home and plunged into it. He was reckless. It was a mad courage not stemming from a lack of fear, rather from a lack of any sense of it or from its failure to develop. He had gone out driven by his lust stirred up at the concept of a woman being raped in the middle of the road, and by his desire to witness that rape and probably share in it. However, he covered that up after the event, when justifying what he did in his zeal to protect the honor of the woman and his anger at her being abused. He also wanted to mark his territory in that area of the edge of the village, so that no one would encroach upon it some day.

I really forgive my father for much of the damage he caused us through his irresponsibility towards life. I do not reproach him for his pathological lust since he was not responsible for it, nor for his intemperance, since he drowned his misery in intoxication. But, as a child, I was unable to fathom that and my mother's remonstrances to him were mine too. The protests became suffering, loathing and helplessness at one and the same time.

Father went out carrying his stick in one hand and the swaying lantern in the other. Through the open door the voices came to us more clearly and sounded more inflamed. The light we had surrendered to empty space was swallowed up and smothered in a circle of all-pervading darkness. A damp smell blew through the door as a result of the clammy autumn rain. We could see Father's blurred shape sinking in the mire and determine where he was from the circle of light moving with him. This was what guided Mother in catching up with him, and we followed her in his tracks.

When we arrived, Zanuba was laughing. She was stretched out on the muddy ground laughing. We thought she was mad, because up to that point we had never seen a drunk woman. Those who had taken her had fled, those remaining being those who had come to help or who pretended that, when Father approached with his lantern and stick. They had by now pulled down her rolled up dress, covering her legs but her long torn underdrawers were still lying near her. She had started singing, laughing and mouthing very filthy words that made Mother shy away and move towards the house, while Father with words of rebuke began trying to put an end to it by asking those present to leave and warning them against perpetrating something like this in the future.

"What business have you with this whore?" a man yelled.

"Your mother is a whore," responded Zanuba.

"Shut up, you brazen hussy!" said another. "Some people have arrived."

Zanuba laughed boisterously and intoned in a singing voice, "Welcome, son of a bitch."

However, she stopped when she lifted her head from the mud and saw Father. Trying to get up, she revealed her genitals saying, "Look."

The men laughed. Then, comprehending the repulsiveness of what she was doing, chided her, "Cover yourself up. Damn your ugly face."

Giving another protracted, drunken guffaw, she flung herself into the mire, raising her legs in the air. This prompted a man to pounce upon her, beating her with his stick while her foul curses due to her pain and anger mingled with the uproar. Father was at a loss to know how he should act, confronted by a drunk woman, men aroused by lust and a distressing scene. He was accustomed to such as her and them, but in regard to us it was a frightful spectacle. We retreated immediately afterwards towards the house. The next day we heard Father relating the details to Mother in terms we did not understand. But we did comprehend that it was shameful and that Zanuba did not die. They had carried her to her house and locked the door on her, leaving her lying unconscious on the floor.

The following afternoon we were destined to see Zanuba from close up. She came slowly and unhesitatingly, as if she had detected our presence in her neighborhood for the first time. As soon as Mother saw her approaching, she remarked, "This is the one they beat up last night." Her declaration had a remarkably upsetting effect upon us. From that time on, I was conscious of embarrassment mixed with unbounded anticipation in regards to her. I hated her profoundly and wished unconsciously that they would beat her again. Mother, with her gentleness, weakness, compassion and serenity, was my ideal of womanhood. She was the angelic side of femininity. I had discovered amid the clamor and commotion in the mud and mire in the darkness of the night that femininity had another side: satanic, that men for some unknown reason chased after. I reckoned that what had happened to our neighbor woman in our distant village al-Suwaydiya would be repeated with this neighbor of ours. The whispers I had heard previously some nights between Mother and Father came back to me, all of it sending shudders of disgust through my soul, a premature curiosity to understand what they had been doing and a resentment of what they did.

Negative hostile feelings towards my father stuck to me for a long time, feelings that I had not sensed even at the times he left us for parts unknown. And because I was unable to talk about what I heard at night, I harbored anxiety and aversion for some unspecified thing and for an obscure act originating with my father and exciting me.

Due to her brutal violation, Zanuba deserved my sympathy. Father's whispers in the night had produced an act that I considered irksome to Mother, and the men who had beaten Zanuba in front of me. It would only have been natural then for me to feel a mutual affection for her approximate to that I felt for Mother. However, what happened to me when I saw Zanuba was altogether different. I was seized with rancor and a desire not to see her again. In my view she was responsible, not them, but it was not clear in my mind who she and they exactly were: what the offense and what the punishment. Why should she be responsible and what had instigated this nervous tension towards her? Instead of the black and blue bruises on her face making me feel sorry for her, they excited me just as if they were the marks of another man on the body of a woman he had attacked. This state of affairs differed very little in subsequent reevaluation of my early childhood feelings. In fact, these hostile sentiments confronted by stories and scenes of lewd women grew deeper and changed from disgust and indignation to a hatred for sexual violence and possibly a loathing for the perpetrator. I have always desired lofty, poetical things, not due to my staid conservatism, but due to an unequivocal romanticism I was born with, a romanticism that sees even in the utmost sensuality of sex a sublime human experience. It makes one want to scream when this experience is degraded to an unpleasant banality.

Zanuba was approaching our house. She was coming in curiosity to investigate. This little mud house had been locked up. It may have once belonged to the storehouse guard and probably had been given to Father on that basis. If that mysterious event had not occurred when the young boss was slapped by his brother and they disappeared one after the other the same as they had appeared, both of them or one of them would have spoken to Father about the matter of the house and guard duty. We might have been thrown out, because the one who gave us permission to live in it was a man from the village as far as I can make out. The overlord reckoned that it was his brother who had settled us in it. Therefore, it would have been in keeping for him to be harder on us than he had been on his brother, taking his revenge on him out on us by driving us away.

The *fellahin* talked at great length about the cause of the quarrel between the two bosses, making conjectures about it without being absolutely certain. They traced it back to the sale of a piece of land, to the younger brother's claim to his inheritance from his father, to his desire to go to France to study and, as if it were a secret, one of them announced his opinion in a whisper: "The quarrel is over a woman!"

The news spread, not because it was true, but because it was a secret attached to a woman. When this was the woman of a boss she became someone fascinating, provocative just like the inside of his mansion was because she, like it, was something hidden from view, an object of the imagination in keeping with the most magnificent images of folk tales about the world of palaces and the beauty of women in them. The sky was a blue screen set up on high; the sun was the mouth of a smelting oven; and in the middle of the screen that shaded the spectators there was a hand moving the mouth of the burning rays, reflecting them at sunset in a horizantal position and making them show a golden film before the invention of films. And pictures were reflected on the blue screen above. I myself saw a picture. I stared at a picture as they advised me to do. I gazed at the sky until the picture was imprinted in the heavens. The *fellahin* stared at the pictures that their imaginations stored up and then, gazing up into the sky, saw them imprinted there. A loaf of bread, a field of wheat, a silver Ottoman coin, a woman were in all the drawings. The most beautiful things in the pictures were those that were white: the loaf, the coin and the woman, and especially the woman, the boss's wife living in his palace; the princess they dreamed of and saw on the blue screen spread above them like an awning whose edges extended to the horizon.

Zanuba was approaching our house. She too was a woman but a brown-skinned woman from a hut, not a palace. When she was drunk, they quarreled over her body lying in the mud. Her image was not reflected in the horizon because she was real, not in the horizon where only fantasies live, things that can be visualized in the most tantalizing colors and enchant because they are distant specters, very distant indeed.

Father was a realist, not one of the surmisers. "The dispute between the two bosses is over the grain in the storehouse, not over a woman...this grain that the whole village has toiled for a whole year to reap. The younger one thinks it best to sell it now and the older one, the actual owner, is insisting on delaying it. He is a merchant who likes to hold a monopoly and had beat his brother for the sake of money," he declared to Mother.

"And you?"

"I'm not the third brother!"

"I mean which one do you think has the right!"

"The devil has the right!"

"God forgive me...the devil..."

"Don't revile him...he's our neighbor. He lives in the storehouse...inside the sacks."

"You've frightened the little ones..."

"To teach them to learn not to be afraid."

"And what is he doing in the storehouse?"

"Guarding it!"

"From the *fellahin*?"

"The *fellahin* don't rob the boss's storehouse. A *fellah* steal from a *fellah*. He knows he'll get away with it. But stealing from the boss...it happens sometimes. When it does, the police arrive with guns and whips accompanied by the boss. Here in this courtyard, a *fellah* was killed. The boss accused him of theft and killed him. They covered his body with a sack, so that the others might see him and be frightened..."

Zanuba was approaching our house. It wasn't an observation tower, nor was Father a guard. After the younger boss discovered us in it, he gave us permission to live in it. It was empty and near the storehouse. When Father asked him to allow us to remain in it until we left the village, he had no objection. He charged him to take care of the mulberry grove, gave him permission to raise a box of silkworm eggs, drank the coffee he had brought him, and promised him a sack of wheat at harvest time or if he thought of it. He never returned to the village.

Through time, we cleaned up the house. We brought water to splash on the dusty floor and make it smooth. We tramped it with our feet and beat it with a wooden mallet used for washing clothes.

130

When it dried, a skin of clay was formed on top that kept down the dust. Mother spread a mat over it on which we sat, ate and slept. On the opposite side, we placed our belongings around the hearth. Father repaired the door, provided it with a lock and bolt and announced to Mother that he was going to work night and day to gather some money so we could leave.

Autumn was half over; the sun's rays had weakened; the cold wind had begun whining in the mornings and evenings, participating in the yearly obsequies for the departed summer. A yellow epidemic blight moved through the trees poisoning the ragged many-colored leaves and withering them. A certain moroseness spread through the atmosphere, doubling our sense of being lost strangers and our fear of the specter of approaching winter.

We went into the open countryside to provide for ourselves. We had to work in the *durra* and wheat and could gather a handful or so of olives every day. In the evening, we would grind the grain to make loaves of bread and use the olives as a condiment and save some for the winter. No *khayriyya* ever passed us by. We came to be well-known, my sister and I. When we reached the site of the votive offering, they would give us meat and *hareesa*. If we didn't show up, they would miss us and send someone to call us, and just like little beggars we would arrive in the crowd of people of all ages, clothed in tattered garments of many descriptions and afflicted with all sorts of infirmities. A crowd that would put a gypsy gathering to shame, robbing it of its peculiar features, giving it the stamp of the lowest sort of beggars, the decrepit and the deformed. As soon as we arrived, we would crowd together around the cauldron or stand aside, overpowered by a sense of poverty and misery until one of the fellahin who knew us would hurry to us with our share of what was being distributed.

Zanuba was heading for our house. Last night, she had discovered for the first time that there were human beings[3] in her neighborhood as they had told her. This description of us as human beings was not to make any distinction in our standard of living or work, but to point out that we were from the city. Human beings lived in the city where houses were built of stone, the streets paved

---

[3] The *fellahin* would call themselves *nas*; the term they used for the author's family is *bani Adam*, the sons of Adam, or proper, good people.

with asphalt, where there were automobiles, electricity and women with bobbed hair and short dresses that showed their legs.

Remorse! Remorse in the sun eclipsed; a confiscated garden with its trees smashed; a cat that stole its owner's food so it was beaten and thrown out; a dog that failed to retrieve the game that the hunter sent him after; Father's face the morning after an unsuccessful journey or a drunken bout when as a consequence he slept on the side of the road. But Zanuba's remorse was not a mask. Zanuba did not veil her face. She didn't bother to veil it but in visions of recovered consciousness she recalled that she had exposed her immorality to us, had uttered obscenities we had heard, and Father had gotten something out of her, therefore we might refuse entrance to our house.

At the doorstep, she extended us a preemptory greeting betraying her reluctance and feelings of guilt. We were flabbergasted by her appearance on the doorstep. She tried to smile, to act like a normal visitor but failed. Father wasn't at home so Mother stammered a return greeting, confused about how to act in front of a strange woman, whom she had seen last night in the mud, as drunk and unrestrained as possible. Mother was by nature conservative. She never condemned any woman, but it grieved her whenever she was obliged to associate with a woman of a questionable reputation. She became cautious, conscious of a lack of inborn courage when confronted by an imagined boldness in a woman who does not conform to the rules of common decency. Her compassion that weakness engendered by an excess of womanly tenderness spilled out. She was sociably polite to any person who came to visit us or keep her company, without any pretence. In the same manner, her timidity would make her tremble in the presence of strangers or the supposed powerful until she became acquainted with them, when her good nature would resume its serenity and we would act spontaneously, sharing it generously with others.

She returned Zanuba's greeting in embarrassment that in no time was suppressed under a willingness to respond. She was anticipating asking her something, saying something to her, entering into a conversation with her about the reason for her visit. But Zanuba contented herself by sitting on the doorstep, looking at us in deliberate contemplation as if she had come to see who we were and what we were doing, why we had left the city, whom we had in this village and what connection we had to the landowners, the owners of the storehouse. All these questions, as Mother recalled, she flung at us afterwards during subsequent visits, since she was unable to deduce them from our situation due to her failure to induce my sister and me to come near her on our own doorstep.

Night fell. The lamp was hanging on a nail in the corner. The door was locked and bolted. We grew more apprehensive, and Mother was beset with feelings of remorse over the stand she had taken with Zanuba. We dreaded her return, imagining that she would be resentful towards us and might harm us. When Father returned, on time, bringing something he had bought from the village shop, he scoffed at us. He made our delusions look foolish, saying that she was a poor soul and, in consideration of her being our neighbor, we should treat her decently and not boycott her or treat her as an enemy, since she had done nothing to harm us. Under the pretext of searching the garden and around the house, he went out that night and left. We stayed up waiting for him to return until drowsiness overook us and we slept. Mother stayed awake alone, listening to the wind moving through the trees, and the dogs barking in the nearby fields, struggling with fear mingled with intuitive jealousy and apprehension aroused by suspicions about Father's intention in going out at night. Mother understood that he was driven by the riotous lust in his blood to take risks and she suffered silently on account of it.

I was tormented that night too. I was sleeping in my mother's arms and was awakened in the night by whispering and quarelling in the darkness. Holding my breath, I heard faint screams, suppressed and tormented, futile pleading to be left alone and Father's curses followed by successive movements. It aroused me, kindling a fire of resentment in my blood. Then a cough. The subdued voices stopped, and Mother, covering me, took me in her arms and we slept.

Chapter 16

I was destined to see Zanuba after a few days in another guise, in contrast to what she had been the previous time. The remorse, shame, and contrition that had marked her face and movements on her first visit had disappeared.

Her cheeks were quite rosy and her low fez with its wide headband was tilted over her forehead. There was laughter in her eyes, and her medium-sized compact body displayed an unnatural mirth. Her ample breasts held in by a flowered chintz were shaking with laughter. Her thick tongue was firing off pointless chatter that was talking just for the sake of talking. When she ceased talking, she sang heart-rending songs that were charming like her dancing that she claimed was for us.

As soon as she crossed the threshold, we could smell the alcohol on her breath. It was bad drink, liquor made from figs. As Father would say, it was strangling stuff with a repugnant, sharp smell. It would make a camel drunk. They had actually made one drunk on it once, the same day they intoxicated a rooster and a viper by pouring the alcoholic liquid into the mouths of these animals. They got great fun out of the spectacle of their shaking and stumbling.

Father made Zanuba welcome. He knew her well by now. His nights were colored with drinking and sex in long unintentional encounters with this woman, whose neighbors we had become and whose lover he had become. He was her twin brother in drunkenness, lust and indifference towards family life and family responsibility. This abrupt change threatened the family. Mother would cry over it. But Zanuba suddenly by some means gained access to her affection, becoming like a kind aunt to us when she was sober. Her proximity was a blessing and a necessity. Her intoxication was a diversion that banished the gloom of our loneliness and isolation and dispelled the anxiety gnawing at our hearts. Her courage overwhelmed Mother, who never stopped talking about her.

We made room for her where we were sitting on the mat, but she stuck to her place on the earthen floor, sitting cross-legged as though on a rug. When she used improper language in asking for a cigarette, Father reprimanded her.

"Behave yourself or I'll throw you out."

"You..." (She was so drunk she blinked her eyelids.) "You are going to throw me out?"

"I told you to behave yourself..."

"What have I done?" She turned to Mother. "What did I do, my sister? Last night this husband of yours..."

When Father got up angrily, she got up scared and said no more. However, she resumed talking with one idea in mind: she was happy, she loved us, she respected us but she was happy... She wasn't drunk, she was happy... So why were we angry?

"Have I said anything to anger you?"

"No, Zanuba," replied Mother. "You are good, a good neighbor. We aren't blaming you for anything."

Zanuba was jubilant. She struggled to her feet. We laughed. We knew what she wanted. Father didn't interfere. Going to Mother, she kissed her hand. This kiss was the indemnity she paid whenever she got drunk. There was no use resisting. This act was the beginning of her clowning. We would die laughing at her and jump up as she raced around behind us. Mother's turn to be kissed came first, then sister's, then lastly mine. She would kiss our hands one after the other, then go back to her place, radiant and animated, to resume her talking with greater freedom. Kissing our hands was not an apology as much as it was her way of enlisting us into her clowning and extracting from us her right to let down, to sing, to dance or to swear and make slanderous remarks. Father would be forced to rebuke her and induce her to leave and go back home because we were simply going to bed.

After the aversion I had towards her, I got used to her. I danced with her, aped her, sang like her. Her best song was *"Daluna"*[1]; her singing was soft and sweet when she was sober, lying in the shade of a tree in her small garden that we were astounded to learn belonged to her. She made it public property for everyone. We considered her figs and pomegranates delicious. When she got to know us, she gave us the right to pick them. Father began helping her to care for the garden, but in the middle of work she would leave off what she was doing, saying she was going for something she needed and would return without delay. She would stay away until the af-

---

[1] A famous Syrian song.

ternoon, or until night and sometimes until the next day. She would return with the shakes or dead drunk. In that state, she wouldn't stop over at our place. She would make for her own house and sleep for a whole day.

There in her house while she was drunk, they would hunt her down. They would get into her house through the door or window, if they were not locked, or manage to open either one of them by some means, often tearing off the wooden window frame or smashing it, and in the light of matches rush in at her. Her voice would arise in the darkness of night, laughing boisterously, cursing and screaming, creating an uproar and fights. She would cry or give up, becoming as lifeless as a corpse, not paying any attention to what they did to her. If they tore at her flesh, to avoid the pain in her body she would run away, with them chasing her and catching her. They would fight each other over her, blood would flow and some-one might be killed. Then the whole village would curse her and ostracize her. At night, they would lie in wait for her to sin with her. Despite all they did to her, she would stand up against the village men, and when she was sober they stood in awe of her, en-raged at her cursing and fearing her boldness that turned into rash-ness if she became obsessively angry with one of them.

When Father had put in an appearance in the mud, Mother's fear for him was quite justified. This wanderer, adventurer, drunk-ard, with no sense of fear, this damned lecher was her husband. Mother, who understood him, would relate to us after many years all his doings as entertaining stories, passing reminiscences, or as old memories evoked by recent events.

Zanuba's small, laughing eyes, which her high cheek bones made look sunken, were held fast by a pair of wolf-like eyes (my father's). Framed by a face the color of ripe wheat with wine-col-ored lips, the fleshy lower one slobbered with lust. This failure in his family and working life was a success in his love life. Being like that, he refrained from talking on the subject. He drank but did not talk about drinking. His intoxication alone compromised him. He would make love and not remember the woman. His affair with her was as insignificant as his leave taking. He didn't keep keep matters secret nor did he brag. He lived spontaneously, an-swering the call of lust just like the call to drink or to set out on a journey. He lived the act in a most natural way.

Zanuba became his mistress just like the widow in our village al-Suwaydiya. He became her lover, and, in contrast to what he had been with the widow, he was now in nothing other than a temporary marriage. Mother was disgusted. Picturing Zanuba inebriated made her nauseated. She refused to acknowledge his lapping from this turbid vessel. That he would embrace an unwashed body reeking of alcohol, depravity and lust was too much for her. But he desired Zanuba for just these same reasons: she was a brothel person like him, tarnished with everything that roused his natural impulses.

Death was lying in wait for him. Mother said that they shot at him one night. He denied it, maintaining that what she heard was just a stray shot in the dark. Is it conceivable that he did not hear the aimless stray shot behind him?

Isn't it conceivable that the eyes of the men full of sensuous desire who had vied with each other over Zanuba were turned towards him in enmity? Wasn't he destined to run up against one of them? All that was uncertain. The quarrelsomeness in his blood had died down. The aroma of one inebriated body with another inebriated body had seeped through his veins and he had surrendered to it. As usual, he leaped before he looked. He proceeded without heed for the risk, the squalor, or the disgrace and she was infatuated with him for some inexplicable reason that still hasn't come to light. Most likely his amiability seduced her or the risk he took for her; his licentiousness and his indifference towards life around him gratified her. In addition, she undertook what he did not ask of her: she refused all other men, deferring to one man. She loved him and consequently loved us. She improved herself and her conduct for his sake and did all that was in her power for us.

The merciless winter that year brought back the image of the bygone winters in al-Suwaydiya. We remembered them with regret. Bitterness becomes sweet when the drinker tastes something more bitter. Al-Suwaydiya's bitterness was sweet in comparison to the *colocynth*[2] of al-Akbar. There Mother could go to the *mukhtar.* We were his hired laborers, in debt to him, and our sister was a servant in his house. He would give us, very niggardly, barely enough to keep body and soul together. But he gave to us. He did that so we wouldn't die, so we would live to repay the debt. But

---

[2] A vine of the Mediterranean area bearing a small bitter fruit.

here we weren't anyone's hired laborers. We were free from bosses but were the slaves of want. Our servitude here was worse. We wished that that boss, the owner of the storehouse, would hire us, but ever since the affair with his brother he had vanished. We felt as if we had come to live in an ownerless hut and a small abandoned field, barren and neglected, no one caring for the cattle that pastured or took their midday nap in it.

The one fortunate aspect of it was that Father did not leave, and fear and hunger did not gang up against us. The specters of thieves sneaking in through the roof, the door or openings in the clay walls in al-Suwaydiya were gone here. Father was with us. How good it is for children to have their father with them. Father was working. He gave up shoemaking: the red Moroccan leather, the rubber soles and the other materials were lost in the unsuccessful venture. His advice to the *fellahin* to soak the shoes in water to enlarge or straighten them was no use. Moreover, he put the responsibility on them, on their feet, and their innate peculiarities. "They are stupid," he said to Mother in self-justification, "...it's better for them to go barefoot. No one could possibly, even in the city, make shoes to fit feet such as these."

Mother replied that the feet of people in the village were the same as people's feet everywhere and that the fault was in the shoes with rubber soles curved like boats. They were ugly, flat, too narrow or too wide and, in short, could not be worn. Therefore, they carried them under their arms just to say they had shoes.

Father laughed unexpectedly. We laughed with him. He glowered and resumed his cursing. "It's better for them to carry them than to wear them," he said. "That way they'll remain new. In al-Suwaydiya I saw people carrying their new shoes, made in Antioch itself, and going barefoot. The important thing is to say they have shoes!"

He recommenced his cobbling inside the house. As it was wintertime, he set up his wooden box and anvil just inside the doorstep. It was hoped his cobbling trade would improve with the rain and the cold. Some of the *fellahin* did bring their rotted shoes to be repaired. He would take them from them, turn them over and declare in complete despair that there was no way to fix them. They had no others, so Father was obliged to do something. He would lay them aside, promising to do his best to sew or to patch them. Getting that over with, he would enter into a long conversation with the owner of the shoes while Mother, in the center of the house, would be consumed with rage that he was talking, not working, and because the *fellahin*, whose shoes he had or who found his conversation strange and entertaining, would keep coming back and sometimes stay until evening.

Therefore, when he announced one day at the end of winter that he was going to give up cobbling and go back to making *mushabak*, she didn't object. She only asked where the necessary money was going to come from for buying the flour, sugar and oil. He dared not disclose to her his intention of going to the city to borrow on our servant sisters' wages. He claimed he was going to get a loan from the *mukhtar*. Some days later he maintained that he was setting out for another village for some purpose and that he would be back by evening. He left but did not return. He set out secretly for the city. This was his second trip there since we had come to al-Akbar. We had nothing in the house to eat, but of more concern was Mother's fear here. For some reason I don't understand, it was worse than in al-Suwaydiya. It seems she was afraid for herself. She charged us not to let anyone know of Father's absence and we did so. She would lock the door as soon as night fell, put the bolt in place, then sit on the bed with one of us on either side of her. In order to amuse us and banish her anxieties, she would tell us old stories and sometimes sing. I believe that after we dozed off she would cry as she had in the past.

Zanuba found out he was gone. After two days, she was convinced that he had carried out his intention to leave on a trip that he had hinted about to her. On the third morning after he had stopped going to her, she came to us to ask about him and to assure Mother he had gone to the city to get his hands on a little money in order to have a small capital to launch his new, old, enterprise *al-mushabak*. Zanuba reassured Mother that he would come back in a few days and that in that interval Mother could rely on her, Zanuba, not only to ward off harm, if that should happen, but to ensure our livelihood no matter how long his absence. Despite Mother's misgivings about Zanuba's words and her desire to get rid of her lest she bring us trouble, the other told her that she would not get drunk, indeed she would not touch a drop of *arrack*, and that she was asking as a favor from Mother that she be allowed to sleep at our place on the threshold. If Mother hindered her, she would sit up all night in front of the house, never closing an eye and in this condition, "When Zanuba isn't drunk, the men scram. I'm stronger than the men!"

Was she telling the truth? Mother told us afterwards that she was. She kept her word and did not drink. She was strong, courageous and generous, contrary to what we had imagined. She brought us provisions, we don't know from where, and sat up with us dispelling our worries with her laughter and singing:

> Zanuba, oh you *arrack* of figs,
> Oh you ornament of gardens
> Cry and wail you poor thing
> Over your separation from Zanuba

She would dance and I would dance with her. When we went to sleep, she and Mother would sit up in the dark, talking. She told Mother her story, disclosing her husband's murder at the hands of the older boss, the owner of the storehouse, who had struck his brother. Her only son had died of a strange illness as a young man. She was left alone, so sad that she almost lost her mind in sorrow. She consoled herself in alcohol, became addicted, and indifferent to everything, as there was nothing left in this world to care about.

Father's absence was not protracted. After a few days, he returned at sunset. However, as usual, he was a miserable failure, in the depths of despair. He didn't go to Zanuba that night, he didn't laugh for us. For the first time, I sensed that something had happened that my sister and I shouldn't know. Mother broke out weeping. After being patient with her for a short while, he scolded her. Then they both kept silent. We lay down in the darkness, trying to sleep, but every once in a while Mother would throw out a question concerning our oldest sister who worked as a servant in the city. In the morning, our parents got dressed in their best, saying they would be away all day because our sister was sick and they were going to the city to see her.

I pleaded with Mother to take me with her. She gave me to understand that it was impossible. I clung to her so she wouldn't leave, but she took no notice. Leaving me with my sister, she locked the door upon us. Our tears were of no avail, and in vain I tried to open the door to catch up with her. When the door was opened for us from the outside after a short time, it was Zanuba who opened it. She told us she was going to stay with us, that our parents had gone to the city and would return in the afternoon bringing us some good things.

We stayed, awaiting our parents' return all afternoon. I was not much concerned with my sister's illness. I wanted Mother back. This was the first time she had gone far away from me. I went to the edge of the field where I sat on the raised borderline overlooking the road, my eyes fastened on the bend around which our parents would come into view on their return. My sister joined me, and we remained nailed to the spot until nightfall. Had it not been for fear of the dark we would not have given in to Zanuba who came begging us to come into the house. She led us back bawling loudly. That night, I experienced feelings of being an orphan, of lonesomeness and of being cut off from everything dear and secure. I never worked as a servant child; I wasn't plucked from my parents' side like my two sisters, destined to live far away from them. That night I could appreciate in my imagination what they endured in their alienated exile, and therefore I extol their suffering and that of all children who have been deprived of their childhood through death or poverty.

Zanuba, who had instilled in me feelings of loathing as she lay in the mud and also a sense of sexual excitement towards her even before I recognized sexual arousal, was washed that night in my childhood tears. She, like all females, was lifted out of the mire of social disrepute from associating with despicable men to the peak of human glory where the glory is in the spirit, the loftiness in the nobility of the deed; and the woman is judged by her goodness that washes away every stain, giving sweet fragrance to every breath of her reputation.

I slept in her arms. Mother and child. I wasn't her son and she wasn't my mother, but in the warm tenderness radiating from her intrinsic nature she was a mother and made me a son. She was the same to my sister. She patted our heads, restrained our tears and made us feel that we were blood kin and more. Thus, the night passed calmly and silently with me awakening only with the sun.

Mother returned in the evening. Her sick daughter did not recover. Oh, the sorrow of a mother whose daughter is sick and does not recover. It is a long illness. We don't know its name or cause, but we know that it is serious and that we have to forget it and forget our sister who suffers from it. Years go by, and she is not mentioned in the house.

She is not mentioned in the house; only in the heart.
At our house there was a mother, and that mother had a heart.

Chapter 17

Three years passed by with us still in the village of al-Akbar.

The child that I was grew, and his powers of discrimination concerning the tribulations and the things he witnessed increased with his age. He was now closer to understanding things when observing them and more equal to grasping them when recalling them.

The gleam of light in recovering those lost years flashes like lightening through the soul and is as suddenly extinguished. The flashing gleams of light illuminate the ancient ruined subterranean vaults for the roving eye. Memory's lens is the eye of a fish under water in a storm. A car's lights pierce through the fog with their yellow light, and pictures of the past that time has wiped out present themselves in the fog.

However, two pictures defy time; they have defeated nihilism, looming up in all their brilliance. Two pictures of Mother and Zanuba remain intact. I loved both of them with all my being. My hate for Zanuba had changed into love ever since the night I slept in her arms. Perhaps, unconsciously, they were one and the same, but consciously the love was innocent, deep-rooted by what happened to her and flaming with boundless admiration for her unrequested and unexpected sacrifice. However, it could have been a latent reaction, unleashed and activated by a challenge.

Zanuba stood by us during those three years. A heart overflowing with human kindness is always seeking an outlet to express the potential of this love deprived of expression. Zanuba had found a channel for her capability to love in a rivulet flowing in our direction.

Mother, my sister and I drank from the stream of her love with such feelings of gratitude that I don't understand now how we expressed them. These feelings were more apparent and more self-expressive in the impatience with which we awaited Zanuba's arrival when Father was away from home.

Father would be absent once every few months whenever he was broke, possessing no longer the price of a loaf or a tin of tobacco. He would leave for the city to borrow from our two servant-sisters' wages. When we had only one sister left working, the loan dwindled and from this loan he paid the cost of going and coming plus the expenses of staying in the city. A stay that lasted for days, while he managed to convince sister's boss that we were hungry and in urgent need of some money and that he wouldn't show him his face again for a long time during which the loan would be covered by sister's wages. But he would go back again after a while to borrow again, to take up his position in front of the door, repeating the same words he had used previously in his entreaties, unconcerned about the age of the child he was mortgaging for additional months each time.

I recall these trips of his were made mostly in the winter. In the summer we gathered our bread from those ears of grain we gleaned from the earth during the harvest. During this season, the village shopkeeper would give us some of our necessities on credit. He would receive full payment from the grain we gathered from gleaning: an exhausting, humiliating job that our family was destined to pursue those three summers, but that I wasn't to experience until the last summer.

I experienced it when Mother agreed to take me with her to the countryside when the harvested ground was close to the nearest outskirts of the village.

The harvest began during the first months of summer. The barley was harvested first, then the wheat; in the fall, the maize corn and, last of all, the olives were picked. Mother was appalled, as she told me later, at being a gleaner: snatching, pushing and shoving, her back bowed and her feet and hands bleeding for the sake of a handful of ears of grain that had fallen from the reapers and gatherers. Ears short of stalk, of scanty grain and empty kernels. But she was forced into it, accepting this reality in suffering and tears, enduring the burning sun, the dusty heat and the barley beards. All that often getting the better of her, she would cry secretly or openly in the rough, blazing hot countryside.

At first she and Father went alone, apprehensive about my little sister sharing in such harsh work. Then, under the pressure of need, she took her along. In this situation, I had to stay home alone. Having feared that, I resisted with tears and by hanging onto the hem of Mother's dress but to no avail.

It being impossible for me to stay alone in the house, Mother asked Zanuba to take me to her place. Zanuba, who was accustomed to locking her house and wandering off at will to no one knew where, found it trying to be tied down by the whole day. However, for days she devoted herself to me just as if, in the loneliness of her life, I had become her companion, and, in the emptiness of her house, a child she knew was not her son, but who, in exchange for her early bereavement as a mother, became a son to her.

She would come to us in the morning and, if she found me sleeping as my family who had gone to the fields had left me, she would sit on the doorstep silently and motionlessly waiting for me. Sometimes, if I overslept, she would waken me, help me to dress, give me something to eat or take me to the village shop to buy some sweetmeats for me. She would then take me back to her house where we would sit together on an old mat spread over the smooth earthen floor while she told me curious, colorful stories about kingdoms and treasures, jinns or ghouls. Or she would sing as if she were rocking her drowsy child, trying to put him to sleep so that she would be free to attend to her household duties.

As Zanuba did not have enough housework to fill her spare time, she would lock the door and lie down beside me on the mat. A tranquility would settle down over us; we would succumb to that shadowy cool atmosphere that made us sink into a sleep lasting until the afternoon. When we woke up, we would eat something before going out to the garden where she did some work. In the evenings, we sat at the edge of the garden from where I would go to watch the path, yearning for my parents and my sister. It was an agonizing need within me, for their absences stirred up feelings of anxious longing.

When the family returned from the fields at sunset, I would run barefoot, like a rabbit escaping from a cage, into the dusty path to meet them. I would savor Mother's welcome, her smell and her kisses. Even though she was tired out, she often carried me on top of her load the remaining steps to the house, where she would put down her load and lie down exhausted, asking me to bring her a cup of water to quench her thirst and restore some of her strength.

I was no less delighted to see my sister than I was my mother. Sister would take me into the garden to tell me what they had run across during the day and how she had gleaned a pile of ears of grain, for which Mother had praised her, promising her a dress and shoes. Or she would tell how one of the reapers, taking pity on her, had given her half a sheaf. Or the steward had asked her for a cup of water and asked about her family and then said, "Go and pick out the biggest sheaf and take it." Or how a bird had flown out of the underbrush in front of her or a snake had slithered through the dirt, and she had jumped and run away, shouting at the people to kill it.

She only mentioned the amusing, cheerful side of it. Her talk egged me on to entreat Mother to take me with her. I imagined the people would give me sheaves of grain in pity and affection, that the steward would pat my head as soon as he saw me, and that a colored bird would fly up in front of me. I didn't have the courage to picture the snake, despite the fact that Father told me it wasn't anything to be afraid of and wouldn't bite unless it were stepped on.

Mother, giving in to my persistent entreaties, decided one day to take me with her gleaning. When she announced that in the evening, I was so overjoyed that I became over-excited and, as a result, could not sleep. In my mind, the countryside spread out in one continuous land surface, unbroken by boundary lines. It appeared to me as an area of land planted with golden grain on whose borders were luxuriant green trees and in their midst streams of clear water sparkling over a bed of many colored pebbles. There were birds in the trees and wild fowl moving through the bushes. Partridge with their charcoal-brown feathers barred with white and their red beaks were the ones that took my breath away. I had only seen partridge once in the pouch of a hunter who passed by our house. I reckoned I was able to run after a partridge and catch one or hide behind the bushes and throw a stone at it and then chase it. Even the streams I pictured flowing through the fields teemed with fish that I envisioned in different shapes and forms. I thought that if I took a basket with me and put it in the brook, the fish would get caught in it and I could lift them out alive flopping about on each other in the basket. I was prepared in my mind for all these images that sister's talk drew for me about the gleaning, the sheaves of grain, the rabbits that hopped around them, and the birds that took to flight with such alarming but delightful movements. The cold terrifying vision of the snake alone aroused my fear. I made up my mind to be very careful so as not to step on one lest it bit me, as Father had said.

I don't know how I managed to fall asleep that night. Of a certainty, my sleep was troubled. When Mother awakened me in the morning, I jumped out of bed, hurriedly washed my face and got dressed. She gave me a chunk of bread the same size as sister's and tied up the provisions that were our food for the day. Father picked it up and set out in front with us bringing up the rear.

The village was awake. The *fellahin* were sending their animals out to pasture through the main square to join the flocks the shepherds would take to graze. When we passed by Zanuba's field, I turned around, wanting her to see me going with my family to glean. We cut through the village to the eastern outskirts, where we met the sun rising in all its magnificent glory, making the tree shadows long and thin. Father urged us to quicken our pace, before the sun rose higher and it got hotter. After that, we crossed over harvested land, sometimes walking along the ridges, at times among the stubble, and along narrow dusty paths where we passed flocks of animals, raising clouds of dust in our faces, until we looked down on land at whose edges the *fellahin* were gathered. Mother said that the harvesting in this field had ended yesterday evening. Today, they would release it, so we must stand with the others, waiting for the go-ahead to begin the gleaning.

We took up our positions in the crowd, composed mostly of the poorest *fellahin* from our village or from the adjoining one. There were men, women and children all barefoot, in threadbare garments, with disheveled hair, their children's faces dirty, unwashed in the morning. Among them were the elderly, the deformed, and the beggars, talking in loud voices, pushing themselves in, trying to get onto the harvested land or start gleaning around the edges. The steward would shout, rushing at them with his stick, driving them back to the waiting crowd. In no time they would try it again or shove their children onto the land to glean the ears. The steward would go back to them, cursing them or beating them with his stick, shouting at them to wait until they were finished gathering the sheaves, then they could rush in as they liked.

I lost my enthusiasm, standing there beside my sister, disappointed at my expectations of the picture my imagination had drawn of the gleaning. There were no trees, no streams, birds or wild fowl. The countryside was bare and bleak. There were brambles and thorns on the ridges. In the forenoon, when the sun's burning rays poured down on us, Mother took out a couple of rags to wrap around my sister's head and mine. I was happy when the steward came up to Father to speak to him, hoping he would allow us to begin gleaning, but the steward said that the land wouldn't be released until around noon, because they hadn't finished loading he sheaves, and the reapers had left some scattered patches of grain behind them, so they must go over it again to reap them. After that, they they would comb the stubble to gather the grain that had fallen while the sheaves were being lifted and loaded on the animals. He then let Father in on a secret: a rumor that other land near by was being harvested, that he would be there and would let us glean around the edges before it was released.

We were delighted when Father told us that. We felt that God was helping us by making people compassionate towards us and that this steward, like others whom my sister had told me about, sympathized with us and pitied us because he was acquainted with Father. He considered us to be strangers from the city who were compelled by necessity to do such unaccustomed and unsuitable work.

I was overwhelmed with embarrassment and thrown into confusion just like the day sister and I went in the company of the *fellaha* to the saint's tomb to get some *hareesa* and meat. I wished I had stayed with Zanuba. Feeling envious of the way sister boldly mixed with people, I hid behind Mother, waiting for us to be permitted onto the harvested land so I could run to gather the grain as others did.

Those gathered there were distributed along the length of the boundary of this land, waiting hopefully and restlessly for the anticipated moment. As soon as the steward gave the word, they pounced upon it, women, men and children in wide rows, their backs bent, their eyes boring the stubble and their fingers as sharp as claws. They tried to outdo one another in gleaning the stalks of fallen grain, advancing with a quick pace from the boundary we had been standing on to the other one at the opposite end of the field. Some of them filled my hands with stalks as they bound them into bundles and gathered them together in a designated spot in the field. Each family knew its own bundles from the mark they put on them.

They called this quick combing the first meal of the gleaning. It was the richest meal because the stalks of grain left behind by the reapers' scythes were more plentiful. When they finished that, they went back over it helter-skelter, trusting to their luck and the sharpness of their sight, heedless of the thorns, stones and all sorts of crawling things. They continued wandering across the reaped land from edge to edge, until there wasn't a fallen or lost stalk of grain among the thistles. When they finished that, they would move to other harvested land or where the reaping was in progress and it was about to be released, scattering over the countryside to pursue their gleaning until evening.

This work was not only difficult, it was harsh. Attachment to my family in whatever part of the land they went relieved me of my embarrassment and confusion, as it segregated me somewhat from the crowd. However, the stubble, the thorns and stones hurt my feet and hands. Getting scratches on my palms, I tried at first not to bother about it. Running hither and yon, I happily gleaned the grain stalks, collecting them in my small hand, then running to Mother to give her what I had gathered. Her encouragement goaded me to work harder.

That went on for about two hours, until the day was almost half gone and the blazing sun had roasted my head and my face. When there was not a stalk left on that land, Father proposed we should take a break to eat the bread, and we had to supplement it with what was in the haversack. Then we would go to the land the steward had informed us of.

We sat in the shade of a thicket, where Father had gathered our bundles of grain and tied them with a rope. After eating from what we had brought, we drank warm water from the clay jug we had with us. Father smoked a cigarette, we rested for a while, then set out again in the direction of the land we were bound for.

This countryside where there was neither tree nor water was now ablaze with the heat of the midday sun. Despite my obstinacy and endeavor to endure what my family endured, the walk exhausted me. I began lagging behind the family, forcing my sister to lag behind with me. Taking me by the hand, she urged me to quicken my pace. Failing in that, she called Mother, who stopped and came back asking how I was. She kissed me, encouraging me to go a little farther as we were about to reach our destination. However, the land we were making for was still at a distance, I was worn out, my head was on fire and Mother realized that she had made a mistake in giving in to my entreaties to go with them to glean. I heard Father blaming and chastising her. At her wit's end, she poured water from the jug to wash my face and did her best to distract me until we reached a bush or thicket to rest in its shade.

But, after a few steps, I felt dizzy and sat down the burning ground, crying.

We stopped walking for a few minutes. The sun's heat was unbearable, sweat poured down our faces. Mother took some of the bundles of grain, sister carried the water jug. Father, taking the rest of the bundles in his hand, carried me on his back and we continued on our way over the uneven harvested earth until we reached our destination.

There were no people there like there had been at the first place. The gleaners reckoned that the harvest on this land would not be finished until tomorrow, and gleaning behind the reapers was forbidden. However, the kind steward, in pity for us, allowed us to do that along the edges from where the sheaves had been gathered.

There was a wild azarole tree[1] that the steward had made into something like a tent for himself. He advised Father to put me there in the shade. He brought me a bowl of *eiran* [2] that I drank and then went to sleep. When I came to, it was late afternoon. My parents and sister had gleaned a great deal of grain. The steward going behind the reapers selected a large sheaf, called Father to come get it, saying it was for the little chap who should not be brought out to the fields in this extreme summer heat.

---

[1]Neapolitan medlar (crataegus azarolus).

[2]A kind of grain juice used in preparing food.

150

Chapter 18

Summer ran its course and with it the harvest.

The autumn in that rural area donned a twofold placidity: no wind, no clouds, and no rain. The sun lost its strength, the leaves on the trees, especially the sycamore, turned yellow early, falling quickly.

Mother, with her ever-present sense of fear, smelled the feel of winter in the autumn air. She could smell it and lived in tormented anticipation of the turbulence of the coming season, envisioning the cruel winter, its rain and darkness with us in this remote village in this mud hut without much warmth, schooling or security.

Was she the ant or the cricket? Did she even know the story of the ant and the cricket? It is doubtful she had heard of it, but in order not to be a cricket singing the summer away and starving in the winter, she had worked during the summer so we would have enough to eat in the winter. The grain harvest being over, she was thinking about condiments and decided we should go out to glean olives.

During the weeks she took us to a small river behind the village that flowed through a hilly area between the rocks. There we gathered firewood and lit a fire under a copper boiler we had borrowed from Zanuba. Mother washed from morning until afternoon, not leaving a piece of clothing or household linen unwashed. She was happy despite the toil, delighted at the abundance of water and being able to get as much hot water as she wanted. Father cut down oleander branches to make screens we could bathe behind. Mother cooked *mujaddara*[1] for us, out of which we made a hearty meal. In the evening, we gathered up our things and returned home.

I will never forget that day with its water amongst the stones, the oleander bushes standing along the curves of the shoreline, the stone pipe trees around it, the pleasant warm sun on our almost naked bodies, bathing and eating the *mujaddara*. That day was one the reasons for my great love of nature. Sitting there on the bank, I felt I was capable of helping Mother, so I begged her to take me along to glean olives as she had taken me to glean the grain. Due to

---

[1] A dish made (in Syria) of bulgur with lentils, onions and oil.

her experience with me in gathering the stalks of grain, she refused me unequivocally.

With the onset of winter, the work in the fields ceased. We returned to our hut to gather dry branches to pile up as fuel for the cold weather. We now had food to eat. Mother applied herself to boiling wheat to make bulgur and grinding the remaining for making bread. She arranged things so that we couldn't eat our fill, yet would not go hungry. She helped Father dig up an area in the garden that she sowed with radishes, onions and spinach. Zanuba came to work with our parents, then Father went to work with her digging up her garden and planting the vegetables. The vegetables would also be ours, for Zanuba seldom cooked. She had now become very close to us, always in our house, affectionately devoted when sober; boisterous and brazen when drunk. It appeared that Father had her completely under his thumb: she feared him and never crossed him. For certain, she bestowed upon him the best she had, like a woman not short of sex but of love. Despite the men who used to take her in her drunken state, she needed a man of her own to feel affection for her and protect her. That man was our father.

The winter was bound to pass with no more change in our life in the village than in Father's affair with Zanuba. Clouds, wind, rain, and gloom woven from the fabric of the sombre atmosphere and of the soul, filtering through the grey light enveloping everything around us. Huddled around the fire we lit on the cold nights to keep us warm, Father would tell us stories of his adventures and sights he had seen during his journeys. In the light of our situation in al-Akbar, our reminiscences about al-Suwaydiya made it a different place, not as bad as it had seemed when we were in it.

Our hut became our small closed world, isolated, harboring our disappointed hopes and all our expectations of deliverance born in the morning to be snatched away by the fingers of the nights. Just like the dreams that lift the slumbering dreamer out of the real world, creating a different reality embellished to make it pleasant and attractive, Father's stories about the world he took us into made us forget our world, exchanging it for colorful imaginary visions that delighted and solaced us. For that reason Father was generous with those stories that he intoned to the beat of the continual rain on many of those nights.

152

After that winter, during which we reached the lowest standard of living of all the days of our exile, when summer drew near we were on the verge of starvation.

One day a son of one of the *fellahin* came to play. He grabbed me and we started wrestling. He threw me. I tried a second time and he threw me again and the third time too. At that I said exaggerating: "Wait until the summer...until I get enough to eat, like Mother says, I'll be stronger and beat you."

The next day he brought me a loaf, but I refused it. Feeling insulted, I refused: "We're waiting for the summer," I told him, "when we'll gather the ears of grain, grind the wheat and make the bread."

Shrugging his shoulders, he ate the loaf and left me hungry.

He felt me dreaming of summer...eating in advance. It was a bill of exchange, a stone in the pot. And Mother, acting like the Bedouins, fooled our stomachs with a stone in the pot.

Summer was the stone...but the distracting deceptive pot would contain black dirt instead of a stone. The hope that sustained us all through the winter and spring that year would vanish like fog before the glare of the sun. The thread of forbearance would be severed by a sharp knife, in one blow making us reel from the shock and sink into the depths of poverty and fear. It was a disastrous summer, hiding within its folds a terror that would thoroughly confound the whole family, leaving it with no escape. That was the year of the locusts, the year of our calamity... We didn't know that it would be the year of our calamity, therefore the surprise really shook us.

By the end of spring, Mother's belly was noticeably protuberant. I had seen her cutting up some clothes and sewing small clothes from them by hand. She told me I was going to have a brother, that he would arrive one day from somewhere unknown but that we would not be aware of his existence until he was in the house with us.

He arrived in the middle of May. That night my sister and I were to go to Zanuba's house.

After lighting the lantern, Father took us there and stayed with us. He was silent and glum like he was the morning after he returned drunk, when he would be ashamed in the daytime of what he had done at night.

153

We slept on Zanuba's mat. When we woke up in the morning, Father wasn't there. Zanuba told us we had a sister and that she was very tiny. She took us home to see her.

Mother was in bed with a swaddle beside her containing a bit of red flesh. She uncovered her face saying: "Your sister!"

Saying that, she kissed me. Her love and concern for me had increased. She had hoped I would have a brother and her hope had been dashed. Our baby sister hadn't infringed on anybody's rights, but our parents assumed her to be guilty.

Her crime was that she came, and her arrival in our harsh circumstances doubled the crime. Our elderly neighbor's attempts at condolences never succeeded with Mother. Zanuba never stopped laughing as she said, "Give me the baby and I'll raise her." Mother shook her head, thanking the Lord and asking Him for good health for the suckling child's sake.

Zanuba said she was going to get drunk at night and dance. Father forbade her: "Leave us alone," he said.

But he was drunk that night before her. He told Mother he did it to forget what had happened to us. Mother, who was in such a weak state that she could do nothing but commiserate with everyone, herself most of all, sympathized with him.

Throughout those days, Zanuba was like a sister to Mother. She washed for her and cooked. Catching two of her hens, she killed them and brought us provisions and money. We knew where the produce came from, but the source of her money remained a secret. Mother gave it back to her. Hurling it on the mat she left singing *Daluna*, and we didn't see her face until she returned drunk in the evening.

A month later Mother discovered that our baby sister was blind. Her pupils had a white film over them. "Your sister's eyes have flowers on them," Mother told us. We didn't understand what the flowers were; nevertheless, Mother shared her crushing sorrow with us this time. Imitating her, we would wave our hands across the baby's eyes to test her sight. The baby cried but didn't see. Mother cried and lamented, reproving God in her usual way: "Lord! What have I done to deserve this?"

"Don't lose your faith over it, woman," said Father. "God knows best. It could have been worse."

In her terror of the greater misfortune, she prayed for the Lord's forgiveness. She lived so much in fear of His wrath and the

154

great calamities He had let befall her that to her He became fate. She bowed her neck under His yoke even though she protested to Him. And when she became conscious of her protestation, her apprehension grew worse.

At any rate, the fate of the greater misfortune was not long in descending upon us, dragging his hooded cloak across the whole village along with us. That summer the locusts appeared in June, entirely destroying the young crops, the plants and trees. Panic spread through the village at the thought of famine that father said would be comparable to the days of the *Safar Barrlik.*

The locusts flew in swarms like a low expanding cloud in the sky, shutting out the sun shining from behind as if it had been veiled. The swarm would alight upon the ground or garden to gnaw. Their gnawing sounded like a wide surging flow as if there were thousands of tiny scissors all cutting at the same time.

During the first days of the locust plague, I saw a swarm of them lighting on a mulberry tree in our garden. After an hour there wasn't one green leaf left. The tree branches were bare, heavy with elongated reddish fruit that looked to me like a necklace of gluttonous eyes glistening out of tiny horselike heads. When the sun grew hot, they flew off and came down, their beating wings making a faint disturbing drone that was sometimes a buzzing sound as they flew lower just over our heads, spreading out in the air over the whole countryside, destroying the greater part of the crops.

On the evenings of the third and fourth days of the locusts arrival, the village warden, upon orders from the *mukhtar* who had returned from a meeting of the *mukhtars* in the district administrative center, went round to all the houses one by one, informing everyone, men, women and children, that they must go out to the fields and lands to combat the locusts.

Father went to the *mukhtar* and threatened him with imprisonment, informing him that the police would patrol the houses and if they found anyone in them who had not gone to fight the locusts, even a child, they would hold the father responsible.

"We are poor strangers," Father said to the *mukhtar*. "We have neither a field nor land in the village, and it is not fair to compel the whole family to do such onerous work as this that they have never been used to."

However, the *mukhtar* insisted, saying that he would be on a certain land where he wanted to find our family, so we would be directly under his supervision.

In the morning we left for the land assigned to us. There were many *fellahin* there, each one holding a large palm branch or a straw broom with which to catch the locusts as they landed on the ground and kill them. The children's job was to gather the ones that were killed in containers and empty them in a trench that would be filled in with earth when full.

We began the battle when the locusts were in flight. They advanced, swarm after swarm, filling the air with the rustling of their whirling wings. Sometimes, they landed on heads or shoulders, making the women and children jump with fright, running barefoot over hundreds of enraged locusts with needle sharp wings. The sun rose higher and higher, and the locusts increased with the heat. The police shouted at the people, threatening, warning and waving their whips at the nape of their necks and in their faces, surrounding them in a circle so they would kill the locusts or be killed. There was no escape.

I saw Mother, a woman convalescing from childbirth, carrying her straw broom, beating the ground, advancing or retreating like the others, then stopping, panting and wiping the sweat pouring from her brow. Looking at my sister and me, her heart broke with pain at the sight of us and from fear we would get fatal sunstroke.

I ran, carrying a small basket over that dusty, thorny, stony countryside where reptiles abounded, gathering the dead locusts, some of them still alive, some crawling with broken wings or legs. Blood stained my hands and that disgusting, loathsome sight filled me with as much terror as did the police.

At noon, Mother went up to a policeman to tell him she was going back to the house, as she had left a blind, suckling child there. Threatening her, he returned her to her line. Father entreated him also and when he wouldn't budge he yelled at him.

"You're cruel; you are heartless!"

The answer was the lash of a whip.

"I'm not going to drive you back to prison, you dog," the policeman swore at him. "There you could rest, I'm not going to drive you there... You'll stay here to fight the locusts and after that we'll settle our account."

Father didn't reply. Words were useless. I saw him defying the policeman with blazing eyes. He stood still for a moment, looking at my sister and me who had rushed to him, crying. Taking our hands, he said: "Why are you crying?... Never mind...let's go back to work."

Mother regretted what happened, fearing that Father, who kept a nervous silence that became very tense, would immediately take off. But Father didn't leave. This work was forced labor, too. He didn't flee from it as he had in the days of the *safar barrlik*. He may have felt it was his duty to help in the combat against the locusts; he may have feared they would take out their revenge on us; or he may have accepted the humiliation so as not to leave in these crucial times. At any rate we went back to work, remaining out in the countryside until the successive swarms of locusts let up in the afternoon. Upon our return home, Father lit the fire; Mother, absolutely exhausted, heated water for us to bathe and nursed our poor baby sister.

This went on for several days. One evening, we heard that a detachment of soldiers had arrived in the village and were billeted in the *mukhtar's* house for the purpose of taking steps in the battle against the locusts. At their head, was a sergeant from Iskenderun, a cruel merciless person. The news about him came to us, exaggerated from neighboring villages.

"We can't do anything," Father remarked to us in bitter dejection. "Don't be afraid of the soldiers, they're no crueler then the police. We must do as the others. Inevitably, there will be a way out."

Zanuba arrived that night also, not quite as drunk as usual, with a small glass of *arrack* for Father along with something to eat. She cursed the police boldly, unrestrainedly, saying she would do such and such to them and entreating Father not to quarrel with them lest he, being a man, would be punished severely. However, they wouldn't do anything to her, Zanuba, a woman, and if they beat her she would shoot the one who did it. She swore she would.

"Whoever does all that won't run and hide?" father joked.

Zanuba let out a laugh, "I didn't run away," she replied. "...I went and worked like the others...but on land that I chose to go to, not the *mukhtar* ...that son of a..." (She cursed him slanderously.) "That one who in the daytime uses the police to control us and at night ingratiates!"

Zanuba's arrival revived Mother. She was delighted with her talk as she, like Father, was finding courage and support in it and compensation for the abuse they had received. Mother told her that we would eat supper together. Father drank the foul smelling *arrack*, and at the end of the evening went out to see Zanuba to her house.

"Don't be late," Mother cautioned him.

He was late, but she didn't call him to account. She wanted him to drink and forget, so she didn't call him to account. In the morning, we went out to the combat. At noon, something happened that entirely changed our situation.

One of the *fellahin* called to Father by name. Thereupon, voices were raised shouting his name all together. We saw a soldier with a whip in his hand, advancing from a distance. In alarm, Mother lay down her broom and rushed towards Father to protect him, with us running behind her, filled with fear of the soldier coming towards us.

"Are you so and so?" asked the soldier.

"Yes..."

"The sergeant wants to speak to you."

"What does he want?"

"I don't know."

The soldier yelled at the *fellahin* that had collected around us: "Everyone to work... The locusts are taking over as you stand here!"

The *fellahin*, turning around to see what was going to happen, dispersed, leaving us alone with the soldier. Father bowed his head in bewilderment, sensing some unknown cursed oppression. He was besieged: besieged by us most of all. If it had not been for us, he would have fled from the entire village, walking all the way to Iskenderun, even if it took days. In Iskenderun, neither police nor soldier could apprehend him: he would not have to combat locusts or be humiliated.

"Come on...," the soldier said.

"Stay where you are...," said Father, turning to us.

The soldier was sympathetic to our situation. "The sergeant is over there," he said pointing towards the trees. Then turning to face us..., "He won't be long coming back to you. Take your time at your work...why don't these two youngsters take a break?"

"But what does the sergeant want with me?" asked Father.

"He'll tell you what he wants," replied the soldier. "I told you I don't know. If you please."

Father went with him, leaving us where we were, watching him.

"May God go with you," said Mother. "Don't leave us in suspense... Let us know what happens to you... Tell him we are poor, that you are a stranger and have a family."

She stammered out the last words as if her tongue had been weakened by paralysis. The look of defeat on her face bespoke silent suffering and helpless protest. I wanted to take her hand, to kiss it, to speak words I did not know how to express because in my aching heart they were reacting with sorrow that was mute like the sun is subdued, overshadowed by this dust cloud, subdued in this hellish plague that had befallen us. She was anguished and felt that the whole damned world was going to hell.

Father went with the soldier while we waited. And from under the shelter of a tree upon which guns and whips hung, the sergeant also waited, sitting on a stone. As soon as he saw Father approaching, he rose yelling at him from a distance.

"You? What brought you here?"

"Abdu! My God...," yelled Father at the same instant.

He trembled... They hugged each other and Father almost cried, unable to control himself from the great force of his emotion. The sergeant, having put his mind at rest, went on to enquire about him and us. He had dismissed the soldiers before listening to his story, so they could not hear what father was telling him about the situation we had gotten into.

This sergeant was a relative of ours. He was the godfather of my sister who was fighting the locusts in this dust-laden countryside. When he asked about her, Father replied: "Over there!" (pointing towards us).

"And your wife?"

"With me...combating the locusts, too."

"What brought you here? Since when? How? My God!"

"Fate...we were desperate, Abdu... The times have done us in, Abdu."

He was talking with his head averted. Confronted by this relative, he felt the need to open up and confess unashamedly. The sergeant was troubled and bewildered, faced with a situation he hadn't met up with before. He had questioned the village *mukhtar* about the village and its families, about the inhabitants and the number of *fellahin* in it, about the feudal lord who was one of the biggest landowners. The *mukhtar* had told him, incidentally, that there was a family of strangers in their midst, people from the city, and that the man's name was so and so. He did not give any further information. However, the sergeant, concerned with what he had heard, decided to make enquiries the next day about this displaced family and did so.

We saw Father coming back, accompanied by the soldier. He was pointing towards us, but we didn't understand what he wanted. Then he shouted to Mother: "Leave the work... This is Abdu...our best man Abdu. Come on, bring the children. Bring the girl to see her godfather..."

I did not know the meaning of the words "godfather" or "best man," but I felt that heaven had sent down something to ease my aching heart, that the sun had been eclipsed and that my soul had been inundated with peace because someone from there, from the city, knew us and might be able to rescue us and prevent the police from beating Father.

We went to him, Mother ashamed to appear before him in the state we were in. Hoping she would not weep in front of him, I hesitated, hiding behind her. Coming to meet us, he shook hands with Mother and picked up sister to kiss her. He kissed me, patting my head.

"Go to the house right away," he said to Father. "I'll come to you in the evening and we'll talk."

Then, stopping him, he asked, "Who ordered you to go out to fight the locusts?"

"The *mukhtar*!"

"Didn't you explain your position to him?"

"Yes, indeed, I did explain... I didn't want him to excuse me... I entreated him to excuse my wife only and to have mercy on the blind baby in the house."

"A blind baby?"

"Yes, godfather," replied Mother. "We have a baby with a flower on her eyes... She can't see at all... What a calamity."

"You'll eat with us, godfather," said Father. "Don't be late."

"Food isn't important... Don't expect me for supper... I'll eat at the *mukhtar's* with the soldiers."

We left for home, our parents talking along the way about their best man, the sergeant, mentioning things about him, his office and his importance. Father said that he had attained this high rank through his own diligence and that, with his authority over the detachment of soldiers, he would help us to get out of the situation we were in.

Mother suggested cooking a chicken for him and Father agreed, saying that if he didn't eat with us that day we could prepare food for him for the next. Upon reaching home, we felt that the crisis had passed and everything was opening up before us. We set about cleaning the courtyard and preparing everything to welcome our distinguished guest. Mother even swept the road and we sprinkled it with water and washed the linens for the bed he might sleep in. From the afternoon on, our eyes were fixed on the road.

The sergeant Abdu did not come that evening. Some of the eminent *fellahin* of the village came. Their visit and the courteousness expressed by it perplexed us. They explained, however, that it was for Father's mediation.

Sergeant Abdu, a man of few words, a strict disciplinarian whose reputation for cruelty had preceded him, had done something that proved everything said about him and worse.

The *mukhtar's* treatment of us having enraged him, he remained the whole afternoon sitting or leaning in gloomy silence on the ground at the edge of that garden. In the evening, he returned to the *mukhtar's* house where the detachment that had taken over from the police was billeted. There, he maintained his silence, sitting on the mat on top of the bed provided for him. When they placed the tray with the supper on it in front of him, he requested them to bring in the *mukhtar*, the elective committee, and the village notables to talk with him. When they arrived and were assembled around him, he put out his foot and kicked the supper tray containing bread, *leban* and bulgur. Rising up in front of the *mukhtar*, he yelled "Do you think I'm a beggar, you cuckold...asking for alms, you son of a..."

He slapped him once, then again, then picking up his whip rained blows on those who interfered to rescue him. He ordered the soldiers to hold him in custody in preparation to driving him to prison in the morning.

Those present interposed in defense of the *mukhtar*, but the sergeant called out his soldiers. He was as ruthless as death itself.

161

"Don't you think I'm receiving my courage from my uniform and rank. Here I stand without my rank (tearing off his sergeant's insignia). Let any man of you stand up to me... This *mukhtar* of yours is pitiless: he bullied a stranger in your midst, having no mercy on his sick wife and her blind baby girl or the homeless family, forcing them all into combat against the locusts while his family, the owners of the land and your families, members of the elite and landowners, remained at home. The police disregarded it... I won't disregard it. From tomorrow morning, your families will go out to the combat and we'll settle our account, you..."

When Mother heard what had happened, she feared the outcome. The sergeant would stay for a week or two, then leave. At that time, they would take their revenge on us. In self-defense father told those who had come to him: "I didn't egg on the sergeant; I didn't say anything to him. Despite the fact that the *mukhtar* did us wrong and the police beat me unjustly, I didn't say anything to him. Ask the soldiers... I'm prepared to talk to the sergeant and request him to free the *mukhtar* but I'm not responsible for what happened."

Father was being truthful. The *fellahin* knew that the *mukhtar* was a churlish evil man. Some of them had gone to him entreating him to leave our family alone, but he had refused. He had caused many of them hardship. They cursed him for that and in their hearts wished he would be taken to prison and be stripped of his position as *mukhtar* that he had held for many years.

However, the sergeant was not thinking of the *mukhtar's* evil treatment of the *fellahin*, nor had he any intention of getting mixed up in the matter of the *mukhtar* ship. Had it not been for our mistreatment, he would probably have shrunk from uncovering any other incident or punishing the *mukhtar* and through him the village by compelling it to comply in expending every effort in the fight against the locusts to gratify him and his soldiers.

He came to us that night with his gun slung over his shoulder as a precaution, refusing the company of any of his soldiers just as he had refused to eat a bite from the table hurriedly prepared for him at the *mukhtar's* house. They had brought him eggs and chicken instead of the bulgur that he had left for his soldiers. He had gone out alone, his face lined with anger, determination and its usual calmness. Steering clear of talk of the incident, believing we hadn't heard of it, he threw himself down on the mat placed on

162

the ground in the courtyard, saying without any preface: "If you have anything to eat I'm hungry."

While eating with our parents, he again inquired about their situation, listening attentively to the long story father told concerning the circumstances that forced us to leave Latakiya for al-Suwaydiya and thence to this village. Before the story was finished, Zanuba's voice arose in obscene curses against the sergeant, instigated by some of the village notables, who having made her drunk, turned her over to us to revile him in this manner.

"Is this Zanuba?" asked the sergeant.

"Yes...do you know her?" replied Mother. "May God cut off her tongue... She is good when she is sober, but when she is drunk..."

"From where did you get to know her?" asked Father in surprise.

"I heard about her... The fellahin told the soldiers... And I know why she is cursing..."

"I'll shut her up," said Father.

"I'll shut her up myself," responded the sergeant. "Let her come here..."

Zanuba arrived with her hands on her hips, seemingly in a state of vulgar arrogance. Indifferent to both Father and our guest, she said to the sergeant: "You son of a..."

However, the sergeant, who had turned over on his back still stretched out on the mat, addressed her calmly as if he hadn't heard her curses: "You are Zanuba!"

"What do you want?"

"I'm going to sleep with you, tonight!"

Father sat up straight. Mother bit her lower lip.

"You and all your soldiers brag," laughed Zanuba.

"I'm going to sleep with you tonight," stated the sergeant emphatically, unconcerned with her mockery.

"Did you hear?" Zanuba asked Father. "Is this your relative and your guest... Tell him who Zanuba is."

"Shut your trap and get out," ordered father. "Why did you come? Who sent you here and told you to curse?"

"No one...and you! Don't you want me to come? Have you got too important for me? Are you afraid of the sergeant? Are you afraid of what he'll do to me?"

"I'm going to sleep with you, tonight," repeated the sergeant.

"The sergeant is joking with you, Zanuba," said Mother... "His wife is as beautiful as the full moon, and he isn't thinking about you or anyone else... Please come and sit down... Have you had your supper?"

"I'm going to sleep with you, tonight," reiterated the sergeant as if he hadn't heard what Mother had said.

Zanuba recommenced cursing, but the sergeant didn't turn a hair. He went on repeating his statement with masterly assurance while she stood there in disarray, as if she realized that the sergeant was not joking.

His silence and calmness alarmed her. Faced with his eyes looking right through her clothes, she sobered up, sucked in her lips and went and sat down beside Mother. After that, she stretched out, pretending to have dosed off. Then, she actually did go to sleep. When Mother roused her so she could go home, she refused, declaring she was going to sleep at our place.

And she slept.

Chapter 19

We did not go to the fields to fight the locusts the next day. The *mukhtar* came to apologize to Father, and we were treated respectfully on all sides. However, the sergeant advised Father to leave the village saying: "It's a shame for you and your family to be displaced in this countryside. Go back to Iskenderun and work there. You can arrange your affairs somehow or the other... After my departure, the *mukhtar* will take revenge on you. Watch out. If anything like that happens, let me know. Aren't you afraid for your wife and children?"

Father bowed his head in thought. The harvests were ruined, meaning there would be no way to glean grain or olives. The *fellahin*, who were facing famine, would not find a *piastre* to have shoes repaired or to buy sweets. Living in the country would be impossible this year and it was impracticable for us to go back to the city. A curtain as dark as an overcast winter night hung between us and any gleam of light in the picture of the future.

It would take some thinking on Father's part to find a way of escape, besieged as we were by the obstacles of poverty, hunger, exile and the lack of any means of moving.

But he left the matter to what the coming days might offer.

The sergeant remained in the village, not leaving us, after he discovered us, affording us protection, hope and comfort. His hovering around Zanuba was noticed and understood by Father, who may have spoken to him regarding the matter. He may also have forbidden her to come to our place, for she stayed away completely. When the sergeant asked about her, Father told him that she was a wanton woman, a heavy drinker, and that no one knew where she went or when she returned. Since he was embarrassed in front of Mother, and Father stayed away from the issue, the sergeant decided not to try to find out about her from us or mention her name. We considered he had forgotten her or put her out of his mind until the middle of the night a week later, when we heard shrill screams and Zanuba's voice at times resounding with curses and at others with Father's name in supplication for his help. I was awakened suddenly by this loud screaming. I was sleeping in the courtyard on the mat. A *fellah* came running towards us shouting for Father to come and rescue Zanuba from the sergeant. Father got up with a stick in his hand, telling Mother he was praying God would let this night pass without mishap. I sensed that he hated the sergeant and wished he would get out of the village despite the fact that his departure would be a catastrophe for us.

When Father reached Zanuba, she was bleeding, leaning in exhaustion against a tree, her shoulders bare and with bruises on her body and face. In the light of the lantern one of the *fellahin* carried, Father could see the blood trickling from her. He told Mother that she was having a miscarriage, but Mother said that the blood was from a wound in her thigh or stomach. They argued about that. We learned from the *fellahin* that they had come running upon the sound of shrill voices calling for help, rending the silence of the night. Picking up their weapons and sticks, they had rushed in the direction of the noise. There, they had seen the sergeant trying to rape Zanuba. He had broken a window to get in. He had to break it, because Zanuba had refused to open the door to him. At first, he tried to win her over, to rouse her desire, spending a long time without success. Becoming desperate, he threatened her and punched her, wanting to ravish her by force. In resistance, she opened the door in an effort to run away, but he caught up with her at the tree. There, ripping her clothes, he threw her down to the ground and rolled around with her. However, she didn't let him take possession of her nor submit to him. By the time the *fellahin* reached them, he had got up off her, pulled out his revolver, threatening anyone approaching him. Then he retreated under cover of the darkness to the adjacent fields.

Father helped Zanuba to get up. When some of them tried to oppose him, Zanuba resisted them. Father said the sergeant wanted to punish her for cursing him, and that he would speak to him the following day. Warning them against going to extremes in rashly inflating the affair, he took Zanuba inside her house, locking the door upon her. He came back, saying to Mother: "I'm afraid of treachery against the sergeant. If the *fellahin* find the sergeant, they will most certainly shoot him. If I knew where he went, I would go warn him to keep out of sight or bring him to hide him in our house... I can't go to the *mukhtar's* house to inform the soldiers. That would be a bad provocation whose price we would pay."

"I never thought our best man would do a thing like that," remarked Mother. "God damn the devil."

166

Father shook his head in pity over Mother's naivete and good-ness of heart. He had realized from the first night that the sergeant desired Zanuba, that he wasn't joking. Knowing that Zanuba would not comply with the sergeant's wishes, he appeared angry at what the sergeant had done and happy, or at least not sad, at what had happened. Zanuba had established her faith-fulness that night.

"Zanuba is truly her father's daughter," he stated in praise of her.

"May God never uncover a woman's head," retorted Mother.

"Zanuba is like a man," said Father.

"If she wouldn't get drunk!" said Mother. "What will people say now!"

"Let them say what they want... Her drinking is nobody's busi-ness..."

After that, silence reigned in the serenity of the night that had previously raged with the waves of uproar. The stars above us resembled distant glittering lanterns strewn about in a disorderly fashion. The universe in all its splendor, as pure as a breath of mountain air, was sleeping the soundless sleep of a child. Father was recklessly smoking a cigarette that glowed in his mouth when-ever he took a drag on it. I would see his face through the grey veil of smoke for an instant, then not be able to discern it. I could see Mother's black bulk beside him, both of them silent, awaiting the unseen.

After a while Father stirred in his seat and threw away his cigarette in preparation to getting up. When Mother asked him what he saw, he replied, "There's an indistinct shape over there." She in turn got up in alarm. The one approaching cleared his throat in the darkness.

"I'm Abdu!" His voice came from a distance.

Our parents ran to meet him, asking him how he was.

"There's nothing the matter! I'm fine," he answered abruptly.

He came over and sat with them on the edge of the bed.

"Bring me a pillow and cover," he commanded Mother. Then he said to Father, "Had it not been for you, I'd have burned down this damned estate."

"I beg of you, sir, to exercise patience!" replied Father.

I don't know what happened after that. It was said that a del-egation from the estate went to Iskenderun to lay a complaint; that the boss, the owner of the grain storehouse beside our hut, intervened with the authorities; and also that the sergeant, fearing assassination, took off.

Father ridiculed all these conjectures spreading through the village and conveyed to us by Zanuba. He knew more about it than anyone else. The sergeant had conversed with him the following nights, telling him that he had to visit a number of villages where the fight against the locusts was not being carried out as it should. He said that the waves of locusts had let up somewhat and were about to end; that there was nothing left in the village as the crops were all lost, the locusts having eaten every green thing.

Knowing that the sergeant was a stubborn, bold, silent man who never talked about anything except what he did and sometimes acted and said nothing, Father believed what he said. The sergeant could have, had it not been for us and his compassion for us, made an example of the estate without paying any attention to rumors of their intention to harm him. Father advised him not to go out alone at night.

"If only one soldier accompanies me, they'll think I'm afraid," he replied scowling.

He intended going out alone at night without his gun, content with his revolver. The day after the event, he sent for the *mukhtar*, the elective committee, and some of the notables, making them wait for him until he had finished his supper and seen to the affairs of his soldiers. Then he met with them, scowling, silent, warning them without words. When he thought he had put the fear in them, he said sternly: "Which one of you sent Zanuba to curse me?"

They proceeded rashly to swear on the most solemn oaths that they knew nothing about it and hadn't heard of it. They said that Zanuba was a drunken, wanton woman, when she drank she quarreled with the high and the low, that he had given her what was coming to her and that all of them were in agreement with what he had done to her, admired it, only wishing he could cut out her tongue.

"And these rumors about me?"

"God forbid... Zanuba deserves it... Ah, if you had only killed her and rid the estate of her."

"I heard that some of you want to attack my soldiers... OK...from tonight I'll send every soldier into the road unarmed and let anyone of you dare pelt him even with a flower..."

He dismissed them without returning their farewell. Going out alone without a soldier, he said to Father: "If they gave me a kingdom to rule over, I'd discipline the ants crawling on the ground. So do you think this estate is going to get the better of me?"

Father was greatly impressed by him. The day he left, he came to us, kissed Sister and me, and advised Father to quit the village, telling him to ask for him when he reached the city. Father told him he was going to leave the village and would only stay in it long enough to arrange for our departure.

Chapter 20

However, the matter of traveling didn't arrange itself for Father.

After the sergeant's departure, we experienced feelings of fear from the vacancy he left behind. Mother exhorted Father not to go out at night and asked Zanuba to forget what the sergeant had done to her, begging her to defend us against the village men when our name was mentioned. Zanuba smiled but did not say anything. She bowed her head to express something that wasn't clear to us. She may have merely been offended by our doubts of her love for us, or she may have felt sorry that Mother even now fathomed her and did not understand the other side of her personality: her goodness, her generosity, her courage, and the subjugation she endured from the tyranny that had befallen her, that she refused to forget or complain about, but that drove her to drink to forget it for a little while.

To be on the safe side, we did not go out to the fields. Summer was coming to a close; the October winds were raising the dust accumulated in summer and in the evenings it blew stronger, rattling the door and windows, making us imagine that the villagers were taking them off to get at us. Father scoffed at Mother's misgivings; however, as he was not so confident as before, it became difficult for him to take off and leave us. Not because in his absence we wouldn't have food to eat, but because his attachment to Zanuba was very strong and he was afraid for us, dreading the *mukhtar's* vengeance erupting against him for what the sergeant had done during the days of the locusts.

This last idea that kept him awake at night was not disclosed to Mother until later years. At the time he held it in, lest it increase her alarm. Putting out the light, he would sit up in the dark, perhaps sleeping a broken sleep for a short while. When day came, he tried to work as a cobbler, but none of the *fellahin* brought him shoes. Zanuba was the only one who helped us from time to time with provisions. She would swear to Mother that no one thought ill of us, that they realized that the sergeant was a government agent and all government agents were cruel like the police. She said there was nothing for us to fear and that we could remain in the village quite secure.

With the arrival of winter, there was nothing to eat. They even gathered and ate the plants that grew along the brink of the water after the locust plague. The village shop was closed. The hens, whose eggs were gathered with extreme care, could not be exchanged for any kind of grain. Meat, which had always been scarce, disappeared completely. No one slaughtered an animal even for a votive offering.

The only place that held any grain from the previous year was the boss's store house beside us. It was a large storehouse, and the boss who used to come with wagons to transport what was in it to Iskenderun had ceased coming. Father noticed that the *fellahin*, emaciated from hunger, were hovering around the storehouse like vultures around a carcass in the desert. However, they would just eye it and retreat; they didn't come close to it, touch it, question Father nor say anything to him about the matter.

The old lady beside us died one cold day. It was Zanuba who discovered the decomposing body. Some *fellahin* and *sheikhs* who gathered round along with the *mukhtar* examined the hut and took her out to bury her in the afternoon with no one to mourn her except Mother. She refused to let us leave the house that day, telling us that our neighbor had died and we must stay away from the hut lest we see her in our dreams.

In obedience to her command, we spent the day squatting on the bed or around the hearth. After closing the door early in the evening, we were delighted at Zanuba's arrival. Our dear Zanuba, whose mere appearance in our house brought us peace of mind, new life and confidence.

She told us in detail how she had smelled the stench from the old lady's hut, ripped off the door and entered. The villagers and elderly *sheikhs* being afraid to touch her, the old lady had almost been buried unwashed. Zanuba washed her, arising to the occasion as if the old lady had been her mother, without so much as taking any of her household goods. After the burial, the village *sheikh* said to her: "You deserve the very best, Zanuba, most of all, the Lord's forgiveness and His best merit. At any rate take her bed... The rest of her things will be distributed among the poor through me."

Zanuba did not answer or take anything. She knew, as she said, to whom the late old lady's things would go and she didn't care. She had nothing to do with such issues. Had the dead woman been a drinker and had on hand a bottle or even half a bottle of *arrack*, she would have taken it. The *arrack* alone would have been of use to her, the rest of the stuff was of no interest to her. She said she had only done what she thought necessary, with no expectation of any reward or forgiveness. She did not care for anything, since matters, after this year of the locusts, had arrived at such a bad state.

A few days after this, Father discovered traces of wheat, barley and *durra* around the large storehouse. He followed these traces to the adjoining field. Upon going to enter the hut of the old lady who had died, he found the door only closed. The lock had been removed and on the inside were some kernels of grain. The thieves were hiding in the hut, robbing the storehouse by night. He thought they were getting in through one of the sides, not through the main entrance that hadn't been touched. He made the rounds of the walls, tapping them with his stick, hoping to chance upon the hole that was opened at night and closed by day. Everything was in order; the walls had not been touched either. Had they broken through the walls they would have left traces of dust on the ground. In the darkness, they couldn't possibly have swept up the dust and restored the walls and ground to their original state. When he let Zanuba in on his misgivings, she laughed.

"You keep out of it," she advised. "The estate people are hungry."

"They're robbing the storehouse, then?"

"Why not, they're doing it so they won't starve."

"And if the owner finds out about it?"

"The *mukhtar* and the guard will be responsible."

"What about me? I'm the only one living beside the storehouse."

"They won't suspect you... You're not doing it... If they search your house they won't find one kernel of grain... Just say, 'I don't know anything.'"

Father was worried and Mother was afraid. The owner would arrive shortly, the theft would be uncovered. The news may have already spread to the *mukhtar*, who would have informed the owner, who would call in the police. They would arrest Father, beat him so he would confess and not believe him no matter how he swore to his innocence. Even if they were convinced he hadn't stolen, they would ask for the names of those who had. They would say, "Your house is beside the storehouse so what have you seen or last heard? Whom do you suspect? Haven't you noticed anything? Why didn't you inform the *mukhtar*?"

Mother suggested that we take off, that we sell all our household goods to secure the hire of a cart to move to Iskenderun. It was futile for us to remain in the village; it was now the beginning of winter and we were without food; Father was unemployed and without hope of taking up any trade or finding any source of income. Everything was against us, famine had settled over the sky like a flock of vultures. This harvest season belonged to the vultures. People would die and along with them animals; the plague would spread. Even if we escaped all this woe, we would not escape the damage the boss, the storehouse owner, would do us. Getting away from it, fleeing once more, was the only way of escape.

However, Father, despite his conviction that what Mother said was right, found the door of escape shut in his face. Our departure would merely strengthen doubts about us, confirming the accusation against us. No matter how far away we went, the hand of the law would reach us. And on top of being starving vagabonds, we would end up in prison.

Once again, probably for the seventh or eight time, we were up against a solid stone wall. To whom could we appeal? Who would hear our cry? The air was impenetrable and the daggers were at our breast. Our faces were all eyes, eyes that were full of tears, that were invisible ink for our written and unwritten grief. We saw it, lived it and ate it. Grief was our daily bread. It was our only food. Our bodies grew emaciated, our eyes sunken, our cheeks hollow, nothing but skin and bones.

"If you would just inform the *mukhtar*, it wouldn't be our responsibility at least," Mother said.

"I'm not going to squeal on anyone."

"But they are stealing!"

"What are they supposed to do during this famine? Bide your time...people will eat each other when winter comes. They aren't to be blamed. During the *Safar Barrlik*, mothers ate their children. They became like cats and ate their children... What good will sticks or guns do? They'll only hasten death and bring people relief... Let's be patient... A way out may come from some unknown source."

173

Zanuba alone remained unconcerned, keeping up her dissipated life with cold disdain, mocking the world in the same manner that the world mocks people. In fact, her wantonness had become depravity. She cursed the world; she blasphemed God unrestrainedly, regretting not having killed the sergeant. She said that in her view everything was now permissible. If people were going to die of hunger, why not die before they grew hungry. By way of provoking the men and disparaging them indiscriminately, she took to denouncing their masculinity, saying that they were already dead; they were no longer good for anything. She ridiculed them, claiming they were a bunch of eunuchs who were of no use to their wives, in fact they had grown as skinny as their wives. She would yell at Father challengingly: "And you?"

Father wouldn't say anything. If the village men were helpless in the face of the disaster, what could he do? In accordance with what one in his situation would say, the bitterness he was enduring was no worse than that of others. He even loathed his own existence. Circumstances had gotten beyond irresponsibility and, in the face of these circumstances, responsibility imposed itself upon him without giving him room to escape. His situation probably made him hate himself and feel ashamed that he was a man. He no longer approached Zanuba despite her provocation. He did not visit her, refusing to keep her company at night, pleading tiredness or drowsiness. I was surprised at his manner of speaking, his rudeness to her, his silence in answer to her words and his disregard of her cursing. I was ignorant of what was going on, but I felt the increasing gloomy dejection, like black despair that was proceeding at will to overlay the floor and walls of our mud hut.

One day the boss, the owner of the storehouse, arrived on a horse along with some carts and *fellahin*. As soon as the storehouse door was opened, we heard his burst of anger. Mother locked the door in fear, endeavoring to prevent Father from going out. Yelling at her in reproof, he opened the door, telling her we were innocent, having had no part in it. If they were going to swallow us up unjustly, locking our door wouldn't do any good. On the contrary, it would make us look suspect. The best thing was just to remain as we were and leave things in God's hands.

The boss came out of the storehouse in a raging fury. Ordering that everything be left just as it was, he mounted his horse and rode off to the center of the village to the *mukhtar's* house The news having spread through the village just as quickly, the *fellahin* gathered around the grain storehouse while we stood in our doorway silently watching what was taking place before us. Father was scowling and Mother was trembling and mumbling prayers under an overcast sky threatening thunder storms, while the cold December wind blew over the muddy ground. The terrible thing we had been anticipating was happening, making us shiver worse than the cold did.

The *mukhtar* arrived on foot, racing ahead of the boss's mare with some men following behind them. The *mukhtar* sent the village watchman to the district administrative center to summon the police. We watched them entering the storehouse, coming out, circling the large rectangular building and pointing to the roof. Then, following the traces of grain, they stopped in front of the old lady's hut, went in and came out again following the traces. The *fellahin* flocked in while the children ran around in the courtyard. Some of the boss's men were keeping them from entering the storehouse, some advanced, poking their heads in, but immediately retreated... The boss was talking loudly, threatening and menacing, and the *mukhtar* was pointing in our direction. The boss shouted to Father: "You! Come here..."

Father went with Mother at his heels. My sister and I ran after them.

"Who robbed the storehouse?" asked the boss.

After saluting him, Father replied politely: "I know nothing about it sir."

"You know nothing about it and you are living here? Right beside the storehouse? Liar! Thief!"

"By God, sir," interceded Mother in a choking voice, "we know nothing about it... We are poor. We lock ourselves inside at nightfall."

"Who let you live in this house?"

"Your brother..."

"How much do you pay?"

"We don't pay anything."

"For what reason, then, do you live in it? To guard the storehouse... That's quite clear. But you don't guard it... Its protectors are its robbers, you bastards."

"We have never robbed it," replied Father. "Ask the *mukhtar* about us... Ask the people of the estate..."

The police arrived in the afternoon... They eyed the place, wrote a report...arrested Father and some *fellahin*. The sacks were being moved to the carts and the investigation began in the courtyard... After handcuffing those under arrest, they shut them up in the old woman's house. In a short time they called them out one by one... They would ask the *fellah* a few questions, then rain blows upon him with a stick... The fellah would scream, plead with them while the police continued beating him... The boss, the storehouse owner, sat watching, whispering in the ear of the sergeant who was bellowing at his men: "Beat them within an inch of their lives...and don't worry about that even... To hell with them... I'll kill them if they don't confess."

One of them denounced Zanuba. We saw the police mounting their horses to set out looking for her. In a short while, she was brought before the sergeant.

"Are you stealing from the boss's grain, too?" he asked.

"I haven't stolen" she replied. "Who do you think you are? God? Why are you imprisoning people and beating them? What about this criminal sitting beside you? I have an account to settle with him... An old score that he knows about. Don't think I've forgotten... I'll kill him with my own hands so that the whole estate can witness it..."

"You whore..."

"Whore? And your wife?... And his?... Ah, you husbands of unfaithful wives!"

"We!"

"And your government also!"

"Are you reviling the government?"

"I'll revile the Sultan himself...as far as your arm can reach..."

The sergeant was a giant of a man, a brute with paws like a winnower's fork, fingers like sticks of firewood. Shaking with anger, he slapped Zanuba as hard as he could. He smacked her cheeks, hit her on the chest, making her reel and fall, then finishing off the beating by kicking her thighs, her hips, and her head as she screamed: "You cuckold...you scum."

The sergeant ordered that she be strung up by her feet to be *bastioned*. The men intervened, requesting the boss to advise the sergeant to let her be.

"This is going to be the lot of all of you," he yelled at them. "I'll kill you one by one... The grain must be brought back. By God

176

I'll ruin you all, I'll lacerate your skin to shreds and impale your flesh on stakes until you confess and bring all the stolen goods."

Mother went into the house, weeping and slapping her sides, cheeks wailing: "Oh my God! Ah Zanuba...you poor thing, Zanuba... They will kill her, and when your father's turn comes, they will beat him. They will drag him to prison... When will you withdraw your wrath from us, God?"

She went out again, weeping, and we followed her, also in tears. She went and kneeled in front of the boss, who shoved her in the chest to get rid of her, while the sergeant, who had finished with the investigation of a *fellah*, yelled: "Bring another one..."

They brought another. He was shackled, an old barefoot man who appealed for mercy on account of his advanced age.

"When you robbed the storehouse, you didn't feel your age or weren't ashamed to do it," stated the sergeant. "You hid the grain in your house; tell us who brought it there."

He named a certain *fellah*.

"And the others, his accomplices?"

"I don't know them... I swear by God I don't know them... I was hungry... They told me to take that bag and put it in my house... They gave me a little from it... We were hungry and we ate. Yes, sir, we were hungry. We hadn't tasted food for three days."

"You eat stolen goods?"

"Die, if you eat stolen goods," yelled the sergeant.

"Why don't you tell yourselves that?" suddenly exclaimed a *fellah*. "You eat both the lawful and the unlawful... You don't leave an egg or a chicken on the estate!"

"You bastard," shouted the sergeant, "you are the ringleader, you viper..."

"Call me what you like," said the *fellah*, who was arrested and beaten on the spot. "I robbed the storehouse. I'm telling you I stole and I don't care... I fed my children.. Do what you want to..."

"We'll do what we want... Just wait, you son of a bitch... You don't know me..."

"We know you," exclaimed another *fellah*. "You threaten us because you are a government employee. If you were in our place..."

"Seize this dog," the sergeant yelled at his men. "...Seize them all."

The police charged the *fellahin* with guns and sticks. Some fled while other held their ground. The father of one of those ar-

177

rested came to blows with the first policeman he reached... A tumult ensued, and I heard shots being fired in the air. Night was falling. The whole village, which had congregated in the courtyard and along its edges, closed ranks around the police and the boss, the owner of the storehouse. Shouts arose, one of the prisoners escaped and the others, trying to do so, caused confusion.

"They are going to attack us," shouted the feudal lord to the sergeant. "...Open fire...open fire!"

Successive shots rang out. The crowd ran to the right and left. Screams and wailing, the weeping of women and children could be heard and the sounds of feet running in all directions. We rushed with Mother towards the house through the running, shoving crowd.

The battle in the courtyard continued. Bullets resounded amid the cursing and shouting. We could no longer tell the difference between objects and people. It appeared for a moment that the whole village was taking part in the battle, that bullets were raining down on all sides. We heard raging hoarse voices, the moans of the wounded and shrill sobbing wails, then a hoarse frightened voice exclaiming: "Fire...look at the fire...the storehouse is burning..."

It was then that we saw, in the glow of the flames ascending from the storehouse, the terrible spectacle of the blazing fire and the battle that had reached such violence. We could no longer distinguish the police from the *fellahin*. The uproar intensified, erupting at the big door of the storehouse, the door they fell upon with axes, sticks, and their feet, tore down and toppled. The people stormed the storehouse amid the smoke and flames that were beginning to spread through it and were pouring out of it. The wind caught the blaze, carrying the fire and illuminating the adjoining gardens. We could see the *fellahin* leaping through the flames in a mad frenzy, pulling out the sacks. Some of them pounced upon the loaded wagons with knives in their hands, ripping the sacks open so that the grain in them spilled on the ground. The women and children shoved and pushed one another in a rush to gather what had spilled, scraping it up with gravel and dirt amid cries of greedy delight and squabbling.

In the midst of the fire and the riot when the police lost control of the situation, they shot directly at people and the battle changed into a carnage. The shrieking and wailing increased. No one any longer paid attention to the darting flames or thought of putting them out. It was a fearful sight, watching some of the *fellahin* carrying a policeman to throw him in the fire; to hear him in mortal fear, calling for help, lowing like an ox being slaughtered.

Zanuba, who had climbed to the roof and lit the fire after escaping from the police, was urging the men on, begging them to burn the boss and not let him escape. She was standing on the edge of the roof, her clothes torn, her hair disheveled, laughing boisterously like a legendary demon, while the smoke and flames curled around her. Those down below were yelling for her to come down, to jump down before the roof caved in. However, she kept up her hysterical laughing, holding up the bottle of kerosene she had used to light the fire through the opening the thieves had made in the storehouse roof, sprinkling the remainder of it on the roof, the ground and people in a fit of barbaric insanity. All the while, the blazing wood was snapping and cracking and falling. The red tongues of flame from the collapsing rafters were falling in all directions, making the people draw back to avoid them. Then, they would attack with renewed force, incited by this demonic play with death.

After that, the terrible thing that was the culmination of this riot occurred. A policeman shot at the roof from behind a tree. With a shriek coming from the roof like a roar and resounding above all the other screams, Zanuba's body fell like a bundle of rags blown by a strong gust of wind, landing in the front courtyard of the storehouse. The voice of this unfortunate soul was silenced forever. On all sides, arose raving and terrifying shouts on this fearful night, lit up by the fire that burned the storehouse to the ground.

A detachment of police arrived at midnight to occupy the village. Using their whips and rifle butts on bodies and doors, they drove people in groups to the district administrative center and to the city. Some of the *fellahin* fled to the mountains, becoming fugitives of the law. The houses were confiscated and everything in them turned topsy-turvy. The village was under seige for several days, during which time Father returned from the city, not having been convicted of either theft or of taking part in the riot. Upon entering the house, he announced that we were leaving. I don't know how or from where he got hold of the price of hiring the cart he brought from the city to move us away.

It was a one-horse cart with iron-rimmed wheels like the ones we had come in to the village with three years previously. Putting our few meager belongings in the middle of the cart, we sat on top of them around Mother, holding our little blind sister, while Father sat beside the driver, speaking only rarely.

Night was falling. We were on our return journey. It was winter...darkness, wind and rain.

The road was long. We kept silent. I buried my head in Mother's breast. Covering us with a blanket, she said: "Sleep my little ones... We are going to the city."

Interlink World Fiction

The best way to learn about people and places far away

This series is designed to bring to North American readers the once-unheard voices of writers who have achieved wide acclaim at home, but are not recognized beyond the borders of their native lands. Interlink World Fiction series publishes the best of the world's contemporary literature in translation or original English.

FROM SYRIA

Just Like a River
by Muhammad Kamil al-Khatib

Thought by many Syrians to be the most influential novel of its time, this first novel is a riveting examination of Syrian political and social life during the 1980s.

ISBN 1-56656-475-1 • pb $12.95 • 128 pgs.

Sabriya
Damascus Bitter Sweet
by Ulfat Idilbi, trans. by P. Clark

"Sabriya is a haunting, accomplished novel about the lives of women in 1920s Syria... Idilbi's stately prose is relentless in its exposure of Sabriya's despair... [This novel] reveals Ulfat Idilbi as the possessor of a singular, passionate voice which is all her own."
—Financial Times (London)

ISBN 1-56656-475-1 • pb $12.95 • 128 pgs.

I saw Ramollah"

FROM PALESTINE

A Balcony Over the Fakihani
by Liyana Badr
trans. by P. Clark & C. Tingley

"An excellent, moving account of the effects of conflict..."
—Journal of Palestine Studies

ISBN 1-56656-104-3 • hb $19.95
ISBN 1-56656-464-6 • pb $12.95 • 128 pgs.

A Woman of 5 Seasons
by Leila al-Atrash
trans. by N. Halwani and C. Tingley

This novel vividly explores an Arab woman as she seeks to win
independence and fulfillment.

ISBN 1-56656-416-6 • pb $12.95 • 208 pgs.

Wild Thorns
by Sahar Khalifeh
trans. by T. LeGassick & E. Fernea

_"Khalifeh's compelling novel is rich with
insights into the unspoken feelings of Palestinians... "_
— Middle East Journal

ISBN 1-56656-336-4 • pb $12.95 • 208 pgs.

A Lake Beyond the Wind
by Yahya Yakhlif
trans. by M. Jayyusi and C. Tingley

"Yakhlif's meticulous picture of mid-century Palestine..."
—Publishers Weekly

ISBN 1-56656-301-1 • pb $12.95 • 160 pgs.